THE HOLLOW ONES

The Blackwood Tapes Vol. 1

Guillermo del Toro and Chuck Hogan

GRAND CENTRAL
PUBLISHING

LARGE PRINT

Copyright © 2020 by Guillermo del Toro and Chuck Hogan

Cover design by Will Staehle. Cover copyright © 2020 by Hachette Book Group, Inc.

Grand Central Publishing
Hachette Book Group
1290 Avenue of the Americas, New York, NY 10104
grandcentralpublishing.com
twitter.com/grandcentralpub

First Edition: August 2020

Grand Central Publishing is a division of Hachette Book Group, Inc. The Grand Central Publishing name and logo is a trademark of Hachette Book Group, Inc.

The publisher is not responsible for websites (or their content) that are not owned by the publisher.

The Hachette Speakers Bureau provides a wide range of authors for speaking events. To find out more, go to www.hachettespeakersbureau.com or call (866) 376-6591.

LCCN: 2020933579

ISBNs: 978-1-5387-6174-8 (hardcover), 978-1-5387-6173-1 (ebook), 978-1-5387-5216-6 (large print), 978-1-5387-5223-4 (intl. mass market), 978-1-5387-5323-1 (trade pbk. Can.)

Book design by Marie Mundaca

Printed in the United States of America

LSC-C

10 9 8 7 6 5 4 3 2 1

CH:
For Richard Abate

GDT:
For Algernon Blackwood, Lord Dunsany, and Arthur Machen

Astute readers may recognize in our main charac- ter's name a tribute to one of our most admired authors and the originator of the "occult detective" subgenre, Algernon Blackwood. While some reli- gious rites detailed herein have been embellished for dramatic effect, any errors of fact are uninten- tional. We would like to note, however, that grave robbing in New Jersey, for occult purposes, is not at all fiction or a thing of the past. It's happening. Right now.

PRELUDE: The Box

Wedged between two buildings in the Financial District of Manhattan—namely 13 and 15 Stone Street—exists a sliver of a property that officially stands as 13½ Stone Street.

Roughly four feet wide and composed of a colonial stone running the space between the buildings, capped off at thirty feet above the ground, this property serves no apparent purpose but to hold an unremarkable cast-iron Edwardian mailbox.

The Box has no ornaments, no distinguishing characteristics other than a large envelope slot, and there is no door or key to retrieve the mail once it is deposited.

Behind The Box, a solid wedge of stone and mortar.

The deed on this minuscule urban mystery dates back to Dutch colonial times, and the taxes on it have been punctually paid by the firm of Lusk and Jarndyce since 1822. Before that time, its property records exist only in reference, but all are in perfect legal standing.

The oldest recorded mention of The Box goes back indeed to a pamphlet published in what was then named New Amsterdam. *The most complete narrative of the vicissitudes of Jan Katadreuffe and his Final, Virtuous Elevation to the Kingdom of Our Lord.*

In said pamphlet—published by Long and Blackwood, 1763, Folio, four pages—a wealthy spice merchant makes a deal with a demon in order to secure the arrival of his ships and cargo.

The ships are delivered, but henceforth a foul spirit runs amok and tortures the merchant—every nightfall—biting him savagely, scratching his back, and riding his body like a jockey while the wretched soul screams in abject misery and commits sinful acts of great violence.

In the drama, a layman, trying to help, tells a learned priest of a possible solution:

"*...The iron box on High street, your woes is there to greet. Sealed letter bears the Blackwood name. And in a forthnight thee shall meet...*"

The priest praises the Lord and the sacraments as the only solution to pursue. Katadreuffe pays for a litany of masses and is liberated from his torment only hours before passing away, purified.

A small, unassuming gravestone memorializes the passing of Katadreuffe. On the Rector Street side of Trinity Church, the tombstone reads:

HERE LIES THE BODY OF JAN KATADREUFFE, LATE
MERCHANT OF SPICE AND WOODS WHO DEPARTED
THIS LIFE THE 16TH DAY OF OCTOBER 1709—
AGED 42 YEARS. BEHOLD AND SEE THEE PASS BY.
AS THEE ARE NOW, SO ONCE WAS ME, AS I AM,
YOU SOON WILL BE. PREPARE FOR DEATH AND
FOLLOW ME...

Over the centuries, 13½ Stone Street has withstood many a litigation: zoning, corporate, and otherwise. Every one of these legal battles has been won at great expense. And so The Box stands: a mystery standing in plain sight. Most people pass by without even giving it another glance.

A decade ago, a large insurance company across the street installed three security cameras. A dedicated observer could attest that, even though a few letters arrive to The Box—approximately one every three weeks or so—no one ever picks them up, nor does the mailbox ever overflow.

Of this small mystery, one thing has been corroborated time and again over the decades: Every letter that arrives at The Box is a letter of urgent need—a desperate call for help—and every single envelope carries the same name:

Hugo Blackwood, Esq.

2019. Newark, New Jersey.

Odessa set down her menu and looked around the Soup Spoon Café for a list of specials. She found it, a whiteboard near the hostess station, written in block lettering with a red marker. Something about the handwriting triggered a long-forgotten memory of her days at the FBI Academy in Quantico, Virginia.

A Behavioral Sciences lecturer drew up homicide definitions with a squeaky red dry erase marker on the big board in the front of the auditorium.

The differentiation, the lecturer explained, had nothing to do with the homicides themselves—severity, method, or manner—but rather the cooling-off period in between.

The Serial Killer's hallmark is their cycle. Weeks, months, or even years may pass between homicides.

The Mass Murderer kills in one setting, within a fixed time frame, totaling a minimum of four homicides com-

mitted in close succession with little or no downtime in between.

The Spree Killer murders in multiple settings, usually over a brief period of time, the duration lasting anywhere from one hour to several days or weeks. Related: a Rampage Killer, a single person who murders multiple persons in a single homicidal event.

The last two classifications allowed room for overlap. One case that was difficult to properly classify—and was generally considered to be the first rampage killing in the United States—had occurred just seventy-five miles south of the café in which she now sat.

On September 6, 1949, Howard Unruh, a twenty-eight-year-old World War II veteran, departed his mother's house in Camden, New Jersey, dressed in his best suit and a striped bow tie. He had argued with his mother over breakfast, prompting her to flee to a neighbor's home, frantically telling them she feared something terrible was about to happen.

Unruh walked into town armed with a German Luger pistol, carrying thirty 9-millimeter rounds. In a twelve-minute span he shot and killed thirteen people, wounding three more. Locations included a pharmacy, a barbershop, and a tailor. While the desire to murder was proven to be premeditated—Unruh was later found to have kept a list of enemies in a diary—his victims were a mix of preferred targets and people unfortunate enough to cross his path on that clear Tuesday morning. Victims and eyewitnesses alike described the look in Howard's eye that morning as trance-like, dazed.

To anyone other than a law enforcement professional, the classification of the crime matters little. The only truly important fact of the matter was that, for more than sixty years, Unruh's shooting spree stood as the worst rampage killing in New Jersey.

That is, until the night Walt Leppo ordered meat loaf.

"Is it cooked fresh?" Walt asked the young server after his return from the men's room.

"Oh, absolutely," she answered.

"Would you do me a favor, then?" he said. "Could you look and see if there's maybe a slice or two left over from the lunch rush? Preferably set under a heat lamp for a few hours? Really dry with toasted edges?"

The server held his gaze for a few moments, as if unsure whether or not she was being put on. She was a student probably, likely at one of the nearby law schools. Odessa had put herself through her third year of law school in Boston waiting tables, and she acutely remembered the uneasy feeling she got when certain male customers made vaguely creepy, borderline fetishistic food requests—usually loners, men who she suspected wished that they could order women off menus, not just food.

The server glanced at Odessa sitting across from Leppo. Odessa offered an encouraging smile, hoping to set the fellow young woman at ease.

"Just let me check," she said.

"Thank you," he said, closing his menu and handing it to her. "By the way, I prefer the end pieces."

She left with their orders. Walt added to Odessa, "We used to call the end pieces the heels."

Odessa nodded as though fascinated. She said, pleasantly, "Serial killer."

Walt shrugged. "Because I like my meat loaf the way my mother used to make it?"

"Oh God. Add one oral fixation."

"You know what, Dessa? I got news for you: Everything can be sexualized. Everything. Even meat loaf, apparently."

"I bet you like your toast burnt, too."

"Like a slice of charcoal. But didn't you get the regulation about rookies not being allowed to profile veteran agents?"

Both their heads turned when the first drops of rain began tapping at the other side of the picture window at the front of the Soup Spoon Café.

Leppo said, "Oh great."

Odessa checked her phone. The weather app radar

showed a mass of precipitation in shades of jade and mint approaching Newark like a cloud of toxic gas. She turned it around so that Leppo could see. Her umbrella happened to be locked next to the Remington 870 twelve-gauge shotgun inside the trunk of their car, parked half a block up the street.

"Jersey rain," said Leppo, unfolding his napkin. "Like hosing down a dog. Everything gets wet, nothing gets clean."

Odessa smiled at yet another "Leppo-ism," looking outside as more drops strafed the window. The few people outside moved more quickly now, with a blurry sense of urgency.

Things speeding up.

At the very same moment Leppo was asking about meat loaf (as later chronologies would bear out), a dozen miles north of Newark, Evan Aronson was on hold with his health insurance provider, listening to soft 1970s rock while waiting to question a surcharge for a recent emergency room visit. At his ten-year Rutgers reunion a few weeks before, Evan had torn his left biceps during a re-creation of his Greek brothers' traditional late-night porta-potty leap, as he attempted to catch his former fraternity house roommate, Brad "Boomer" Bordonsky, despite Boomer having packed on a solid thirty pounds since graduation.

While enduring another one of Styx's greatest hits, Evan looked up from his desk in the Charter Airliners office at Teterboro Airport and watched as a late-model Beechcraft Baron G58 taxied out of the nearby private aviation hangar. The pilot, tall and in his fifties, climbed out of the cockpit of the million-dollar twin-engine piston aircraft. The man wore gray track pants, a long-sleeved pullover, and sandals. He disappeared back inside the hangar, leaving the aircraft engines running outside. A hangar attendant exchanged a few words with him and then moved away.

Moments later, the pilot returned holding a very large wrench.

Pilots, but especially owner-pilots, do not perform their own aircraft repairs. Not with the plane's twin three-hundred-horsepower engines still on, propellers rotating faster than the eye can track. Evan stood out of his chair to get a better look at the pilot, standing there with his left arm in a sling, his right arm holding the telephone receiver, connected by a cord to the base on his desk due to airport radio frequency regulations.

Under the whine of the turbine, Evan heard a loud pop—and a simultaneous crunch.

He heard it again, struggling now to see the pilot, who was apparently working behind the Beechcraft's fuselage. The tall man came around to the near wing, and Evan watched as he swung the large wrench at the running lamp—popping the seal on impact, crunching the red plastic casing, pieces of which fell to the tarmac as the lightbulb went dark.

Evan gasped audibly, so obscene was this act of violence against an aircraft worth millions of dollars. Evan stretched the phone cord to full length, the soft ballad "Lady" providing a weird counterpoint to the sight of a plane owner vandalizing his own property.

These high-end private jets were both babied like pampered pets and rigorously maintained like race cars. What this man was doing was tantamount to putting out the eyes of a champion racehorse with a screwdriver.

This couldn't be an owner at all, Evan decided. Someone was causing thousands of dollars of damage to this aircraft...and perhaps stealing it.

"Mr. Aronson, I have your file in front of me..." came the insurance representative's voice—but Evan had to drop the receiver, letting it clatter against the floor, its cord recoiling to the desk. He rushed out the office door straight into the needle-sharp drops of cold rain, looking left and right, hoping someone else was seeing this and could help him.

The tall man finished with the last lightbulb, the

aircraft now cloaked in darkness. A small emergency light backlit the scene.

"HEY!" yelled Evan, waving his one good arm. He jogged a few steps toward the scene, yelling "HEY!" a few more times, both at the tall man and in either direction, hoping to rouse somebody with two working arms.

A hangar attendant approached the pilot, trying to stop him. Three downward wrench blows caved in the right side of the attendant's head—the attack lasting only seconds. The attendant collapsed on the ground, rattled by death spasms.

The pilot crouched and went to work on the rest of the skull, like a caveman finishing his kill.

Evan froze. His mind could not process such violent terror.

The pilot tossed the wrench to the side with a great clanking and walked perilously close to the left propeller, rounding it, climbing up onto the wing, settling inside the glass cockpit.

The aircraft jerked forward and started rolling.

The only light in the plane was that of the cockpit avionics, a cool green-blue LCD Garmin G1000 display. Evan thought it lit the pilot's face like an alien's.

He was transfixed by the dead look in the man's eyes.

Mechanically, the man reached for something in

the cockpit beneath Evan's line of sight. Suddenly there was an explosion of sound and flame, shattering the right-side window. Rounds from the AK-47 semiautomatic rifle ripped into Evan's body like hot nails, buckling his knees, his body collapsing, his head smacking the tarmac, knocking him instantly unconscious.

As the darkened Beechcraft turned toward the taxiway, Evan bled to death peacefully.

Odessa had the steak salad. No onions, because she didn't want the taste in her mouth all night. She ordered coffee because it was the middle of their shift and that is what FBI agents drink.

"Did you know," Leppo said after the server left, "there is more trace amount of human feces on menus than anywhere else inside a restaurant?"

Odessa brought a tiny tube of hand sanitizer out of her bag, setting it upon the table as though she were attacking on a chessboard.

Leppo liked her, she could tell. He had a grown daughter of his own, so he projected and understood. He liked taking her under his wing. There were no assigned partners in the FBI. He wanted to show her the ropes, teach her "the right way" to do things. And she wanted to learn.

"My pop sold kitchen supplies everywhere in the five boroughs for thirty years until his pump gave out," he said. "And he always said—and this might be the most important lesson I can teach you as a third-year agent—that the hallmark of a clean restaurant is its bathroom. If the bathroom is hygienic, orderly, and well maintained, you can be assured the food prep area is safe, too. Know why?"

She had a guess, but it was better to let him pontificate.

"Because the same underpaid Chilean or Salvadoran immigrant who cleans the restrooms also cleans the kitchen. The entire food service industry—and you could make an argument for civilization itself—hinges on the performance of these frontline workers."

Odessa said, "Immigrants, they get the job done."

"Heroes," said Leppo, proposing a toast with his coffee mug. "Now if only they could do a better job cleaning menus."

Odessa smiled, then tasted onion in her salad and made a disappointed face.

The first emergency call came from Teterboro, saying a private jet had taken off without tower authorization. The aircraft had banked due east, over Moonachie and across Interstate 95 toward the Hudson River. The aircraft was assumed stolen and flying in an erratic pattern, rising and falling a few thousand feet in altitude, occasionally disappearing below the range of the radar.

The Port Authority of New York and New Jersey issued an emergency alert. Teterboro was shut down in accordance with FAA regulations, suspending all pending flights and redirecting inbound air traffic to Linden Municipal Airport, a small airfield in southern New Jersey used primarily for sightseeing tours and helicopters.

The first citizen 911 call came from the operator of a tugboat in the Hudson River, less than a mile south of the George Washington Bridge. He claimed that an airplane with no lights had flown very low between the tug and the bridge, making "popping noises" in the rain. The operator said it sounded like the pilot was throwing firecrackers at his boat, and feared it was the start of "another Nine Eleven."

The second 911 call came from a fashion executive driving home to Fort Lee on the George Washington Bridge who reported seeing "a large drone" headed toward the Upper West Side of Manhattan.

There followed a flood of emergency calls from Manhattan residents, claiming that an aircraft had buzzed their apartment building or place of employment. The airplane was spotted over Central Park, heading due south along Fifth Avenue, but difficult to eyeball as it was flying dark. The pattern of the calls traced a flight path cutting diagonally across Lower Manhattan over Greenwich Village, then back toward the Hudson.

The Staten Island Ferry was cruising within sight of the Statue of Liberty when the Beechcraft swooped down on its stern. The only lights were the bursts of flame from the muzzle of the automatic rifle firing out the right side of the cockpit. Rounds picked at the orange hull of the MV *Andrew J. Barberi*, some cracking through the windows of the passenger space. Two commuters were directly injured by gunfire, neither gravely. Seventeen passengers were more seriously injured in the ensuing panic, causing the ferry to turn around and return to the Lower Manhattan terminal.

Three bullet holes were later found in the copper exterior of the crown and torch of the Statue of Liberty, but no injuries were reported there.

The Beechcraft made a hard turn west, back into New Jersey airspace. It was spotted over Elizabeth on a course heading toward Newark, New Jersey's most populous city, knifing through the evening rain.

Newark Liberty International Airport was closed, and air traffic diverted.

Reports followed of a second aircraft over southern New Jersey, but these were later confirmed as sightings of the same aircraft.

The aircraft's altitude dipped as low as one hundred feet at times. An eagle-eyed bus passenger on a bright section of the Jersey Turnpike noted the N number on the plane's fuselage and texted it to the state police.

Twin F-15 fighter jets were dispatched from Otis Air National Guard Base on Cape Cod, flying toward Manhattan at supersonic speed.

Police sirens pierced the night all across the metro Newark area as cruisers raced toward airplane sightings, but ground municipal deployment was completely ineffective. Within minutes the aircraft was sighted over the Pulaski Skyway, then Weequahic, then Newark Bay, then the MetLife Stadium in the Meadowlands.

"How's the meat loaf?" Odessa asked.

He responded with his mouth full of it, "Best I ever had."

Odessa shook her head, then caught the server's attention with a shake of her empty coffee mug. She was going to need the caffeine. They were working on the Cary Peters corruption case, the former deputy chief of staff to the governor of New Jersey ensnared in a widening scandal. Peters had resigned three months ago in what now looked like an attempt to squelch the investigation and keep it from moving inside the governor's office. The active part of the case had only recently died down. The ensuing scandal had rocked Peters's personal life, as well as his professional life. (Reimbursing oneself $1,700 for a night at Scores gentlemen's club from your boss's campaign fund will do that.) Taking a bullet for the governor had come at a great cost. Television news and tabloid reporters swarmed all over his and his wife's and family's lives as they were going through a white-hot breakup. It got so bad that the city of Montclair, where they lived, established NO PARKING zones outside his house on the advice of the police department, in order to keep the zealous press away. Peters had since gone into a tailspin that included being booked for a DWI earlier in the month. One online news site maintained a counter on its homepage estimating the number of days before Peters cracked and cut a deal with prosecutors to save his own skin, turning on the governor in this rapidly widening scandal.

For the FBI, and specifically for Leppo and Odessa, the investigation had entered the paperwork stage. The FBI headquarters at Claremont Tower was working around the clock thanks to recently released documents from the statehouse and the governor's campaign committee. Odessa and Leppo had spent each of the previous four nights reading through emails, employee contract agreements, and expense reports. Most investigative work in the modern digital age involves forensic computer analysis and decoding the voluminous digital footprints and fingerprints we all leave behind.

This is why the FBI likes to hire lawyers.

This dinner in this iffy diner in a blighted section of one of the most dangerous cities in America was Odessa's only respite from the nightly document slog. With that in mind, she could have listened to Leppo talking with his mouth full all night.

Their phones, both screen-down on the table, simultaneously began to vibrate. They quickly checked them, knowing that it was never good news when their phones bugged out at the same time.

Surprisingly, it was not a text about work. It was a news alert from the *New York Times*. An airplane hijacked out of Teterboro had buzzed Manhattan with unconfirmed reports of automatic gunfire coming from the cockpit. Live updates scrolled below the headline report. The aircraft had apparently crossed the Hudson River. Its most recent sighting was near Newark.

"Shit," said Leppo. He forked a huge chunk of meat loaf into his mouth while plucking his napkin from his lap. Odessa knew that her coffee would have to wait. It was always better to get moving first, rather than being called upon to respond. Odessa quickly visited the ladies' room, as experience had taught her, while Leppo went to the front cashier with his credit card.

Leppo was already outside in the rain with a free real estate circular tented over his head when Odessa hit the door. At a break in the headlights, they crossed the street under the cold rain, skirting a gutter puddle and striding north toward their unmarked silver Chevy Impala.

With the falling rain and the automobile tires whisking along the wet asphalt beside them, Odessa did not hear the airplane's twin engines until they were almost immediately over her head. The dark plane knifed through the stringy rain, wings pitched slightly to one side, the underbelly of the fuselage passing not two hundred feet above them.

It was there, and then it was gone. Unreal.

"Jesus," said Leppo.

Odessa stopped so fast, Leppo bumped into her from behind.

Sirens replaced the fading roar of the plane's engines. A cruiser went screaming past them into the cross street as Odessa slid into the driver's seat of the Impala.

Leppo was already on his phone, talking to somebody at Claremont. The top six floors of the Claremont Tower overlooked Newark from the shore of the narrow brown Passaic River.

"Where to?" Odessa asked him, watching more blue lights plow through the spit.

"Don't bother trying to follow it," said Leppo, pointing her left at the intersection. Back to Claremont, then.

Leppo punched the phone audio through the Bluetooth of the automobile dash. "Davey, we were on dinner, we just saw it, what's the word?"

"Terror bid," said Davey. "They've scrambled jets from Otis."

"Otis air base," said Leppo, incredulous. "To do what? Shoot it down over Hoboken?"

"If that's what it takes. He's been back and forth across the Hudson, stunting, doing fly-bys, shooting up the city."

"Give me what you got on the 'he.'"

Odessa pulled over for another police cruiser, which went blasting past, going the opposite direction they were.

"Plane is reg'd to the CEO of Stow-Away Corporation. That's a rental storage facility company, those big, boxy orange buildings. Suspected stolen, though. We have one dead on the ground at Teterboro, an airport worker. Hold on, Walt—"

The audio went muffled as Davey put his hand over the microphone, calling out to another agent nearby. Odessa and Leppo looked at each other.

"Stow-Away," she said, feeling a dark ping in her chest.

Leppo nodded. "Not good."

The CEO of Stow-Away, a man named Isaac Meerson, was a major donor to the New Jersey Republican Party . . . and a close friend of the governor of New Jersey, and Cary Peters.

"Can't be," said Leppo.

"What can't be?" said Davey, coming back on the line.

"Stow-Away is getting pulled into the Peters corruption case Hardwicke and I have been working. Any description of the hijacker?"

"The pilot? No. I'll check."

Odessa was at a red light. The wipers worked frantically, making the traffic light look like it was flashing. "What should we do?"

"I don't know," said Leppo. "Can't be related to us. Right?"

"Peters has been depressed and basically off the grid," said Odessa. "There was that thing about the wife in the paper yesterday—"

"Her filing for divorce? No surprise there, though."

"No," said Odessa. "Still..."

Odessa knew Leppo well enough to sense that he was keying in on Peters now. "Stealing a plane? That's way outside his profile."

"He had taken flying lessons," she said. "Remember? Stopped short of getting his license due to anxiety attacks. That was all on his background."

Leppo nodded. He didn't know what to do. He said, "Shit shit shit shit shit."

Davey's voice came back again. "Okay, I've got nothing on the hijacker yet."

"Forget about that, Davey," said Leppo. "What's the plane's last known position?"

"Northwest from Newark," he said. "Over Glen Ridge. That's the latest I got. Hey, Walt, I gotta go—"

"Go, yeah," said Leppo, killing the call.

"Heading toward Montclair," said Odessa. It was all happening so fast. "Do you think...?"

Leppo finished her thought. "He would crash an airplane into his own house?"

Odessa said, "It's not going to be his house for very long. His wife's house."

Leppo nodded. It was decided. "Light it up."

Odessa reached under the center console, flipping the switch that activated the Impala's grille lights, blue and red, front and rear. She punched the gas and started weaving through traffic toward the nearby town of Montclair.

The aerial distraction caused multiple automobile accidents on the streets below, the worst being a seven-car pileup on the Garden State Parkway that snarled northbound traffic in a hopeless gridlock.

After a brief rise in altitude over East Orange, the airplane banked west and dipped below radar yet again. The aircraft's left wing clipped a treetop over Nishuane Park, but the pilot leveled out the plane and flew on. Observers theorized that the pilot was looking for a place to land, or perhaps a familiar landmark to use for navigation.

Minutes later, the airplane dropped completely out of sight.

The first report of a plane crash came from west of Orange. Police and rescue vehicles from surrounding towns were dispatched to the area, awaiting the precise location. But after much searching and radio back-and-forth, the report was debunked as false.

The Beechcraft twin engine had set down on the first hole of the Second Nine course of the Montclair Golf Club: a straightaway, downhill par five. The plane bounced twice on its wheels, the left wing slicing a deep divot in the fairway, turning the aircraft sharply left where its wheel sank into a sand trap, and finally stopping nose-down on the edge of the trees.

Later, an eyewitness would report what he had seen. He had pulled into the golf course parking lot in order to continue an emotional telephone call with his roommate, and was standing outside of his vehicle, pacing and talking, when he saw a man exit the nearby wooded area, walking fast. He reported that the man appeared to be unaware that he was bleeding on the right side of his forehead, looking at the eyewitness with what he described as "dead eyes." He thought at the time that the man was in shock, and called to him, ignoring his telephone conversation. But the bleeding man did not respond, instead striding toward the eyewitness's still-running Jeep Trailhawk and climbing inside. With the eyewitness chasing after him, the man drove out of the golf course parking lot at high speed, not closing the driver's-side door until the Jeep was almost out of sight.

The Impala's flashing lights helped Odessa pass other cars, but traffic was jammed up everywhere. Leppo worked his phone navigation, calling out direction changes, taking them on side roads to Peters's wife's home in Upper Montclair.

They had already decided not to call it in to local PD. "This is a hunch," said Leppo. "Besides, they're busy enough. Last thing we want to do is draw away resources on a bad call."

Odessa said, "You don't think the plane is terror?"

"If so, it will be over soon. The fighter jets will see to that. If not…then it's a guy at the end of his rope. Someone who's got three kids and a restraining order and no way back to the life he once enjoyed."

Odessa went back and forth in her mind about this. It was a long shot—never mind a huge coincidence—that this could be Cary Peters. Chances were slim.

Then again, the airplane was owned by the storage company tied up in his scandal. That alone was a major link.

"Divorce makes you crazy," said Leppo. "I don't think I ever told you this, but I was married before Debonair."

Leppo's wife of nearly twenty years was named Deb, but he called her "Debonair." She was a tiny woman with red Medusa hair who drove a massive red Chevy Tahoe SUV. Odessa had met her exactly twice, the first time just a few weeks after her partnering with Leppo, which was very much a sniffing-out session, Odessa presenting herself in as nonthreatening a manner as possible. Debonair had been sweet to her, outgoing and friendly, but beneath it all was a strength that Odessa responded to, and admired. The second time had been at a weekend thing for agents, a cookout, where Odessa met Leppo's kids and Debonair got to meet Linus, Odessa's boyfriend, and from that moment forward everything was good.

Leppo said, "I was young, we both were. It didn't last a year, but it took me another two years after that to recover. And thank God there weren't any kids involved. Peters, it's hard to tell, but he doesn't seem like the type to go over a cliff like this. Take it from me, though. You never truly know who you are until you get really, deeply hurt."

Odessa nodded. Sometimes the work lessons spilled over into life lessons.

"You know where you are now?" he said.

She took a hard left in the upscale neighborhood. "Almost there," she said.

The streets were empty, a bedroom community if ever there was one. Odessa zoomed past well-tended lawns and brightly lit houses, which reassured her: Nothing very terrible could happen here.

"Oh shit," said Leppo.

He saw it before she did: a Jeep parked up on the curb, its driver's-side door open. The lights were on, the engine still running.

She pulled right up on the rear bumper of the Jeep to block it and prevent it from backing out.

Leppo was calling in the address. They were going in.

Odessa jumped out, her hand on her holstered duty pistol, hurrying wide around the open door. The interior lights showed the Jeep to be empty. The vehicle had come to a stop on top of a street sign it had impacted and knocked down: one designating the NO PARKING zone.

She turned to the house. It was a two-story Tudor Revival with steeply pitched roofs jettied over the first floor. Lights shone inside, downstairs and up. The front door was closed. The driveway, to her left, rose to a half wall made of stone, leading to a side entrance that was unlit.

She was turning back to look for Leppo when she heard the gunshot. Startled, she whirled around just in time to hear the second shot inside the house, and see a burst of flame light in the dormer window of an upstairs bedroom.

"Leppo!" she called, pulling her Glock.

"Here we go!" he said, sounding muffled and far away.

Odessa's ears were ringing, not from the sound of the gunshot, but from the adrenaline surging through her bloodstream, a muffled rhythm, *bhmpp-bhmpp*. She waited for Leppo, only to see him run past her up the driveway. She raced after him, gun aimed down and away.

The side storm door was closed, the interior door open. Leppo went in first. Odessa listened for voices, footsteps, anything—but the noise in her head was too loud. Her own voice rose sharply so that she could hear herself over the din.

"FBI! FBI!"

Leppo was yelling the same ahead of her. "Drop your weapons, FBI!"

Odessa heard no response. She didn't believe Leppo did, either. He pushed on ahead into the kitchen, Odessa following, slowing at a closed closet door.

She shoved open the door with her foot, gun forward. Not a closet but a walk-in pantry. On the floor before her lay an adult female, arms straight down by her sides. Her throat had been cut. The flesh on her palms was slashed with defensive wounds.

Odessa yelled "BODY!" alerting Leppo, but she did not expect him to return. Odessa followed her training to the letter. She went around the spreading pool of blood to check the woman's pulse, finding her throat warm still, but no throb whatsoever, no sign of life. The act of pushing her thumb up under the woman's chin caused the neck wound to open a bit. Air or gas gurgled out of the gap in a big, bright bubble of blood.

A warm wave of nausea surged from Odessa's

torso right up into her throat, and she staggered backward. The sick feeling lingered but she did not lose it. She felt weightless, numb. Odessa was certain she knew the woman's face. It was Peters's estranged wife.

The identification brought her back into herself. One thought occurred to her:

Three children.

Suddenly she was sharp again. She had to be. Her senses cleared—and at once she heard screaming. Coming from upstairs.

Odessa hurried out of the pantry. She made her way through the kitchen, finding the bottom of the stairs, looking up. "LEPPO!" She called Walt's name again, wanting to know his location, and also needing him to know she was coming up the stairs. Friendly fire was something they had drilled on at the FBI Academy every week.

More screaming now. Odessa started running up the steps two at a time.

"LEPPO!"

She scanned the hallway; it was vacant. Blue light pulsed through a street-facing window: local police support arriving out on the street. The cop lights should have been reassuring, but instead the flashing blue gave the second-floor landing a disorienting fun-house effect.

She moved into the first doorway she saw. The

room was peach and pink, all soft colors, ruffle on the comforter of the unmade bed.

Next to the bed, under a bloody sheet on the floor, lay a small human form.

Not real, it can't be real.

Odessa flipped the sheet back from one end, just enough to view a small bare foot, ankle, and thin calf. She didn't need to see the wounded body. She didn't want to see the face.

Back out into the hallway. Hyperventilating, ears screaming, her vision rising and falling like a ship in a storm. *"LEPPO!"*

A second bedroom waited ahead. Inside the open door, a New York Rangers hockey poster hung on the wall, splattered with thick arterial spray. The faint scent of iron hung in the air...

The bed was empty, no body on the floor. Odessa's eyes darted frantically about the small, dark room.

The closet. A sliding door, half open. Odessa shoved it fully open, fast—

A young boy's body was inside, slumped like a rag doll against the rear wall, dead-eyed, staring.

Not real, it's not real—

Odessa spun around, gun up. The room was empty behind her. It was all happening too fast.

A hard thumping against the wall from the adjoining room to her left caused a picture frame to fall off and shatter. Yelling, a struggle—another bump against the wall.

A fight?

"LEPPO!"

Odessa tore out into the flashing blue hallway. As soon as she turned toward the next door, two adult men came crashing out of the adjoining room.

Odessa went into a three-point stance. She made Leppo immediately in the crazed blue light. He was struggling with a male assailant. The assailant turned his head enough so that Odessa recognized Cary Peters's face. He was wearing track pants and there were bloodstains on the knees and the tops of his bare feet.

A knife. The blade glinted, glowing blue. It was a kitchen carving knife with a thick handle. Odessa saw it in Leppo's hand. This didn't make any sense in her split-second read.

A knife, not a gun? Where is Leppo's Glock?

"DOWN ON THE FLOOR—NOW!—OR I'LL SHOOT!" she yelled.

Leppo was behind Peters, gripping him with both arms, one fist gripping the knife. They grappled. Peters was shoving the heel of his left hand up into Leppo's chin and mouth, trying to push him off. His right hand gripped Leppo's wrist, holding back the knife. With great effort in the middle of this life-and-death struggle, the disgraced ex–deputy chief of staff twisted his torso around in order to look at Odessa with an expression she would never, ever forget.

Not the rage-eyed, lunatic aggression that she expected. He looked to her for help. A pleading expression. He appeared bewildered and desperate, even with his wife's and children's blood smeared on his face, on his hands.

He looked at her with the confused, disoriented eyes of a man waking up from a vivid and terrifying nightmare.

He continued to struggle with Leppo, but now it looked like he was fighting off the older man— like Leppo was the aggressor. Odessa only now truly processed that Leppo held the knife. He was wielding the assailant's weapon. Peters, however it happened, was unarmed.

"WALT!"

All he had to do was shove Peters down. He had the advantage. Odessa had Peters at point-blank range. It was over.

"BACK OFF, I GOT HIM!"

If she fired now, the round would explode through Peters and strike Leppo. But nothing she was saying got through to her fellow agent.

Peters turned away from Odessa, losing the struggle, Leppo's knife arm rising by his shoulder. Peters took his hand off Leppo's chin and throat and moved it to his arm, fighting him for possession of the knife.

Peters cried, "Don't...please!"

Odessa screamed: *"LAST WARNING!"*

With a burst of wild strength, Peters shoved Leppo off him, back against the side wall. Leppo was clear. Peters turned to Odessa, holding out his hand, saying, "No—!"

Odessa fired twice.

Peters went down backward, dropping hard. He clutched his chest where both rounds had opened him up, writhing on the carpet runner, arcing his back. Odessa held her shooting stance, her aim staying on his midsection. Peters sucked air, his breath groaning, his chest wounds hissing. His eyes flickered, for the briefest moment, with odd recognition—as if he had just woken and found himself lost—and then the eyes froze, a single tear streaking down his left cheek.

Odessa had shot a man. He was bleeding out. She was watching him die.

She never looked at Leppo.

Peters's body flattened and he lay still. The agonal sounds in his chest became a high-pitched sigh like a tire going flat. His eyes glazed, became dull.

It was over.

Odessa exhaled her own breath, the one she hadn't known she had been holding since she fired.

"I killed him," she said to Leppo but mostly to herself. "I put him down."

It was then that Odessa became aware of two things almost simultaneously: a faint burning smell—like burnt soldering paste—and a girl's voice, crying and calling from another bedroom, faint under the arriving sirens outside.

"Help me! Who's there?"

The third Peters child. Still alive—unhurt.

Odessa found it difficult to take her eyes off Peters's body. Peripherally, she saw Leppo turn and start toward the last bedroom at the end of the hall. Going to comfort the only surviving member of the Peters family.

Odessa started to relax. She straightened and took one step forward, looking over the man she had killed.

Ahead of her, Leppo slowed a moment as he reached the doorway, before entering. Odessa looked up, and as Leppo disappeared into the room, Odessa saw the knife still in his hand.

Odessa's first thought was that this was bad procedure. The murder weapon was evidence and must be treated as such.

She yelled after him, "Leppo!"—calling his name down the hallway over the barefoot killer she had shot dead. The soles of his feet were dirty, almost black, and that made it somewhat more tragic; sordid.

He was gone. And for a moment she was alone in the blue flashing hallway with the man she had shot.

Odessa felt sick. It was different from the nausea she'd experienced upon discovering Mrs. Peters's savaged corpse. Most FBI agents never fire their sidearm in the line of duty. There was going to be an inquest. Thank God she had Leppo as an eyewitness.

Odessa stepped around Peters's corpse, unable to look away as she passed. His bloodstained hands still lay over his chest wounds, his eyes staring straight up at the ceiling and beyond.

She approached the bedroom with her gun lowered, not wanting to scare the surviving Peters child. She stepped into the open doorway Leppo had moved through.

The nine-year-old girl wore warm soft-yellow pajamas covered with images of cartoon baby chicks hatching from smiling white eggs. Walt Leppo stood just behind her, holding a handful of her blond hair in his fist. Her mouth was open but no scream came out. Her body was twisted, trying to pull away from Leppo, but her hair was firmly in his grip.

Leppo's other hand gripped the carving knife, not as one would handle a vital piece of evidence, but wielding it like a weapon, blade pointing down.

35

Odessa's mind tried to bring order to what she was witnessing: *Maybe Leppo is holding the girl in order to keep her from running off. He's only trying to prevent her from seeing her father's dead body out in the hallway, and the bodies of her brother, sister, and mother.*

But this split-second rationalization did not match up with the look she saw on Leppo's face. The doll-eyed menace, his twisted grin. It was almost as though he were showing the girl the knife and its blood-slicked blade.

"Leppo?" said Odessa.

It didn't make sense. Leppo did not seem to even know Odessa was in the room with him. He lifted the knife, turning his head to look at the blade himself, while the girl bucked her head, trying to break his strong grip.

"Walt, put it down," said Odessa. "Walt! Put the knife down!"

She couldn't believe she was saying these words. Odessa found herself aiming her Glock at him. She was drawing down on a fellow agent. It went against every instinct she had.

Leppo looked back at the girl. He yanked her hair back even harder, leaving her tender throat fully exposed. Something was very wrong.

In that moment, Odessa could feel what was going to come next.

"LEPPO!" Odessa screamed.

Without any warning, Walt Leppo stabbed downward. The blade sliced through flesh, bone, and cartilage and got stuck in the girl's clavicle and shoulder—a sickening, muffled bone crack audible as Leppo struggled to disengage the knife and the shoulder popped out of its socket.

The girl screamed.

Odessa fired twice on pure reflex. The Glock jumped in her hands.

The force of the impact pushed Leppo off the girl. He pinwheeled back into a nightstand next to the bed, still holding her hair.

The girl fell with him, bleeding, howling, landing on him. She jerked away, her hair released from his grip. Three thick strands of ripped hair stayed on Leppo's hand.

The girl crawled away quickly on all fours into the far corner of the room.

Leppo's fall knocked a humidifier off the nightstand, the jug coming loose as it fell to the floor, water glugging into the carpet. Leppo crumpled against the side of the bed, sliding down, his body settling, his shoulders and head leaning against the bed frame at an unnatural angle.

Odessa stood frozen in place. She cried out, "Leppo!" as though he had been shot by someone else, even as she stared at him over the barrel of her smoking gun.

Loud voices called out from downstairs. Cops in the house, finally.

Leppo's horrible grin relaxed, his eyes losing their focus. As she stood there staring, unable to believe what had just happened, Odessa saw something...

A mist, looking like a ripple of heat mirage, rose from Leppo's twisted form. A presence in the room, hovering like swamp gas. No color, only—again—the odor of burnt solder, different from the cordite smoke still wisping out of her gun barrel...

Leppo's body sagged perceptibly, as though something, some entity, had fled his body as he died.

When the Montclair cops burst inside the bedroom, they found a young woman sitting on the floor with her arms around a sobbing, trembling nine-year-old girl with a deep knife wound on her shoulder. A middle-aged man lay slumped against the girl's nightstand and bed, dead from two gunshot wounds. The young woman pulled one arm away from the thrashing, wailing girl, showing the armed police officers her FBI badge.

"Agent down..." Odessa said, hyperventilating. "Agent down..."

1962. The Mississippi Delta.

He was briefed on the investigation by a supervisory special agent on the short predawn flight from Knoxville into Jackson, Mississippi. The particulars of the case featured many notable peculiarities, but the fact that the Bureau had chartered an airplane to expedite his immediate reassignment to the Jackson Field Office—he, Earl Solomon, a twenty-eight-year-old rookie FBI special agent just four months graduated from the academy—indicated above all else that this was to be no ordinary inquiry.

A sedan picked him up from the airport tarmac for the long ride north on Route 49 into the Delta. Aside from an initial, perfunctory greeting, the driver, a white agent in his late thirties with a twang in his voice that was just this side of hillbilly, remained silent during the ride, preferring to flick cigarette ashes out his open window rather than dirty the dashboard ashtray. Solomon understood the dynamic. He also understood why he had been dispatched to this tinderbox of civil rights activism and violence. It had nothing to do with his abilities as an agent, nor with his experience, which was almost nil. A disturbing number of lynchings had occurred recently in the Delta, and the Federal Bureau of Investigation was being stonewalled by local law enforcement. They needed to present a black face to the locals.

Solomon was one of the first three black agents accepted into the FBI Academy earlier that year. In his few months in Knoxville, he had gotten along fairly well with his fellow agents, most of whom had military experience and so had previous exposure to integration. Solomon supposed he had endured no more than any other green agent learning the ropes through the most menial assignments. When the call came in the middle of the night for him to report to the office, he didn't know what to expect, but it certainly wasn't a flight to Jackson, Mississippi, to join his first active criminal investigation. His special agent in charge in Knoxville intimated that the reassignment order may have come directly from Mr. Hoover himself. Solomon felt the eyes of the Bureau upon him.

Because this was no ordinary investigation. Another lynching had occurred, this one in a remote, wooded thicket, apparently with ritualistic aspects at the scene. Local law had cited irreligious characteristics of the crime, reported as "satanism," but there were no crime scene photographs yet and local law was notoriously unreliable. That wasn't the most incendiary part of this homicide, however.

This time the lynching was of a white man.

The local agent drove him northwest from Jackson, up Route 49, north of Greenwood, well west of Oxford. The town was called Gibbston, a fertile stretch of land between the Mississippi and the Yazoo Rivers where cotton—and the white race—was king.

They pulled up outside the post office, a small shack that looked like a bait shop with a faded federal shield on the door. The Jackson agent got out and waited for Solomon to join him, though never looking Solomon in the eye. They crossed the street to a clutch of white men in suits without jackets, fanning themselves with their hats, mopping their brows with sweat-dampened handkerchiefs. Solomon was introduced to the local sheriff, two deputies, and the Jackson special agent in charge, whose last name was Macklin.

"When they said they were sending somebody named Solomon to help with the interviews," said Macklin, "I told them we needed a Negro, not a Jew."

Macklin's mouth unzipped a thin-lipped smile that revealed his teeth the way a surgeon's incision reveals interior organs. The other men smiled also and waited for Solomon to respond, so that they would know what kind of Negro they had on their hands here. Solomon looked each man in the eye, letting them twist in suspense a few moments longer than necessary, then nodded and smiled. He needed their help, and he was the low man on the totem pole—if he was even on the totem pole.

There was more idle talk, but Solomon became distracted, his attention tuned to singing in the nearby church. There was, in the congregation's voices, none of the joy he associated with a Southern Baptist service:

He goes before me,
And is beside me,
So I am not afraid.

It was a mournful song. There was great anxiety in the air, hanging oppressively along with the heat and the humidity. Assigning Solomon here showed desperation on the part of the FBI, perhaps at the direction of the White House. Dispatching him to Gibbston to liaise with the Negro community in the Deep South was akin to sending a Communist to listen to the concerns of pinkos.

The service ended and the churchgoers started filing out. Dressed in their Sunday best, they made their way down the steps to the dirt sidewalk, the men replacing their hats upon their heads.

Macklin and the others had advice for Solomon. "Just let them see you here, let 'em get curious. You don't want to scare anybody."

But Solomon knew that Sunday morning from eleven A.M. to noon was the only time the majority of the local black community would or could assemble. Missing this opportunity meant waiting another week at the very least.

He said as much to SAIC Macklin.

"No," Macklin told him, "we'll go around and do some interviews individually later today and tomorrow."

Solomon watched the churchgoers saying their goodbyes and getting ready to disperse. He thought that there was an element of...if not fear, then trepidation, in Macklin's desire for him to avoid this crowd.

"Sir," said Solomon, already stepping into the street, "I'm going."

Solomon got halfway there before he realized the men were following him. Solomon couldn't have that. Why was he here, otherwise?

"Sirs," he said, "I think it best you wait here."

And they did. Solomon continued across the

street, and he saw the congregants watching him come. They saw that he had stopped the white lawmen from accompanying him. They were stunned that a young black man had such authority.

"Good day, ladies and gentlemen," he said, introducing himself to the silent observers. "I am Special Agent Earl Solomon." He showed them his badge and ID card from his flip book, then replaced it inside his jacket breast pocket. He noticed many of them looking past him at the white lawmen across the street. "The Bureau dispatched me here to Gibbston to assist in the investigation of the homicides by lynching."

The pastor emerged from the church doors, stopping on the top step, behind the faithful. He had shed his robe, dressed in an open-necked white cotton shirt and dark slacks, mopping at his brow. A blaze of silver in his black hair distinguished him with the effect of a candle in the darkness.

Solomon nodded to him respectfully, but felt an unusual suspicion in the preacher's manner. Perhaps the pastor was simply unused to another black man compelling the attention of his assembled faithful.

Solomon continued, "You should know that the federal government is interested in hearing your concerns and bringing an end to this violence. Your rights are to be protected. I am here looking for any information whatsoever any one of you might have pertaining to any of the recent murders."

Their faces. Looking back and forth from the local sheriff behind him to Solomon. He stood before them like an emissary from another planet.

A burly man in his fifties plucked at the placket of his shirt for ventilation. "You a company man," he said.

Solomon dipped his head to one side, allowing that. "Yes, I am. The company is the FBI and I am its agent."

"And we are to trust you?"

"I think you have to start somewhere."

Another man pulled off his wire-rimmed eyeglasses, polishing the lenses on his necktie. "I heard 'bout you. The first agents. Read a story in *Jet* magazine. They trying to integrate the FBI."

"Yessir, that's correct," said Solomon.

"He's just a child," said a trim older woman in a stiff blue dress.

"A child with a badge," said another man.

The older woman said, "Now that a white man's been strung up, they send you."

"I go where I'm assigned," said Solomon. "What matters is, I'm here now."

"Get us to snitch," said the older woman. "Make some arrests for the white lynching and vanish out of here."

Solomon took care to nod respectfully to her when he said, "No, ma'am."

Solomon looked to the pastor. No outward indication in his manner, but he knew he needed this man of God's help. The pastor wrinkled up his nose a bit, like sweat from the noonday sun was getting to his upper lip.

"Brothers and sisters," he said, "I believe that this man, Agent...?"

"Agent Solomon."

"Agent Solomon, who shares the name of a wise and wealthy king of antiquity, deserves a chance to prove himself as a man of justice. I am going to step back inside God's house, and in the event anyone has any insight to share with him, they should feel free and unfettered to do so."

With that, the pastor stepped back inside the church and closed the door. Solomon thought it strange that the man seemed reluctant to bear witness to what those among his flock might have to say. The reason for this became apparent after much quiet consultation among an extended family huddled near the older woman in the blue dress—who regarded them with a look of cutting disapproval only one's elder can muster.

A man in his thirties pulled off his straw hat, revealing a glistening bald head and the sweat-yellowed band inside the crown of the hat. He wore a tie pin with a small cross containing a glass jewel where the silver lines intersected. He gave one long look at the lawmen waiting anxiously across the street, before turning his attention back to Solomon.

He said, almost in a whisper, "You maybe need to know about the boy."

The white agent, whose name was revealed to be Tyler, drove, with SAIC Macklin in the passenger seat, Solomon sitting alone in back. They followed the sheriff's official car, a tan-on-white hardtop station wagon with the county star emblazoned on the door.

They rode along a soft country road past miles of sugarcane fields. With the windows down for ventilation, Macklin had to shout his questions back at Solomon over the gusty hot air and road dust and cigarette smoke, but Solomon had no answers for him. He didn't know what awaited them at the address, whether it was a potential suspect, a witness to the crime, or something else altogether. The straw hat man wouldn't say any more, having been silently shamed into submission by his fellow churchgoers.

The sheriff's car slowed to a stop, asking directions from a boy of thirteen or fourteen, walking shirtless and barefoot, whacking at road grass with a thin switch of cut sugarcane. The boy pointed up the road with the stalk, telling them where to go. Solomon noticed Tyler's eyes watching him in the rearview mirror the way an agent dead-eyes a suspect or a complainant.

The sharecropper's house was a low-slung, rambling structure with no foundation, set back from a path in the field. It was constructed of unpainted wood that seemed better suited for tinder than shelter. The structure itself was decades old, though it seemed to Solomon that one good summer storm would shred it to matchsticks.

Solomon looked out his window. No toys in front of the house. A laundry line wired from the rear corner of the house to a tree was empty but for two bobbing black crows. No television antenna on the roof. Curtains in the first-floor windows but no shutters outside. The windows, strangely for this heat, were closed.

"I should go alone," said Solomon.

"Ain't no other way," said Macklin.

Still, Macklin stood out of the car when Solomon exited. Tyler remained sitting in the driver's seat, smoking. The sheriff and others got out of their wagon but only to fan themselves and wait.

Solomon went to the door and knocked. It was opened almost immediately by a young girl wearing a stiff cotton dress, blue with white lace hanging from the raw hem.

Solomon said, "Hello there. Are your parents home?"

She looked at him with large brown eyes, her head barely upturned. "You a doctor?"

"No, miss."

She turned and walked inside. Solomon waited, expecting to hear her call for a parent, but no voice came. No footsteps, either. The hallway inside split left and right, but it was dark, and his eyes wouldn't adjust from the harsh sunlight unless he stepped inside.

The floor was dirt. There was wood flooring farther ahead. A young man stood there with a wax sleeve of saltines, chewing. He was maybe twenty years old.

"You the man of the house?" asked Solomon.

"No, sir."

"Your daddy home?"

"He's out in the fields."

"This is the Jamus house, is it not?"

"Yes, sir."

"Your name, son?"

He selected another saltine. "Coleman, sir. Cole."

"Is your mama home, Cole?"

Cole nodded and turned, starting away, looking back over his shoulder for Solomon to follow him into a side room with a thickly braided oval rug and a few pieces of furniture around it. Near the corner, seated before a window looking out at the sugarcane, was a woman in her forties in a beige housedress, her face in one hand, weeping. She had cried a stain of tears on her waist, more tears running down her wrist and forearm.

Solomon's mouth started to form the word *Ma'am*, but he never uttered it. Getting any information from this grieving woman was a lost cause. She was better left to her emotions.

He looked to Cole, chewing another saltine, looking at his mother like he was used to this.

"He's in the back room," Cole said to Solomon, his eyes still on his mother. "He's chained up."

Solomon found his way there, passing three other children on the way. He came to a closed door next to a back pantry. Solomon heard the unmistakable clinking of a chain, and the creak of a bedspring. A sound he thought was a voice let loose a startling *CAW*, but he realized it was one of the crows on the laundry line outside. He was in that back part of the house now.

The door opened outward. It was more of a storage room than a bedroom, but inside there was a bed, set against the far wall, upon which a thin mattress lay with no bedclothes. Upon the mattress lay a small body, a boy, turned toward the back wall. Medium-weight chains ran from padlocked loops around the iron bed-frame rails to manacles around the boy's wrists and ankles. Blood stained the foot of the mattress from his apparent struggles against the ankle cuffs, his skin there raw, his feet swollen to a man's size.

The sight of the manacles set Solomon's mind racing. They looked like slave chains from a century ago.

He noticed now that the air inside the windowless room was different. There was a changed atmosphere inside here altogether, like an airplane cabin that had been depressurized. He heard a dull, distant sound that was a cross between ringing and roaring, similar to what he heard after a long afternoon training at the FBI Academy shooting range. But it was more than that. He felt disoriented, lightheaded. If his brain were a radio, he'd suspect its reception was somehow being jammed.

All this was forgotten when the boy turned to him. The chains rubbed against the bed frame, iron against iron, and the shirtless boy raised his head slightly, fixing his eyes on Solomon. His eyes. They were steely, almost silver, maybe blue. And wide with madness. The young boy's face was twisted and contorted like an old leather glove worn by a too-large hand. Solomon trembled.

The boy's mouth opened, and stayed open, on the verge of speech, for what seemed a long time.

Just when Solomon believed no sound would come out of it, his dry lips spoke.

"Blackwood."

The voice was faraway, hushed, rawed by many days of mad bellowing. Solomon was shaken, breathing fast and in distress at the sight of this ill boy. *Blackwood?* Maybe he had heard the word wrong.

The boy's eyes bored into him. Solomon recalled the tales his grandfather used to tell, growing up in Illinois, about sailors and merchant mariners he had known in his years at sea who had explored uncharted islands and were lured by exotic women and promises of wealth and magic, only to get mixed up in dark rites. In one awful tale, he and his crew had to leave behind a cabinmate who had attacked them in the night after becoming possessed by a demon.

Indeed, this sharecropper's son appeared to Solomon for all the world to be inhabited by some force of evil beyond the jurisdiction of the Federal Bureau of Investigation.

Before Solomon could speak, the boy's mouth opened again. His tongue was as black as a corpse's. Again, Solomon hung on the words that would come from this black tongue.

"Blackwood."

Was Solomon hearing him correctly?

"What?" asked Solomon, his parched voice nearly a croak.

"Bring Blackwood here."

Overwhelmed and terrified, the fears of his childhood surging back into consciousness with fresh life, Solomon began backing out of the room. His left shoulder struck the door frame, and Solomon shuddered as though he had been attacked. He felt his way back through the frame and into the narrow hall, needing to get out of the room to collect himself.

"Hugo Blackwood. Here."

Solomon somehow got the door closed. The strange name meant nothing to him. He stood there with his chest and shoulders heaving, trying to get breath.

When he turned, he found four young children in the hallway staring at him. Coleman stood farthest away, his crackers finished, his hands hanging empty.

"What happened to him?" asked Solomon.

The children just stared. They didn't know.

"Who...who is Hugo Blackwood?" Solomon managed to ask.

The children had no answer for him. One by one, they turned and walked away.

The answer, however, was forthcoming.

1582. Mortlake, Greater London.

The house by the river at Mortlake, with its many rooms of varying disciplines and moods, was itself an articulation of the great sorcerer's mind.

Its hallways were cool, quiet, contemplative. This door opened to the observatory, the ceiling paned with glass for charting celestial events in service of both astronomy and astrology. Another door opened to a laboratory of navigation and charting, cartography a burgeoning scientific discipline crucial to English mariners who hoped to develop trade routes to Cathay or even the New World, mastering the northern seas. Another door led to a laboratory of cosmography, the study of the universe known and surmised, elements of which—astronomy, geography, geometry—enhanced various other scientific pursuits behind other heavy doors.

A palace of the mind.

No room was more treasured, more hallowed, than the great library. Its contents were the envy of all of Britain, its breadth greater than any university. Shelves and stacks of tomes collected from throughout the educated world: the basal ganglia of the house. Cicero's *De Legibus*, Cardano's *Libelli Quinque*, *The Opera* by Arnaldus de Villanova, and many incunabula—some four thousand arcane volumes of similar import arranged in a system peculiar to, and only fully understood by, their curator: the occult philosopher and British royal adviser John Dee.

In the middle of his sixth decade of life, Dee was famed as Queen Elizabeth's court astrologer, spymaster, and scientist, an influencer of the highest order. He had been entrusted with divining and selecting the date of her coronation, and for twenty years had enjoyed an exalted consultancy in the highest circles of London life. Recently, however, his political patronage had suffered due to a number of disappointing prophecies and rejected imperial recommendations. His mathematical studies continued to be praised and supported, but the world was changing around him. Every scientific advance in the sixteenth century was accompanied by a proportionate diminution of elemental magic.

This schism in the disciplines of science and magic resulted in his diminished influence within court circles and affected the patronage he had come to rely upon—that had, to state a fact, funded his Mortlake manor and subsidized the acquisitions both scholarly and esoteric that made his mind-castle the envy of all of Britain. Purposefully, and perhaps a bit desperately, Dee had of late turned more fully toward an exploration of the supernatural.

His aim was to repair the schism of science and magic, to bridge this divide through the practice of alchemy and divination. He sought an audience with experts in this realm: He sought communion with none other than angels.

This unorthodox pursuit had introduced Dee to an underground league of occultists and spirit mediums. After consulting various mystics who claimed to be in contact with higher realms, he partnered with Edward Talbot, whose real name was Edward Kelley but was using the pseudonym after a conviction for forgery a few years before. Both of Talbot's ears had been removed by a magistrate as punishment for that crime, which was why Talbot wore a monk's skullcap even indoors. Dee, however, overlooked all of Talbot's past indiscretions, so enamored was he with the quality of Talbot's spiritual consultation and the breadth of his knowledge of the uncanny arts, specifically his talent as a scryer.

"We must begin," said Dee. "This is the most auspicious time, Edward…"

Talbot stood now in the center of the great library, his psychic attention focused darkly upon an orbuculum resting in the smooth, cupped palm of a bronze casting of a human hand. The crystal ball was flawless, a perfectly smooth sphere lit from below by three votive candles, giving it the appearance of illumination from within. John Dee wore his customary white gown, his silken white beard falling beneath his mustache in a perfect V, looking like a wizard immersed in a spellcasting. Talbot was deep in a trance, incanting in a language revealed to him and John Dee exclusively by Enochian angels.

There was a third participant in this ritual séance—although whether he was an active participant or merely a witness is known only by those in attendance.

Not much is known about Hugo Blackwood. He seldom spoke, but appeared to be constantly by Dee's side, privately and in public functions. People called him Dee's Shadow but were careful to only do it when he was not nearby.

He was originally presumed to have first encountered John Dee during Dee's 1555 prosecution for treason—Dee had been accused of reading by "casting" (that is to say, tampering with) then

Queen Mary's horoscope—in the Star Chamber where Blackwood was apprenticing as a legal clerk. This theory has fallen out of favor over the past twenty years as contradictory biographical information, however slim, has surfaced, which would place Blackwood's age at the time of the invocation somewhere in his thirties. It now appears that Hugo Blackwood was originally employed as Dee's legal representative, though documents from the time are scarce. One theory, as yet not disproved, is that Blackwood represented John Dee in matters relating to his property and acquisitions.

What is known is that, like many before and after him, Hugo Blackwood was drawn into the famous philosopher's orbit. The reason for his presence at this invocation is unclear. It is not known if he, like Dee and Talbot, had fasted in preparation for the ceremony, though it is presumed that he partook of a goblet of fermented grain beverage, a draught of wormwood, derived from *Artemisia vulgaris* cultivated in Dee's own garden. Perhaps Hugo Blackwood was an interested observer, or, less likely but still possible, perhaps he simply happened to be at Dee's residence on other business on the night in question.

Or perhaps, as had happened many times before, John Dee sensed something in Hugo Blackwood's character that interested him, that Dee judged made him conducive to his pursuit of evidence of an exalted, alternate realm, that prompted him to include the barrister in this ceremony.

Barely any mention of the extraordinary survives in Dee's notebooks, so either nothing occurred that evening that Dee believed warranted special notation, or perhaps he was unaware. Dee lived many more years in search of the ineffable, ambitiously attempting to fuse mathematics, divination, astronomy, and spiritualism into a single discipline, and never succeeding.

But on this night, something did happen. In the act of experimenting with spheromancy in order to summon an archangel to divulge its divine knowledge, a line was crossed. A natural law was broken. A dark boundary was trespassed.

Two men emerged from it unchanged.

One did not.

2019. Newark, New Jersey.

The mass murder scene investigation went all night.

Odessa was a while explaining to the first responders exactly what had happened, offering a preliminary ID on Cary Peters as the assailant of the two dead children and their mother, identifying Walt Leppo as a fellow law enforcement member. The girl was inconsolable. Odessa couldn't even get her to say her first name. EMTs took her away.

Odessa met the first pair of responding FBI agents in the girl's bedroom and took them through the story. She had dealt with eyewitnesses herself and spoke as clearly and succinctly as she could. But when she got to the end, she couldn't make them understand that it was she, not Peters, who had shot Leppo. At first, they thought she misspoke; then that she had been traumatized and didn't know what she was saying; then they told her a supervisory agent was on the way.

Odessa told it again to the supervisory agent. Again, her account was met with disbelief. This time she heard herself describing the part in the hallway, when she found Peters and Leppo struggling, but Peters was unarmed and Leppo held the knife. And then after she shot Peters, Leppo walked with the knife into the girl's room without a word. She understood that what she was saying did not make a lot of sense. She said that Walt must have lost his mind. But the supervisory agent was looking at Odessa as though she had lost hers.

The agents watched Leppo's body as it was being photographed. His gun was in his holster. They looked down at their fallen comrade, killed in the line of duty. Then they looked back at Odessa.

Odessa found a bottle of water someone had offered her earlier and drank all of it at once. She felt more than self-doubt. She actively questioned her own sanity in that moment. She felt shaken to her core.

After conferring with the first two agents, the supervisory agent returned with some follow-up questions for her.

Where were you standing when Walt tried to stab the girl?

Where do you think he got the knife from?

Had Walt been acting strangely at the restaurant before the shooting?

Odessa realized they thought she was inventing part of the story to cover up a bad shoot. That maybe she had accidentally shot Leppo, mistaking him for a second assailant in the dark bedroom. Odessa didn't address or refute it. But she knew what was happening.

The girl would vouch for Odessa's story. She was the only living witness. The wound on her shoulder, from the blade of Leppo's knife, was clear evidence of justifiable force.

They draped a sheet over Walt Leppo's body. The sheet dropped over his unblinking eyes.

Walt, what happened?

Odessa was led out of the bedroom.

Odessa rode back to Claremont in the responding agents' car. Nobody spoke.

The Newark field office was among the FBI's largest, with more than 350 agents and including resident agencies stretching from Atlantic City to Peterson. They had jurisdiction over most of the state of New Jersey, with the Philadelphia field office responsible for a corner of South Jersey.

Up on the sixth floor of Claremont, in a windowless room still imbued with the faint redolence of cigarette smoke from a vanished time, Odessa told the story again, twice. Exactly the same, but for a few details that came back to her upon each retelling. The thumping noises she heard overhead as she moved from the Peters kitchen to the stairs, like sounds of a struggle, for example. The beep-beep of a passive "door open" signal as they entered the Peters house. Leppo requesting leftovers from the lunch rush instead of a freshly made meat loaf.

Odessa started to cry. Once she began, she found she could not stop. She could still speak, but the tears fell and her nose ran into tissues pulled from a box she held in her lap. This was a room normally reserved for interrogating suspects.

Her questioners' faces were expressionless. She had never been on the other side of this. A few questions raised her antennae.

Did either of you drink any alcohol at dinner?

Are you on any medication right now?

She surrendered her sidearm for ballistics testing, which was standard procedure. They suggested she give a blood sample, claiming it was for her benefit. The way they said this didn't sit well with her. But the blood test never came about anyway.

The sun rose, the morning shift arrived, and agents who never gave rookie Odessa the time of day came by the sixth floor just to get a look. That was when she knew—really knew—that she was in trouble. Even though it was justified, she was still implicated in a bad shoot. A fellow agent was down—and she had done it.

★   ★   ★

Around ten A.M., word came down that Odessa should be sent home. When she stopped at her cubicle to get her phone charger, the thought crossed her mind to retrieve whatever else she thought she wanted from her desk drawer in case she was never allowed back in here. *Ridiculous*, she told herself, but was it? From the window she could see down to Center Street, where television trucks were set up for live reporting.

Nobody told her Linus was waiting for her. She saw him in the lobby, wearing a suit without a necktie, as though he had dressed quickly and half for work, not sure what to do. He looked up from his phone and jumped to his feet when she approached, and she held him and broke down a little. She had no idea they had called him.

She had met Linus Ayers in law school in Boston, where he was from. They dated until graduation, broke up, and within a year were living together. It was love but it also made great financial sense for two young attorneys, one drawing a government salary from the FBI, the other a second-year lawyer in a white-shoe firm across the river in Manhattan.

"Thank you," she whispered in his ear.

He rubbed her back reassuringly, still holding her.

"They called me. I thought something happened to you—you were hurt."

She shook her head and buried her face one more time in his shoulder.

"It's bad," she said.

"You need a lawyer," said Linus.

She pulled back a bit to swipe away her tears and look at him, his fair brown skin and concerned eyes. "I have a lawyer," she said. "You."

He almost smiled.

They walked out an unmarked door on River Street, past a television reporter scrolling through her phone with her earpiece dangling from her blouse collar between broadcasts, unnoticed. The rain had cleared out the humidity overnight, cooling the air. Odessa leaned on Linus on the short walk to Newark Penn Station, where they caught a PATH train one stop into Harrison. They didn't speak much. Odessa didn't remember much of their short journey. Exhaustion was starting to hit her now.

She thought she might feel relief upon closing their apartment door on the world outside, but it didn't happen. Linus asked if she wanted to eat anything, but she sure didn't. She climbed into bed with her clothes on, something she had done once before in her adult life, when she had the flu.

She was in a dark funk. Linus set a glass of water

on the nightstand for her. She heard him fumbling with something on the dresser, then realized he was unplugging the coaxial cable from the television. He didn't want her to watch.

But she had her phone and charger still. She looked up the news and watched as much as she could bear. Cameras were outside Leppo's house, recording Walt's wife weeping as she loaded their kids into the car and drove away.

Linus came in to check on her and discovered her on her phone. He made her promise to unplug and sleep. She nodded, but then he remained sitting on the edge of the bed. He wanted to talk. Or rather: He wanted to listen.

She told him an abbreviated version of what happened. One thing she shared with him that she'd neglected to tell the FBI: She said she thought she saw something flee Leppo's dying body. She told him this to gauge his reaction, to test out how bizarre this sounded. He didn't give her much facially, but after a few moments of silent consideration, he told her that he thought she should speak with someone else, in addition to a lawyer. He meant a therapist.

Her spirit sank. She wanted this to make sense. "I saw it," she said. "I smelled it."

"Saw what, though?" he said. "A heat mirage, you said?"

"Not quite that. But like that. A ripple. Something."

"I think you were—understandably—distraught, and your senses played a trick on you."

"I know it's funky," she said. "It's really hard to explain."

"What did they say about it?"

"I didn't tell them."

Linus's eyes widened a bit. Then he nodded. "Maybe you should keep it that way, going ahead." He was assessing it as a lawyer should. "There's nothing factually wrong with omitting it."

"What could have happened to Walt?" she said.

Linus had nothing for her there. "It's all so crazy. Nothing makes sense right now."

Odessa's phone rang. She sat up, but Linus looked before she could.

"Your mother," he said.

Odessa sank back down. "I can't."

"Then don't," he said, pulling her charger plug from the wall and standing. "Sleep."

She nodded. He left.

Later in the day, the twenty-four-hour news channels were obsessively tracking the "last flight" of Cary Peters, patched together from cell phone footage, eyewitness reports, bullet holes, and FAA reports. Odessa watched the coverage on her laptop, a cold mug of tea on the table next to her.

Peters had killed five people: two men at Teterboro, and three family members in Montclair. Odessa paid close attention to the man whose Jeep was carjacked at the golf course parking lot. His description of Peters's cold facial expression and distant eyes—attributed to the head wound Peters suffered upon crash landing on the golf course— matched exactly the look she had seen in Walt Leppo's face.

Peters was said to have been shot and killed by law enforcement, and an FBI agent had been killed in the exchange. As of yet, they did not have the complete story. But Odessa knew it was only a matter of time.

The news was trying to make sense of Peters's killing spree just as Odessa was. Financial pressure, family strife, professional ruin. His life was a shambles, no question. But his actions went beyond. He was not a violent man, and there was nothing in his past that hinted at such a frenzy of viciousness.

Same for Leppo. Odessa kept going over their dinner together. It could not have been less remarkable. And the drive to Montclair: Leppo being Leppo, playing a hunch, at the top of his game. Entering the house that night: the veteran agent taking the lead. Odessa getting waylaid by her discovery of the mother's corpse. She wished she had a clear memory of the noises upstairs.

Was there a struggle? Why hadn't Leppo fired his Glock? How did he wind up with the carving knife Peters had taken from the kitchen?

Her cell rang. It was Claremont. They were sending a car. They wanted her back in for another interview.

Linus said, "Let me get you a lawyer."

Odessa said, "I can't afford a lawyer."

Linus said, "You can't afford not to."

She showered and dressed and went in for an interview accompanied by a Bureau lawyer. Dessa's interview was video recorded, and she got through it without becoming emotional. She was not asked about the condition of Walt Leppo's body after he fell. She signed some forms after the lawyer reviewed them, and was informed she could expect an interview with the Office of Professional Responsibility, which was the FBI's internal affairs unit, within the next few days.

She thought they were going to ask for her badge and credentials. They already had her gun. She was officially reassigned to desk duty during the OPR investigation—standard procedure. She asked how long she could expect the investigation to take.

"A matter of weeks. Or longer."

The way the supervisory agent said "or longer" convinced her she was going to be fired. Of course, it would come at the end of a prolonged investigation wherein small, inconsequential violations of procedure would be cited as cause. But the real reason would be that she had shot and killed a fellow agent—no matter the circumstances—and couldn't expect anyone else to ride with her ever again.

Afterward, she was asked to wait inside the garage for a car to return her home. She was standing alone, waiting, when her phone rang. MOM, read the screen.

Oh no. An electric shiver ran through her. If her mother had heard something—a call from the press, perhaps—Odessa didn't want to talk about it. And if she hadn't heard something—if this was just a coincidental catch-up call, their first in more than a week—then not talking about it would become a huge issue the next time they spoke. *Why didn't you tell me?* The recriminations, on and on. The guilt. Yes, the guilt. Odessa's world was gone and yet, her mother would make it all about herself. *You should've told me sooner.*

Odessa silenced her phone. She couldn't talk to her now. Not now. But ignoring the call and letting it go to voicemail was not enough.

Never enough.

Odessa walked away. She couldn't get in the car

70

right now. As she neared the door to the street, she lengthened her stride, afraid of being seen and called back before she could escape.

She made it onto the sidewalk, moving two blocks north before she felt free again. She texted Linus—she had insisted he go in to work, and wanted him to know she was done with her interview and basically okay—and kept walking. The clouds above were a thick, sweatery gray, threatening hard rain, but only a few needle-sharp drops fell.

She walked due north, staying away from the sketchiest areas near the river, passing car washes and phone stores and bodegas and graffiti-covered vacant storefronts. Just as she began to grow tired of the crumbling sidewalks and faceless streets, she found herself at the entrance to the Mount Pleasant Cemetery, an oasis in a perpetually troubled city. A stone marker near the Victorian Gothic gate said 1844. She walked along the winding roads and rolling lanes, passing funereal sculptures, Romanesque crypts, and elaborate mausoleums. It was a mood.

She thought on a lot of things, but it was all scattered, impossible to dwell upon. Maybe that was a good thing. One image she kept coming back to was Linus's vexed reaction to her confiding in him about the essence...the presence...the *what-*

ever she saw emanating from Walt Leppo's body after he passed. She wished she had the luxury of doubting herself, of discounting what she saw. She wished she could dismiss it.

The hunger pangs came upon her suddenly. She found a Dominican restaurant nearby and sat alone eating roasted chicken and seasoned rice. What she liked best about the place was that it looked nothing like the Soup Spoon Café, where she had spent her last hour with Leppo.

Walt, what happened?

It was still light as she crossed the river back into Harrison. Her legs and feet were tired, and she thought she was thoroughly exhausted—until she saw the gathering outside her building from a block away. It didn't register at first, and then the realization washed over her all at once, with a sickening surge of fight-or-flight adrenaline.

They were reporters. The vans were TV camera trucks, and they were waiting outside her residence on a stakeout. Now Odessa was receiving the same treatment Peters had after his scandal came to light. Now she was the pursued.

Like a bank robber with a trunk full of loot approaching a police checkpoint, she turned on her heel and walked the other way—fearing, with every step, that she would hear her name shouted and be chased. It was out there now: news of the bad shoot, identifying her. Her silenced phone remained in her purse, probably burning up with voicemails and news alerts. She felt hunted. She wiped away tears.

Her world, as she once knew it, was gone. Seeing those lights, the throngs of people outside—waiting—she knew nothing would ever be the same again.

In a bit of grace, she soon found herself walking past the Harrison Public Library. Inside its cool, quiet rooms, between the stacks, she remembered how libraries in the towns she grew up in outside Milwaukee, Wisconsin, were sanctuaries in her youth. The smell of old paper, the coolness of the metal shelves, the smoothness of the tile floors. Libraries were a place for hiding as well as exploring, same as the books they freely offered. She found a chair in a corner and sat awhile. Her phone remained inside her purse like a radioactive stone encased in lead; breaking the seal would expose her to its harmful rays, poisoning her. Numb, she ruminated on her damaged career, on her disrupted life, on Leppo's death. Children walked past her and she had to close her eyes, so shaken was she by the images of the slain Peters children.

The *closing in fifteen minutes* announcement came, and Odessa felt sick. She found a clock and wondered if any of the reporters—at least the television reporters—had given up on featuring her in their newscast. It was dark outside and she walked directly to her apartment building, key in hand. Thankfully, there were no TV trucks and no reporters in sight. She made it inside her lobby without incident, and upstairs into her apartment.

The next morning, she was unable to deal with 90 percent of what was on her phone, but one message got through. Her boss told her not to come in to Claremont for work, but to report to the New York City Field Office instead. Odessa took the subway in to Tribeca, and for the first two days of her temporary reassignment the brass on the twenty-third floor tried to find something for her to do. She expended a lot of energy trying to look busy, but by the end of the second day she was fine just looking out the window. Nobody talked to her.

On the third day, the office emptied for Walt Leppo's funeral. Odessa could not bring herself to attend it. She was certain no one wanted her to go. Sitting at an empty desk knowing her friend and mentor was being eulogized and buried across the river: That was her lowest point.

Her mother kept calling. Odessa communicated with her siblings—there were five, the closest one to her geographically living outside Cincinnati, Ohio—by text, telling them she was okay and promising to call on the weekend. Her siblings were well intentioned, but the mere thought of actually talking to them about what had happened was draining. With her mother, she caught a break. In a rare moment of mercy, Odessa's call went to voicemail.

Mom, it's me. Sorry, things have been just hectic, as you can imagine. It's been a terrible week and I don't know what's going to happen. I'm okay, though. I'm as well as can be expected. I'll try you again later but there's so much to do on my end, I don't know when that will be. Okay. It's Odessa. Okay. Bye.

And then she sat at her empty desk with nothing to do until it was time to leave.

The next day, they found something for her to do. She was dispatched to the Brooklyn-Queens FBI Resident Agency across the East River, in Kew Gardens. A retired agent had recently suffered a stroke, and her task was to clear out his office. Why a retired agent still had an office, she did not know, but she was certain that, as a rookie agent on desk duty currently under a cloud of investigation, questioning the assignment would not be a good look.

True to form, the office manager at Kew Gardens had no idea Odessa was coming, nor did she know anything about the office in question. She fished out a tray of thirty or so odd keys from a cabinet in the copying room and presented it to Odessa, pointing her to the hallway.

Odessa found the office at the end of a back corridor, kitty-cornered with an emergency exit to the stairs. The door was unmarked and indeed locked. Odessa shook the tray of keys and considered the time it would take to try each one—knowing that, by the Odessa Law of Averages, the correct key would be among the last ones selected. The office door was sufficiently hidden from view of the rest of the office wing, so instead she appropriated a paper clip from a vacant desk, removed a pizza delivery joint's business-card-size magnet from the break room refrigerator, and used both to pick the simple lock.

The door opened on a room of stale air. There was no window. She flipped the light switch, and the ceiling fixture, a naked bulb, lit for a moment, then flickered and popped. This office hadn't been used in quite some time.

A desk was empty but for a leatherette desk set; a bookshelf held a few empty three-ring binders, some standing on edge, others lying on their sides; and wall prints featured pale watercolors, which had probably been hanging on the wall when the former occupant moved in.

It looked, appropriately, like the office of a guy playing out his days until retirement. Odessa left the door open for light and moved to the desk, coated by a neat, even patina of soft gray dust. The drawers were mostly empty: paper clips, a tape roll, a letter opener. A nameplate that might have once adorned a similar desk or office door: EARL SOLOMON.

She found old receipts for travel expenses. Lunch in Lawrence, Kansas, in 1994. Dinner in Saskatchewan, 1988. An electronics shop for "tape recorder repair," 2009.

The bottom drawer on the right side was locked. She could tell at a glance that none of the keys in the tray were the correct size for opening it.

Still drafting off confidence from picking the door lock, she assailed the tiny keyhole with her paper clip, but to no avail. A few more tugs on the handle showed her the drawer was tightly secured. She looked again at the desk blotter; the letter opener blade looked thin enough to fit between the top of the drawer and its frame.

She gave it a moment's thought, knowing she would leave a visible trace of forced entry. Then with a glance at the open door to the hallway, she hammered the opener blade in over the top of the drawer with the heel of her hand and gave it a firm sideways wrench.

The interior clasp snapped. The drawer was loose. She at least hoped it was good booze.

The drawer rolled open to reveal a reel-to-reel tape recorder. She lifted it out, placing it on the blotter. Heavy construction, not pure plastic. Beige in color; Sony-branded, though the letters were widely spaced—s o n y—in a compressed, dated typeface; and sporting an old, two-pronged electric plug. The case promised "high-fidelity." The twin spindles were empty. She found a handful of seven-inch tape reels in the back of the drawer and piled them on the desk next to the tape deck. She had a vague memory of her grandfather spooling up tape. She was curious enough to try.

She set one reel on the left spindle, then reversed it, unspooling tape and feeding it through the reader part. The brown tape was brittle; she had to be careful not to snap it. She curled it around an empty reel on the receiving end and figured out how to crimp it in a slot near the bindle so it would not unspool. She wound it a few feet by hand, then plugged the deck into the wall, the prongs connecting to the electric current with a cranky blue spark.

She switched the deck on and then turned the dial to PLAY. It worked! Or seemed to—no sound came out of it at first. She turned the dial again and the tape fast-forwarded with scary speed. She turned it back to PLAY.

The sound of a microphone being bumped startled her. "Testing, testing."

She turned the volume down on a baritone voice, clear but for the scratchiness of the aged Mylar tape.

There was then a radio recording that started up mid-song, also scratchy and distant, then some bumps as the recording microphone was moved closer:

Here come the stars tumbling around me...
There's the sky where the sea should be...

Almost marching music. She got out her phone and thumbed through to her Shazam app.

This improbable method of audio detection—the aged warbling of an ancient device decoded by the algorithmic genius of a modern device—worked. It was "What Now My Love" by Shirley Bassey, featuring Nelson Riddle and His Orchestra. Shazam put the release date at 1962.

The orchestration and vocal performance built to a frenzy and then ended suddenly. A snippet of patter from an old-school disk jockey started but was quickly shut off.

Then—white noise.

And then nothing.

She zipped forward, afraid the tape would snap. But the rest was blank.

Someone testing the machine? In 1962?

She examined the deck, eventually lifting it up. On the underside, burned into the plastic chassis with some kind of hot tool, were the initials ES.

Earl Solomon. That anticlimactic revelation—that the tape deck apparently belonged to the FBI agent whose office desk she found it inside—seemed to end her investigation.

He probably stuck it in the bottom drawer and forgot all about it.

Odessa returned to the office manager. "What am I supposed to do with the agent's belongings?" she asked.

The office manager shrugged. "Any personal items should be returned, I guess? We need the office. Let me see if I have an address..."

Odessa found an empty carton in the printing/burn room and put everything inside.

Odessa cabbed over to Flushing and lugged the carton into NewYork-Presbyterian Queens Hospital. She bounced from visitors desk to visitors desk trying to locate Earl Solomon. She was tempted to use her badge but it didn't feel right, being on desk duty. Eventually she learned that he was out of intensive care, and Odessa made her way to the patient care unit.

The door was open. It was not a private room, but the first bed was empty. She stepped quietly around the half-drawn curtain. A black man lay sleeping, looking all of his eighty-six years. Tubes ran from the back of his hand and his forearm to pumps and monitors working in a hushed symphony. His breathing was shallow, his hair mostly silver, curly, and short.

Odessa set the carton down on the wooden arms of a chair. She had hoped there'd be family members holding a vigil, which would give her an opportunity to explain herself, hand off the possessions from his desk, and politely exit in a matter of minutes. She felt like a trespasser now. She didn't dare wake him. Maybe he was sedated. She might have to use her badge anyway, in order to get information from the nurses' desk, or else wait for the attending to come by on his or her rounds.

A small, flat television played in the high corner of the room. Once Odessa realized what she was watching, her chest went cold. It was a report on the funeral of Cary Peters's wife and children. His own funeral was being held separately. She saw footage of the line of automobiles at the cemetery, a massive outpouring of sympathy and remembrance for the victims. They showed photographs sourced from social media, Mrs. Peters and the children at a water park, at a petting zoo, at a New York Rangers hockey game. Then a familiar photo of just Peters from his days working for the governor. A photograph of their house in Montclair, taken that night, lit starkly by emergency reds and blues of the first responders. And then, without context due to the muted volume, the photo of a young woman with shoulder-length brown hair, wearing a jacket over a white blouse, smiling proudly. Odessa let out an audible gasp when she recognized her own photograph on television: her official FBI identification headshot.

And then back to the news anchor. It wasn't even a local station, it was CNN. Nationwide. Odessa didn't know what they were saying about her...and yet, she did.

"You from personnel?"

The voice startled her. Odessa whipped around, expecting it to be somebody at the door.

It was Earl Solomon. He was awake, if he'd ever been asleep. His eyes squinted at her, then widened. Warm and a little yellow.

"No," she said, short of breath. She checked the television screen but the news had moved on to another story. She looked back at him. "I'm...Odessa Hardwicke. Special agent from New Jersey. Agent...Mr. Solomon?"

"Agent Solomon," he said. "Earl. Put this up a bit, would you?"

He pointed out the bed controller, and Odessa raised the mattress two feet or so, in order that he could see her better. His lips were dry, his tongue pale. "You want some water?" she asked.

He shook his head. He pursed his lips and looked around as though trying to remember where he was. "New room," he said.

Odessa nodded. She was still recovering from seeing herself on television. "Uh...are you comfortable?"

"Not so much."

"You, um...you had a stroke, I'm told."

"Some plaque got loose in my arteries. Lodged somewhere up in my head, blocked blood to my brain. Knocked me off my feet." He patted the bed around his waist, smoothing out the top sheet. "Lucky I had my phone on me when I fell."

"Your voice seems good. Any damage?"

He made a sour face again. "Can't smell, nor taste. Dull tone in my ears. But if that's it, I got off pretty easy. They did a scan, found some more plaque around my heart. And a fungus growing. And that's not good."

"No," she said. "That doesn't sound good."

"You from New Jersey, huh?"

"Correct. They, um..." She didn't want to get into her situation with him. "You still have an office in B-Q."

Solomon nodded, deeply furrowed lines in his

forehead articulating every facial expression. "I don't go in much."

"Apparently not." She tried a smile, but it felt forced. "I don't understand something. Mandatory retirement age at the FBI is fifty-seven years old, correct?"

He nodded. "I guess officially, I'm retired," he said.

"So why do you still have an office?"

"Well, in case I need it."

Odessa nodded, though this made no sense to her. "I'm actually not clear on this. Did they ... forget about your office?"

"They forgot about me." Solomon smiled. His teeth were large and looked loose. "Are you taking over my office?"

"Me, no. Just clearing it out." She pointed with both hands to the carton on the chair behind her. "I brought your things from your desk. There wasn't much."

He never looked at the carton, curious about her. "How is it you drew this errand of mercy?"

She smiled at first, at the expression, then realized she had to come clean. "I'm on desk duty temporarily."

Solomon nodded like he expected this. "Disability or disciplinary?"

"'Administrative inquiry,'" she said, a phrase that kept running through her head. "It was a shoot."

"A bad shoot?"

"That's...really difficult to answer right now."

"I see," said Solomon as he glanced at the television high in the corner. He must have seen an earlier news report about the Montclair shooting. She watched his face as he put it together. His eyes returned to her with great interest and almost a revelatory expression. She wouldn't understand what this meant until much later.

"The governor's aide shooting," he said. "Man turned on his family. Killed them all except one."

Odessa looked down and nodded. "Yes, sir."

"The agent riding with you attacked the last surviving child and you shot him."

She closed her eyes and nodded again. "Agent Solomon, I really don't—"

He cut in. "You don't want to talk about it."

"No, sir. I don't."

"Understood. I have just a few specific questions."

She looked at him with confusion, thinking he was going to let this go.

"First, about the other agent," Solomon continued. "He's a Bureau agent. I assume there were no indications of psychosis prior to this...?"

Odessa shook her head. "No."

"The killer died first."

"I shot him."

"But the agent...was he already acting out of sorts?"

She really did not want to get into this. "You could say that, yes. I don't want to—"

"These are difficult questions, but important. The agent, when you shot him. I'm talking about the moment of death. Was there anything...anything remarkable about it? Out of the ordinary?"

She wasn't sure how to answer. She was reluctant to volunteer anything; in fact, she had been told by the lawyer not to discuss the case with anyone. But this question...so specific...

"I saw a kind of ripple, like fumes, coming off him."

"Any odor? Oily?"

Again, how did he know? "Yes, like burnt solder." She regretted the words as soon as she uttered them. "It was a traumatic moment, I'm not sure of anything..."

Solomon wasn't judging. He was thinking. "Did you find a makeshift altar anywhere in the house?"

What kind of question was that? "There was no..."

"Altar. A shrine. Maybe in the garage or an out-building. An iron pot or an urn—"

She cut him off. "I didn't participate in the investigation because I was part of what they were investigating," she said. "Because of the bad shoot.

And it wasn't his house anymore, or at least he wasn't living there."

"A cauldron—black—cast iron sometimes," he continued. "Might look like a big vase or a trash can if you don't know what you're looking for. And in it you might find hair, human hair, and bones..."

"Bones?" said Odessa.

"And blood, yes...Hard to miss that," said the old man.

"Agent Solomon—" This was too weird. "I shouldn't even be talking about this. I'm here about you."

"Me? Don't worry about me. I can't taste and I can't smell, and I got a fungus growing in my brain, so who knows what's next. I'll take that drink now."

He was motioning to a mauve-colored pitcher on a wheeled tray. Odessa splashed some lukewarm water into a plastic cup for him. He sipped at it with a hand that trembled with age.

"You're gonna need assistance with this investigation," he told her.

"I have a Bureau-appointed lawyer," she assured him.

"Not with your defense. With this investigation."

She didn't understand at first. "Into what happened? I can't go near that."

"You have to. If you want to know what really happened. I know someone who can help you."

"Thank you, Agent Solomon," she said, trying to

strike a balance between politeness and purpose, "but I'm going to let the Bureau do their work, and I'm going to do mine. Speaking of which..."

She made a halfhearted gesture toward the door, anxious to leave.

"What you do," Solomon said, "is write a letter briefly outlining what happened and requesting assistance. You write it on paper. Unadorned prose. State your case. Simply. Truly. Ask for help. You fold it once—exactly once, right in the middle— then seal it in a buff-colored manila envelope. You know the type, six inches by nine inches? They call it booklet size. Address it to—you write this down now—Hugo Blackwood, Esquire. Thirteen and a Half Stone Street. Wall Street area. Know it?"

She waited until he was finished before shaking her head. "What?"

"One of the oldest streets in Manhattan. Listen to me carefully. There is a black iron mailbox tucked away in a narrow stone wall between buildings. Hard to find if you're not looking for it, no number or mark. Nearly invisible—more accurately, forgotten. You deliver it by hand, yourself. An act of contrition, humility. You deposit the envelope containing your letter into the mail slot and then walk away. You wait for him."

Odessa nodded, careful to hold an ambivalent expression now. She felt pity but also an immense sense of compassion for Solomon, realizing his mind had already been affected by the stroke. Their entire conversation suddenly made sense...in that it didn't make sense.

"What was that address again?" she asked politely.

"Thirteen and a Half Stone Street."

"Okay," she said, as though committing it to memory. "Got it."

"You'll do this? Exactly as I said?"

"I will," answered Odessa. "Thank you. How will I know if—"

"If your plea is true—if it is what I think it is—he'll show up."

He watched her eyes. She thought she had him hooked, but as he kept tracking her gaze, she felt herself wither a bit. Another moment of gentle scrutiny and Solomon turned his gaze to the window, looking through the upper-story grime at the gray city sky.

"I know these days are difficult for you," he said. "Just getting out of bed in the morning. Brushing your teeth. I know that, looking at yourself in the mirror, all you can think about is the shooting, and how it could have gone different."

Odessa watched him watching the city. His brain sure didn't seem soft at the moment. He had her mind-set nailed down tight.

"People call it regret, but it's true awareness," he continued. "It's pure comprehension that the actions you take and don't take have direct effect on others. You're complicit. I'm complicit. We're all complicit. The definition isn't 'involved in a crime'; it's more about having done someone wrong in some way. It happens to everyone. So tomorrow morning, when you're in front of that mirror brushing those pearly whites, think about why you do it. Not the oral health benefits. Brushing your teeth, combing your hair, buttering your toast, thinking about what the day will bring you. Everything is an invocation. Little, itty-bitty, step-by-step moments of holy summoning. But here's the thing about it. Sometimes we are not the ones doing the summoning. Sometimes we are the ones being summoned."

Solomon turned his yellowing eyes back to her.

"I was expecting someone to come," he said, "but it sure as hell wasn't you."

He had lost Odessa at the end there. Mentally it seemed that he was going in and out of coherence. All she knew was: She really wanted to leave now. But gracefully.

"Anyway, Agent Solomon, your personal items are right here in this carton," she said. "Do you want me to find room in the closet for them?"

"You can just take 'em back with you," he said.

"I can't, really..."

"I got no family, nobody to give it to, never mind nobody to help carry it all home. If I ever get home. Speaking of which. I know I'm imposing on you, but with the suspension you got nothing but time..."

"It's not officially a suspension, really..."

"My mistake," he said with a gentle smile. "But like I said, I got nobody else in my life. Would you please, if I give you the address, bring my things back to my home? And maybe check on the place while you're there? Turn on a few lights inside— feed Dennis. Damn."

"Who's Dennis?"

"Fish I adopted. Orphan fish. Very sad...He's gonna be *hungry*."

"Oh my God."

"Yeah. Forgot about him. He might be looking for a new home soon, if you know of anyone."

Solomon scribbled down his address, then closed his eyes to rest. Odessa put the address in her pocket, lifted the carton, and said goodbye...but Earl Solomon was already asleep.

1962. The Mississippi Delta.

Rookie agent Earl Solomon tramped through the woods in his leather wing-tip shoes. He stepped carefully; he owned only one pair. The ground was dry on top, but the soil and debris were damp when turned over. His white cotton shirt, under his summer-weight suit jacket, was already soaked through with perspiration.

Sheriff Ingalls wore boots, walking a few paces ahead of Solomon. SAIC Macklin had covered his shoes with galoshes, which he usually kept in the trunk of his car.

Macklin was handing Solomon photos of the lynching. The victim, a white man named Harold Cawsby who went by the nickname "Hack," hung from a noose fashioned of thick twine, the weight of which looked barely strong enough to support the body of an adult male. The limb was thick and low, Hack Cawsby's toes—one shoe on, one shoe off—dangling not more than a foot off the ground.

"Chicken wire around his wrists behind his back," said the sheriff, walking ahead of them. "His pants are down around his hips, but Hack didn't wear no belt. Most likely he fought the noose once he was hanged, kicking and flailing, but that's a fight few men win."

Another photograph showed the man's hands. The camera film had been black and white; the blood coating his palms and fingers looked like molasses in tone and texture.

"Up here, on the left," said the sheriff, slapping at a bloodsucker on the back of his neck. Solomon rarely had a problem with mosquitoes; he was a shallow breather, and attributed his relative immunity to the low amount of carbon dioxide he emitted, which drew the insects. Earl Solomon was a low-resting-heart-rate kind of guy, all the way around.

Sheriff Ingalls stopped before a tree that was measurably larger and older than those surrounding it, resting his hands upon his hips. Solomon held up one of the crime scene photographs, comparing it with the tree. Yes, this was the one.

"Knotted one end around this low branch here," said the sheriff, pointing, "slung the line over that thick branch there, and strung him up."

Solomon took in the area, turning around once, looking skyward. He turned and faced the direction the corpse had been facing in the photograph. The last vision of a murder victim interested him more than last words. Especially the victim of a lynching: He was a young black man in the Deep South, badge or no badge. Forgetting he was being watched, he dipped his head to one side, angling his neck, replicating the final position of the corpse's head. Wondering whom he looked at: who stood here and watched a man die. Hanging parties never leave until the deed is done.

Solomon turned back toward the tree, catching the end of a glance between Sheriff Ingalls and SAIC Macklin. Both men, but especially the sheriff, were predisposed to the characterization of black men as simpletons. Solomon pushed himself not to make the same mistake in his estimation of these two men.

"You have the rope?" he said.

"Sure, yup," said the sheriff with a shrug.

Macklin said, "Common rope, and more so than that, old rope. Could have come out of the barn of any property within fifty miles of here."

Solomon said, "You got the shoe?"

Sheriff Ingalls said, "The what?"

Solomon pointed to Hack Cawsby's stocking foot. "The shoe."

"Yeah, we got the other shoe. Was here."

Solomon nodded. "He either walked here under

duress, was tricked into it, or came on the back of an animal."

Sheriff Ingalls wasn't very interested in being helpful. "We did a search 'round this area. Didn't see no hoof marks."

Solomon looked at the charred debris at the foot of the tree, beneath where the corpse had swung. "Burned some of the ground, though. Maybe to cover up something."

"I don't think they was having a campfire," said the sheriff, already bored. "You wanted to see the crime scene. You said them photographs weren't enough for you. Well—here it is. Now what?"

Solomon kicked aside some of the blackened twigs and leaves, the part that was undisturbed, using the tread of his shoes to preserve the shine of the black leather. As he had noticed on the walk in, the ground was softer and wetter underneath.

The sheriff continued, directing his remarks to SAIC Macklin. "If you federal gentlemen are helpin', I'm all ears. If you're here to stir up more problems, thank you but we got plenty 'nough already. I need arrests and before that I need suspects. There's a conspiracy of silence among the Negroes, and I know how to get people talking if I has to."

Solomon crouched low on the balls of his feet. Preserved in the firm muck of the forest floor were indentations that didn't read well looking down from directly above. But when Solomon reconsidered them from a low side angle, he made out what looked to him like the impression of a child's bare foot.

Not unlike that of a young boy.

Solomon opened his mouth to bring this to the attention of the Jackson FBI official and the local sheriff. But he held his tongue. They were paying very little attention to him anyway. The sheriff was still complaining.

"If the federal government wants to spend some of my tax money on investigating this murder, well, that would be the first time I've ever got satisfaction from Washington, DC. Money well spent. But if you ain't here about the killing, and is more interested in preserving and protecting a certain class of people's civil rights and all that, then I got an actual crime to investigate while you all get wet spittin' into the wind."

Solomon straightened. He wished he had thought to bring a camera. "The victim here, Hack Cawsby, he was a bank manager?"

"He was," said the sheriff.

"And the leader of the local Citizens' Council?"

"Sure. What of it?"

"Citizens' Council is a segregation group."

"A states' rights advocacy group." The coded term came out of his mouth automatically.

"Like I said."

The sheriff smiled at Solomon's impudence. "All right. Have it your way. Sure does point the way toward whodunnit."

"Maybe the color of their skin," said Solomon. "You still have quite a number of suspects."

"Why we have to get crackin' on this. I'll go door-to-door if I have to. Justice demands it. This community demands it. If I don't get to the bottom of this, others will try their own methods. This is a public safety issue."

Solomon took the envelope of photographs from Macklin, who was notably quiet. Solomon pulled out photos of four hanged black men. "You go door-to-door for these ones?"

Sheriff Ingalls looked at the photographs like Solomon was trying to pass him counterfeit money.

Solomon said, "Five lynchings in the past year. Four African Americans, none of them solved. One white man, now you want the county turned upside down."

Sheriff Ingalls screwed up his face with such distaste that, for a moment, Solomon thought he was going to spit on the photographs. "I knew you wasn't here to help solve this." The sheriff pointed a nicotine-stained finger at SAIC Macklin, too. "You all are here to keep me from doing my damn job. To hassle a lawman. When you ain't got no idea what goes on here."

Solomon looked to Macklin, the ranking agent, for help. Macklin was at a loss for words.

Solomon was not. He had a lot more to say to the sheriff. But instead he turned his animosity into a tight smile. "Thank you, Sheriff Ingalls, for your cooperation. I'll let you know if I need anything else."

The sheriff looked to Macklin and back. "That's it?"

"For now," said Solomon.

Sheriff Ingalls turned on his heels and started away. "*God*damn federal government..."

Solomon watched him go. To Macklin, he said, "Thanks for backing me up."

"Listen, rookie," said Macklin. "He's right, you don't know shit here. Sometimes you kick in doors, sometimes you tread lightly. What happens if you need his help?"

"He was never going to give it."

Macklin took the envelope and photos back from Solomon. "I'm saying, try sugar sometimes. Even if you hate the man, you can still use him."

Macklin and Solomon both saw Agent Tyler hustling toward them, slowing when he passed the sheriff, then hurrying up again as he neared them.

Macklin said, "News?"

"Yessir," said Tyler, with a glance at Solomon.

"He's fine," said Macklin. "Go ahead."

"A local reporter filed a report with the wire services and it got picked up," said Tyler. "It's going to be a coast-to-coast story tomorrow."

Macklin sighed. "That's not helpful."

"Worse," continued Tyler, "we got word that Klansmen are coming in from Tennessee. And the story about the lynching of a white man is going to bring in more."

"A tinderbox situation," said Macklin. "You report back to Jackson with this?"

"They know, that's where I heard it," said Tyler.

Macklin turned to Solomon. "You sure you won't need the sheriff's help now?"

Solomon left Agent Tyler in the car outside the Jamuses' house. He knocked on the door and Coleman answered again. "Hello, sir."

"Coleman," said Solomon. "Is your mother in any kind of frame of mind to speak with me for a few minutes?"

"She's sitting with the pastor," he said, stepping aside for Solomon to enter.

Mrs. Jamus sat deep in a soft club chair that was receptive to her wide frame. She held a handkerchief in each hand, one white, the other pale lavender. The pastor, who introduced himself to Solomon as Theodore Eppert, used a folded months-old newspaper to help fan the inconsolable woman. The sick boy, Solomon learned, was named Vernon. He was the youngest of nine-teen children.

"There were these boys," Mrs. Jamus told Solomon as he sat on the edge of a brittle sofa cushion across the room, "white boys, no older than Coleman here"—Coleman remained standing in the doorway, protectively—"come to the door talking about voter-registration this and signing-this-petition that." She mopped her brow and the scoop of her neck where it became her chest. "Said they was going around to everyone in the Delta, writing names in a book. In a *book*." She looked to the pastor, who with a nod confirmed her worst fear. "Not three, four days later Vernon starts show-ing his first symptoms. Not three, four days later."

"Symptoms such as...?"

"Barkin'," she said. "Back talk. Vernon was the star of Sunday school, he weren't no back-talker. Not to me. And talkin' to hisself, and walking around the house in circles. Around and around, mutterin'. All on account of them white boys." She gripped the pastor's hand over the wet white hand-kerchief. "The devil's come to the Delta, I tell you. I am all prayed out."

She started to cry again, and Solomon stood and begged her pardon. He had gotten about all he was going to get out of her. Pastor Eppert whispered some calming words to her, then eased his hand out of her grip and rose to follow Solomon out past Coleman.

"I have sat with that boy," said the pastor. "I have tried to see inside his heart. There's an evil here. The Lord says, When the devil comes, he comes to the best of us. Vernon, bless him, he was the best of us."

Solomon said, "And the doctors haven't been able to do anything for him...?"

"She had Doc Jeffries over early on. Got kicked and barked at—curses too—until he left, said there weren't nothing he could do for him save give the directions to the nearest sanatorium."

Solomon nodded. He was thinking about the small footprint under the lynching branch. "Do you know how long he's been chained up?"

Pastor Eppert asked Coleman. "Day or two or three." Then, in a whisper, "They were worried what he might do to the others in their sleep."

Solomon returned the whisper. "Why do you think some of your parishioners think Vernon's illness is related to the lynching?"

The pastor shook his head. Up close, the silver blaze in his hair was bright, the follicles thicker and coarser than the rest. "I would say they see the devil's hand in this. Have you accepted the Lord as your savior, son?"

"I have," answered Solomon, and left it at that.

He shook the pastor's hand and took two steps toward the door before turning back.

"Do you know, or have you ever heard of, a man named Hugo Blackwood?"

Pastor Eppert looked to the ceiling for the answer. "Can't say I rightly do," he said. "Why do you ask?"

Solomon shook his head. "No reason." He left.

2019. Newark, New Jersey.

Obediah could barely contain its excitement.

Being the last one of the Hollow Ones to have been born made it often more impulsive, more prone to rush decisions. It had made mistakes. Many of them.

But this time it was resolved to do things differently. This time it had a plan.

It had jumped out of the body of the heavyset man—Leppo—and for a moment it contemplated taking the body of the young girl it had just wounded. But it had felt her bone give and crack, felt her clavicle disengage.

No. It could not occupy that body and do what it needed to do.

Still, the temptation was great. It had savored the confusion and the pain in the female agent—shooting her own partner first—and then, it now imagined, she would need to shoot the very girl she was meant to save.

How delightful. Delicious.

Obediah missed the chance. It hesitated just moments too long—and then the room was filled with

EMTs and local police. The female agent left the room, and instead of following, Obediah hovered above the bodies of the humans until a young EMT, approximately thirty years old and in excellent condition, presented himself.

It entered the body quickly, expertly extending its will over the young man's soul and rewiring the body so rapidly that the EMT faltered only a moment.

"Are you all right, Reese?" his partner asked.

Obediah nodded.

"Give me a hand with her," the partner said.

Obediah knew what an EMT would do and how he would do it. Through the centuries it had tried every profession, every science, every art. It couldn't claim to have mastered many of them, but it knew enough so it could stay undetected for long enough if it felt the result would be worth the effort. It could stay hidden in the flesh of its host—so long as his or her work and immediate family permitted selective isolation. Recently, within the past half century or so, most of its violent acts attracted a similar sort of professional—a paramedic, police officer, or firefighter—and therefore most of its interim jumps were well-meaning first responders.

Obediah had intended to enter the female agent, to continue this spree, but instead found something inside the EMT it liked. He was married, with a baby he was eager to get home to. This would be fun.

The couple lived in a modest apartment with thin

walls, so Obediah had to lie in wait until the neighbors left for work.

In the kitchen, the woman had been preparing a meager repast. Obediah selected a meat cleaver from a cheap QVC kitchen knife set: stainless steel, six inches. Not great quality but solid enough.

And just for fun, it decided to do a double.

A double was difficult to control, but enormously satisfying: Obediah hacked the woman in the ribs, twice, and then jumped inside her and forced her to stab the husband. Not mortally, but with enough force to crack a rib and perforate a lung. Then it jumped again and had the husband get her, smack in the middle of the head. The cleaver got stuck—her skull wouldn't release it.

Then it dialed 911, explained the scene at length, and went to work on the fallen woman's body.

By the time the cops showed up—plenty of them—the EMT was parceling the wife's body into pieces roughly the size of a beer can.

The baby was crying in its crib. Obediah jumped into the baby—and was retrieved by a Hispanic officer.

The other officer ordered the EMT to drop the hatchet. Upon failure to comply, he shot the EMT a few times.

The Hispanic officer covered the baby's eyes protectively. It was delicious for Obediah to then overtake the Hispanic officer and walk him past the bleeding EMT and the hacked-apart woman to the open window.

Obediah threw the baby right out the window. Five

floors. Watched it explode on the pavement. Heard the screams of passersby rise up.

The other officer was yelling at him. Obediah turned, reached for a kitchen knife.

The other officer shot his partner, and Obediah jumped into him.

Odessa sat on the sofa next to Linus, eating Indian food delivered by Postmates—costing almost twice as much as the menu price of the food itself, but Linus knew she didn't want to venture out after dark, for fear of being ambushed by some click-hungry blogger with an iPhone, nor did she want to be left alone in the apartment.

It didn't feel like a splurge. Nothing felt special anymore.

Normally they would be watching Netflix on Linus's laptop or streaming a basketball game (if she was feeling generous), but she wanted to stay away from anything that might cause her to trip over a news report. Invisible walls had gone up around her life, and Linus's by extension. She didn't like it, but it felt necessary. Her mood was like the tiny air pocket in a bubble level, supersensitive to any gradient change and impossible to keep centered.

Linus was a sweetheart, filling the quiet spaces

107

with small talk about his day, trying to keep the second hand moving. But inside Odessa's mind, a second voice spoke to her, and it was her own.

You took a life.

She had killed a fellow agent in the line of duty. That point was not in dispute. In her healthiest moments, she ticked off all the events that led her to shoot Walt Leppo; in her darkest moments, she questioned everything about that night, including her own rationality.

Your career is over.

Another fact that was hard to dispute. Everything she had worked for, all the shit she had taken to rate as a special agent of the FBI, the long hours, her ideals: All of it added to nothing. She had a law degree but she did not want to be a lawyer. She wanted to serve her country and in doing so make it a better place for all.

You don't come back from this.

Why delay the inevitable? She wanted to resign, though she knew that would send all the wrong signals. She was trapped in limbo, suspended in a netherworld while a bureaucracy grinded somewhere above her, going through the motions of an endgame, the result not in doubt.

As Linus did his best to retell a funny story from work that day, Odessa's gaze fell upon the carton of Agent Earl Solomon's office belongings on the floor by the door. The spicy food did not register upon her taste buds. The world had lost its flavor.

After letting the New York office know about her morning mission by email, Odessa summoned an Uber via her cell phone, entering Earl Solomon's home address as her destination. As she entered the crossover SUV, the driver, a burly Middle Eastern man conversing via a Bluetooth earpiece, got out to open his trunk. As she thanked him and loaded in the carton of belongings, while glancing up and down the street in fear of an ambush, she understood the look in the driver's eyes. *Another crazy fare.*

She rode southwest to a street just blocks from the Delaware River, which served as the border between New Jersey and Pennsylvania. The car pulled up at a prewar, one-story brick house ringed by a desultorily short—no taller than three feet—decorative chain-link fence. She noticed that other homes on the street had long since added on or built up, but this residence remained stubbornly modest. The driver pulled the carton from the trunk and set it in Odessa's hands as though relieved to have discharged her.

"Good luck, miss," he said.

Maybe he assumed she was going through a breakup. And in a sense—from her career, from her expected life—she was. She thanked him and gave him a five-star review before his vehicle was out of sight.

With difficulty, she emptied the contents of the mailbox into the carton in her hands, then pushed through the short gate and up the walkway to the front door. For security's sake, in case any neighbors were watching her, she dropped a few letters at the door, setting down the carton to retrieve them and, in doing so, retrieving a key from beneath a planter made of blue pottery.

It would take some time to forget her police procedure instincts.

She unlocked the door and carried the carton inside. The air within smelled stale but not unpleasant. She closed the door behind her, called out, "Hello?" just in case, and, receiving no reply, walked through a small living area to the adjoining kitchen. She set the carton and mail down on a small kitchen island, relieved to have delivered the possessions to their rightful owner at last.

The house was quiet, and there was no sign that anyone had been inside for days. She turned and looked at the living area, where a two-cushion sofa faced an old box television set on a wooden cart. An old padded rocker, angled toward the television, appeared to be the favored piece of furniture. Framed advertising signs for Cuban cigars hung on the walls. The décor was very spare, very male. Also, very orderly—which stood out in sad contrast with the current state of Agent Solomon's mind. She shook her head, remembering his nonsensical recommendation to deposit a letter in an unmarked mailbox somewhere near Wall Street.

Dennis the fish swam in a small bowl near the television. He was alive. Odessa carried the bowl near the sink. The water was cloudy and needed to be changed. A shaker of fish food sat on the sill of a window looking out at the backyard. Dennis sipped at the crumbs as soon as they hit the surface of the water.

"There you go, Dennis," she said. "You're welcome."

She opened the refrigerator, and it wasn't bad inside. A few suspect leftovers inside covered Pyrex dishes. Bottles of nutrition shakes and sugary sodas. Not much to throw out.

She walked down the short rear hall, stopping just inside the door of Agent Solomon's bedroom. It was simply furnished, the bed neatly made, a small hamper of worn clothes in the corner. She chose not to poke around, merely sliding open a mirrored closet door, taking note of the old suit jackets inside, and a bright-blue FBI windbreaker.

She profiled an older bachelor, possibly a widower, someone who preferred to keep his home neat rather than be bothered to tidy up after. Solitary living, alone but not necessarily lonely. For whatever reason, she tried to envision herself living in this house near the end of her life. A simple existence, a small universe. These thoughts began to cascade to other thoughts, big life thoughts, wondering about Linus and her future, things she didn't want to sort through now, or ever.

She returned to the kitchen to refocus. Dennis was swimming fast, reinvigorated. Odessa checked the cabinets for a receptacle large enough to serve as a temporary bowl for changing the water. She looked around for a little net. Nothing in the cabinets, nothing in the drawers. She continued to look around, and as she did so, she realized that something about her surroundings was bugging her. It took a few more moments to realize that the dimensions of the house did not seem right.

She opened the front door and walked halfway to the sidewalk, turning to take in the house. There was a window to the right with its interior shade drawn. There should be another room or two on that side.

She returned inside, more energetically this time. She located a narrow utility closet near the front door, recessed into the side wall. Boxes of trash bags sat on shelves, an Electrolux vacuum standing on the floor. There, hanging on a nail, was a fish-net—but she wasn't interested in that anymore.

She knocked on each wall. The back wall beneath the trash bag shelf sounded different from the two side walls. Hollow. She examined the seams and pushed on the right side.

With a soft click and a tiny kickback, the rear wall gave way, swinging left on hinges. The space beyond was dark.

Odessa halted. She took a beat before pushing through. What if it was some sort of sex dungeon? This was how her FBI mind worked.

She entered the narrow passage. The air was not stale but fresh, with a hint—more like a memory—of cigar smoke. Her shoe met a soft carpet. She felt for a light switch and the hidden room came to life.

Bookshelves. Floor-to-ceiling ones, occupying most of the wide walls, with old, textured maroon-and-gold wallpaper covering the rest.

Before her was a small work desk with a wide leather chair. Headphones lay on the desk, connected by a cord to a large reel-to-reel tape player.

To her right, vented out through the wall, whirred a large air purifier. A small humidor containing a few expensive-looking cigars sat next to a standing ashtray. Against the wall on the other side of the desk was a side cart, liquor bottles on the lower tray, thick crystal rocks glasses on the top.

And then she saw them: the tapes.

"Sweet Jesus…"

The shelves contained not books but thin cardboard cartons. Mylar audio recording tapes on seven-inch reels, each narrow spine labeled and dated. Reel number, date, and subject. There were hundreds—perhaps thousands—of them, many of them from multiple recording sessions with the same date, four or five reels long.

The shelves were mounted on sliders, revealing yet another layer of tapes behind—on a wall-mounted system. But this was not hoarding—it was a careful, methodically organized system.

The dates ran to the year 2018. Odessa walked backward to the top shelf of the first bookcase, locating the first chronological recording.

#1001 / Mississippi 1962 / Vernon Jamus

She didn't know what it meant, but of course she thought of the reel-to-reel player from Solomon's office desk, seemingly forgotten. Suddenly she felt like she was trespassing here—not legally, but spiritually. This was a private chamber, and it held secrets—bookcases full of them—that added up to a mystery she felt instinctually that she did not want to solve.

After one last look around at the hundreds of

painstakingly cataloged recording tapes, she turned off the light and retreated back through the narrow utility closet.

Shaken, she leaned against the kitchen island, as though having returned from another world. A long-retired agent who wasn't retired. A secret room inside his house. She remembered his questions to her, and how he seemed to know about the thing she saw—saw, felt, whatever—leaving Walt Leppo's body after she had shot him dead.

A cauldron? Drop a letter in a mailbox on Wall Street?

It was all too bewildering. Instead of changing Dennis's bowl water, Odessa tucked the bowl under her arm to take with her, locked up, and left.

Odessa met with her new lawyer—same firm—behind closed doors at a Midtown office. She had been reassigned to a female lawyer, who asked Odessa to take her through her account again. The lawyer's name was Courtney and she was only a few years older than Odessa, dressed in a simple black-and-white suit, taking notes on her laptop as Odessa spoke, softly tapping on her keyboard while her eyes remained sympathetically on Odessa's face. Odessa imagined Courtney's fingertips were as gently callused as the pads of a cat's paw.

"Thank you," said Courtney as Odessa exhaled, drained, at the end of her recounting. "I think the only thing—or the best thing—you have going for you is the surviving daughter. Her statements indicate that she was certain Agent Leppo was going to kill her and that your shooting saved her life. That is a compelling statement, although we won't know for some time how she presents in person.

Also, she remains seriously traumatized by the event—she is the only surviving member of her family—and so any testimony she gives will be difficult. And as a survivor of trauma, her memory may be challenged at the inquest."

Odessa almost teared up, thinking about the girl. She was torn by a great desire to meet her, imagining that such an encounter could be healing for both of them...and terrified of such a meeting, knowing it might offer no relief, and could even be further traumatizing.

Courtney appeared to be scrolling through her notes, using her track pad. "Is there anything you've left out of your account?"

Odessa shook her head. She said nothing about the heat signature departing Leppo's corpse.

"And you've already stated this, but for my benefit," said Courtney, "you were not under the influence of drugs or alcohol that night. And you are not taking any prescribed psychotropic medicine, and are not currently under the care of a psychiatrist...?"

"Not yet," said Odessa.

"And—forgive my directness—were you and Agent Leppo involved romantically in any way...?"

Odessa looked to the side, at nothing. Trying to control her anger. The stab wounds kept coming, this one dead center in her chest. Was this coming from the FBI? she wondered. Or just Courtney's own suspicion?

"Not in any way whatsoever."

"Got it." Tap-tap-tap with her cat's paws.

Odessa said, "He was the one with the psychotic snap, not me."

Courtney nodded, perhaps a bit embarrassed herself at having had to ask that question. And she should be.

Courtney tapped her track pad, committing Odessa's account to a file. "The FBI wants your badge and your gun, but we are fighting for you."

Odessa felt like handing over her badge permanently. "They already have my gun."

"Do they?" Courtney looked through paper notes in a binder, nodding confidently as though she had found confirmation of this fact, but Odessa knew she was just covering for her own mistake. Courtney had probably received Odessa's case the day before.

Odessa saw more of herself in the beleaguered young lawyer than she liked to admit.

Courtney said, "The FBI has flagged some things for our attention, but I want to ask you about one of them. It has to do with your father...?"

"What are you talking about?"

"It's something that I guess came up in the past—
"

"That was all dealt with in my background investigation."

Courtney appeared to bristle at Odessa's firm tone. "Yes, that is the document I am referring to."

Odessa's head was buzzing. "They pulled my background check as part of this?"

"A summary letter, yes."

Odessa went cold. "Is this normally done in these cases?"

"Well," said Courtney, again looking to her notes for an answer Odessa knew was not there, "I don't know. We handle mostly police officer shootings, like the one on Long Island yesterday. Not FBI shootings."

Odessa looked away. The thought of her father made her morose, but she did not want to show her lawyer any strong negative reaction. Linus was right: She needed a real lawyer.

Then something came bubbling up through the darkness—something she could not ignore. Odessa asked softly:

"Wait…what happened on Long Island yesterday?"

O dessa rode the subway in a mental fog. She emerged onto the street in Kew Gardens with a new attitude. She returned to the FBI Resident Agency, entering with a tight, confident smile for the office manager, returning to Earl Solomon's empty office.

But not before she borrowed an unattended laptop in the copy room, one she noticed had been there since the day before. She closed the office door and opened the laptop on Agent Solomon's desk, sitting in his long-unused chair. She searched for the murder case and found multiple articles relating to a shocking killing in Little Brook, a Long Island hamlet east of Massapequa. A town supervisor, the top elected local official, went "postal" half an hour before office hours ended in Little Brook Town Hall, attacking people with a long-bladed cabinet screwdriver, killing three. The fifty-three-year-old man was shot and killed by a marine patrol safety officer who happened to be there checking permits.

A rampage killing. The assailant had no prior criminal record. Was said to be a pillar of the community. "He just snapped." There were mentions of health concerns, financial pressures. Conditions that affect a great number of middle-aged men. A news item she would normally have skimmed and then clicked away from suddenly had resonance for her.

Then she accessed the FBI directory—nothing requiring a security passcode—for information about Agent Earl Solomon. With the hundreds of archived tape recordings from his house in mind, she searched for case records. No hits. She was tempted to search deeper, but this wasn't her laptop, and she didn't want to get herself, or any other agent, in further trouble. But the impression she got was that an invisible hand had all but erased Earl Solomon from existence within the FBI database.

Never mind the cost, Odessa couldn't stand the thought of Ubering out to Long Island, sitting in the backseat of a car like a child. She looked up Zipcar and downloaded an updated app, entered her email and an old password, and voilà, the car sharing account she had started in Boston still worked.

She drove a silver Honda CR-V east from Queens, her phone copiloting from the passenger seat, taking her along the Southern State Parkway to 27, past Amityville, arriving in Little Brook. She operated with a sense of purpose and also dread, knowing she shouldn't be doing this, feeling she was going to be caught...and at the same time unable to turn back.

The Little Brook Town Hall Annex was an old stone building shouldered by retail shops and a CVS. New York State Police cars ringed the street entrance but no flashing lights, no taped cordon. A female officer in a reflective vest worked the traffic detail, waving cars past. Odessa rolled down her window and badged her way to the curb next to a white van she recognized as an "aftermath" biorecovery service vehicle, or a crime scene cleaner.

There was no officer at the door. Odessa entered the lobby. A plainclothes detective talking on his cell phone eyeballed her, distracted by his conversation. Credentials in hand, she walked past the clerk's window and into the interior of the town building. Cleaners in white bodysuits and rubber gloves were sponging a bloodstain off the wall, the spatter having been dissolved into a wet pink bloom. Farther down the hallway, state police crime laboratory specialists were photographing another bloodstain, this one on the wall and floor where a body must have fallen.

There wasn't much here, and little she could

learn. She approached the crime scene techs and was pointed to an office around the corner. There, a local police officer eyed her with suspicion until she showed him her badge.

"Special Agent Hardwicke?" he said, reading her credentials, suddenly energized. "What can I do for you, Agent?"

The suspect's home was a midsize Colonial with an attached garage at the bottom of a sloping street. A New York State Police cruiser was parked in the driveway, Troop L, Suffolk County. Probably a captain or a major sitting with the widow. Odessa parked down the street a bit—the CR-V did not profile as FBI—and walked back to the house, determined to see this through.

She introduced herself to a pair of troopers on the lawn, offering her creds, feeling their eyes on her as she walked to the door. Dogs barked plaintively somewhere inside the house, probably locked away in a bathroom or basement. The widow sat alone on a large sofa near an old grand piano topped with photographs of her grown children. Her name was Louise Colina and she was probably sixty, older than Odessa expected, though it was likely the photograph of her husband, Edwardo, known as Eddie, on the town website was many years out of date.

The Troop L captain stood when Odessa entered, his wide-brimmed hat in hand. He was a good foot taller than she. But Odessa did not flinch, allowing her badge to lead the way. She shook his large hand firmly.

"Have we met?" he said. "You look a little familiar. What office are you out of?"

"Newark," said Odessa quickly. "But I'm on special assignment to Kew Gardens." She pivoted to Mrs. Colina before the captain could ask another question. "Mrs. Colina, I just want to offer my condolences. This must be an incredibly trying time for you."

The woman looked lost in her own body, the way some nursing home residents appear. She would not recover from this shock for many weeks. "Thank you," she said.

"I cannot imagine what it would be like to watch someone walk out the door one day and...then this happens."

Mrs. Colina nodded. "There was no indication," she said. "I keep thinking it's all a great mistake."

"No indication whatsoever?" said Odessa.

The captain said, "He had gotten into a car accident earlier in the day, struck a stone wall, one-car accident. Didn't report it."

Mrs. Colina said, "Maybe he hit his head. Eddie would never do something like this."

"I am so sorry," said Odessa, again taking the widow's hand, then backing off. "I don't want to interrupt your conversation. I'll just take a quick look around. Captain."

The trooper nodded back to Odessa, curious, but sitting back down, unable to leave Mrs. Colina's side.

Odessa stepped back outside, avoiding the pair of troopers there, following the front walk to the driveway. The garage door was open, the interior cluttered around an old Subaru. She poked through bins of outgrown athletic equipment, storage cartons, a tool bench, a rider lawn mower. She was looking for an iron cauldron like the one Agent Solomon had described. She found an old umbrella stand and a few planters, but they held only dead moths.

Back outside, she climbed four brick steps to the side yard. Angled before a line of trees separating the property from the neighbor's was a garden shed: not one of the prefabricated resin toolsheds sold at Home Depot and Walmart, nor the fancy, cottage-shaped custom sheds, but an old, dark pine wood shed with an old iron clasp, probably built by one of the previous property owners.

Odessa pulled open the door, smelling grease and sawdust. Light from the only window—a single pane of cracked glass—fell over an old hand mower, bicycles, a croquet set and other lawn games, and a cracked bird fountain. She lifted aside a rusty bicycle pump, looking at the cobwebby rear of the shed.

She would never have given it a second glance if she hadn't been looking for it. A fat black pot with a curved rim set in the back corner. It was full of trash: sticks, a string of colored beads, and string. Tufts of brown hair that could have been mistaken for clumps of dead grass. The plastic handle of a long knife set upside down.

She turned on her phone light, wishing she had a pair of gloves. What she had dismissed as sticks...they were bones. Grayed with age. Human or animal, she could not tell.

"Agent?"

The trooper's voice startled Odessa. She saw part of a hat brim through the cracked window.

"Yes?" she said.

"Captain would like a word with you—inside."

"Sure thing!" said Odessa, forcing a cheery note in her voice. "Tell him I'll be right there."

She remained frozen until the hat brim moved on. Quickly she snapped a handful of photographs with her flash on, then backed out without knocking over any of the bikes. She walked down the side of the house to the street and turned to her car, getting in and driving away.

★   ★   ★

"Sorry—I thought you were a reporter."

Odessa smiled and put her credentials back inside her left front pocket. She stepped inside a small office. Photographs taped to the wall around the Portuguese flag showed that the marine patrol safety officer, Mariella Parra, had once been a swordfish boat captain.

She shook Odessa's hand with a manly grip, flecks of gray in her short, butch haircut, the corners of her eyes creased by the years and by the sun.

"My boss is giving me the next few days off," said Mariella, dumping things into a canvas bag. "Just trying to get away from here. Do I have to tell what happened again?"

Odessa shrugged. "I'll take the short version if there is one."

"What does the FBI want with this?"

"We are investigating a rash of similar rampage killings."

Mariella took a surprised step back. "You think there was something more to it?"

"No," said Odessa, "but part of what we do is compile crime statistics in an effort to spot trends." She was bullshitting behind a smile. "I know this has been traumatic for you."

"It's pretty simple." Mariella shrugged. "I had to

check a few permits and stopped into the town hall about twenty minutes before closing. I heard some yelling and I guess at first I thought it was somebody's birthday or something...you know, a celebration. Maybe my ears wanted them to be happy noises. When the raised voices became screams...I think I stood there for another ten, fifteen seconds, still trying to believe it wasn't happening. It's not like on TV, where there's a buildup. Where you know something is about to happen. Suddenly it was happening and I was in it."

Odessa nodded. She understood this much better than Mariella knew.

"When I started moving, my blood was cold, and I had my service weapon in my hand. I was so freaked out. I saw the first body, the lady on the floor. She was bleeding out. The man paying his taxes, he was still clutching his bill in one hand, crawling alligator-style down the hall, leaving a trail of blood. The town supervisor, when I saw him, Mr. Colina—he was stabbing the third woman—that poor, poor woman—in the lower back, just over and over with that long screwdriver. At one point..." She choked up, then continued. "At one point the screwdriver jammed on the backbone and—and kind of lifted the whole body, for a brief moment— maybe an inch or two—and then he pried it loose and went back at it. Mechanically—no emotion there..."

Odessa was riveted, reexperiencing her own trauma as she listened. "What did he look like? His expression?"

Mariella winced and shook her head. "Curious? Gleeful? Somewhat absent? His eyes, they were so bright, kind of exploding. And he saw me, and he let the woman fall, the screwdriver blade coming out of her lower back so slowly. The state police, they asked if I said anything to him. I didn't say shit. I fired my weapon I don't know how many times. I put that crazy son of a bitch down."

Mariella exhaled, having gotten through the account one more time, relieved to be finished. Not counting on Odessa to push her for more.

"And then what?"

"Then...he was down and I went running the other way. I was out of the building so fast. It took the police forever to come."

"I mean..." Odessa tried to put this delicately. "After you shot him. After he went down. Did you run off before he died, or did you...?"

Mariella looked low-eyed at Odessa for an extra beat, and the hair on the back of Odessa's neck stood on end. "I don't know if he was dead. I was too far down the hallway. But I waited until he was still."

"…And?"

Mariella's breathing deepened. "What are you getting at?"

She knew. Odessa could see that she knew. Odessa came closer, her voice quiet. "You saw something—something come out of the body?"

Mariella was scared. "I thought I saw something. My mind played a trick."

"What kind of trick?"

She didn't want to answer. "I don't know."

"It's not part of my report," said Odessa, "if that's what you're worried about. But other survivors of rampage killings such as this…they've reported seeing something leave the assailant's body at the moment of death."

Mariella looked as though she was going to be sick. She found a bottle of water and took two quick swigs. She looked at Odessa, not trusting her…but needing to share this.

"It was…like a presence."

Odessa felt dizzy hearing this. "Go on."

"Not a…not a ghost or anything. An essence."

"Was there a smell—a burning smell?"

Mariella shook her head fast. "I ran. I don't know." She grabbed the floppy handles of the canvas bag and lifted it off her desk. "I'm sorry, I can't…I have to go." Then, as though she remembered she was speaking to an FBI agent: "Can I go?"

Odessa nodded. "Thank you," she said.

With a strange look at her, Mariella stepped past Odessa and strode out of the office. Odessa swiped her own face with her hand, heartened to have her experience corroborated by another...and then newly frightened by the similarity. If it was true...what did it all mean?

Odessa drove back in a daze. Numerous times she blinked and looked at the road ahead of her and realized suddenly she had been driving without thinking about driving for many minutes.

Her mind was pulling her in so many directions. She had to focus.

She texted her friend and fellow agent Laurena to call her. Not sixty seconds later, Odessa's phone rang. She answered, saying, "Hi, you're the best."

Laurena was a second-year agent, but five years older than Odessa, having clerked for a US circuit court judge before applying to the FBI. "Where are you? Are you okay?"

Odessa spent a few moments allaying her fears. Laurena's concern brought tears to Odessa's eyes. "Can you do me a favor?"

"Anything, Dessa. I'm not good at cooking, though."

"I wouldn't be calling you if I needed a meal cooked."

"And I don't clean much, either."

"I want to see crime scene photos from the Peters home."

A long pause. "Why would you want to see that?"

"Not the grisly stuff. But—I want it all. Not for the bodies."

"For what then? Now I'm worried."

Odessa said, "I can't get it out of my head. I want to see what was there—what was in the house. Like, the basement, the garage—everything."

"I don't know. This seems both unhealthy and unethical."

"You can put it in Dropbox for me. Copy them in and send me the link separately. I'll look and I promise I won't download. No link between us."

"There's a link between us if the Bureau needs to look at it."

Odessa said, "They won't. Please, Laur."

Silence except for a tapping sound, Laurena's pencil against her desk. "I'd rather cook you a meal."

"Thanks, Laur," said Odessa, quickly.

"But I didn't say yes—"

"You're the best." And she hung up.

*O*bediah had been expelled from the town supervisor much too prematurely. There had been so much more to do. Despite the always pleasurable frenzy of ejection, the experience ended unsatisfactorily.

It passed from the Little Brook Town Hall Annex, eager to locate another suitable vehicle. She was a woman in her fifties, carrying a yoga mat, climbing into the driver's seat of a tan sport utility vehicle. Obediah took the woman, and the automobile, for a fast ride north to Route 495, an east–west interstate. It pushed woman and machine to their limits, achieving speeds of ninety miles per hour, using her manicured hands to weave in and out of traffic on screeching tires.

It was looking for the right place, the right moment. Like a peregrine falcon timing a dive for an unsuspecting dove or a distracted wader.

It swung right, veering hard into the rear left wheel of a small sports car, sending it pinwheeling across two lanes and off the unrailed side of the highway, *coming apart upon impact with trees. A box truck was struck and spun all the way around, suffering a head-on collision with a delivery van, both of which were subsequently rammed by a Mayflower moving truck.*

The SUV skidded a long arc from left to right across three lanes of highway, still traveling at over eighty miles per hour when it smashed into Jersey barriers made of concrete and stitched together with rebar. Obediah's human vehicle died upon impact, and the entity was forcibly sprung loose like a spectacular firework exploded from a shell. It was ecstasy.

After the other vehicles skidded to a stop, the silence was pure, smoke rising from the crumpled engines. Obediah felt fulfilled, moved, as from the final movements of a great symphony—only instead of applause, all he heard were car doors opening and anguished voices of witnesses unable to accept the carnage before them.

Obediah wasted no time. It entered the body of a young woman in her twenties, a Good Samaritan standing out of her sporty Jeep. It took her back into the vehicle, starting up the engine, knowing from experience that if it didn't leave soon, it might be stuck in a terrifically anticlimactic traffic jam for some time.

The Good Samaritan's boyfriend, caught by surprise, barely made it back into the passenger seat before the Jeep sped away. Obediah's first inclination was to repeat the event, to experience another spectacular crash. But it became first distracted, then annoyed by the boyfriend's protestations, his questions, his concern.

Why are you driving so fast? What's wrong? Why do you look that way?

He reached for her arm, and Obediah lashed out, smacking him across the face, cracking his eyeglasses in two and opening a gash over his left eyebrow. As he was holding his forehead and crying out in pain, Obediah had the Good Samaritan reach over and unlatch his seat belt, then open his door and swing the car violently right, then left.

The irritating boyfriend rolled out of the car and bumped along the highway asphalt until his body, viewed in the rearview mirror, lay still between two lanes, only to be run over by the left tires of an Amazon Prime delivery van.

The sight was oddly satisfying, and for a moment, Obediah considered the same fate for the Good Samaritan, rolling out of the speeding vehicle.

But another impulse commanded the entity's attention. An awareness, a sudden cognizance. It felt it the way animals perceive changes in barometric pressure presaging a change in the weather.

The foe.

He was near.

Obediah was incapable of fear, of anything other than hunger, than the hunt for pleasure. But here was a source of potential pain. Here was the end of the Hollow One's raucous joyride of gluttonous annihilation.

There were four Hollow Ones. There had always been four Hollow Ones. But Obediah was the only entity still free.

It pushed down heavily on the gas pedal, driving the Jeep west toward the city of New York.

Toward Hugo Blackwood.

Odessa returned to Earl Solomon's hospital room, finding him sitting in a padded chair looking out the grimy window. The sky was baby-blanket blue, and she wondered what it looked like to an aging man who'd had a significant health scare... if he was even seeing the sky at all.

"Is it time?" he said before turning. He had been expecting a nurse. "Oh. Agent Hardwicke."

"Hello again," she said, stopping by the foot of his empty bed. The corner television was on mute. "How are you today?"

"I've been better." He turned back to the window. "I can barely see past all the city soot on the glass. I had to shadow a window washer once. In Manhattan. Late '60s, but the buildings were still tall then. I tried going out on a platform. They didn't clip in back then with them... what is it, the clips?"

"Carabiners?"

He turned back to her. "No such thing. Not when you got so little sand left in the hourglass." He scratched at his neck over the top collar of his hospital gown with fingernails like dulled arrowheads. "What's on your mind?"

"Maybe you saw on television, there was another rampage murder. This one out on Long Island."

"A local politician," Solomon said.

Odessa nodded. "Another person who just snapped, no history of violence or aggression. Killed three innocent bystanders before being shot."

Solomon pursed his dry lips. "You see similarities to your case."

"Don't you?"

He smiled, closing one eye—not in a wink, but to get a better look at her. "They always happen in threes, these things. All bad things, actually."

"Always?" asked Odessa. "How many times have you seen something like this?"

"You went out there, didn't you," said Solomon.

She couldn't tell if he approved or was simply amused. "I did," she said. "When I was here before, you asked about cauldrons at the crime scene. Why?"

"I was curious."

"It's a very specific, and strange, detail."

"I know. And you looked at me like I was headed for the loony bin. And then you went out to this spree killer's house in Long Island..."

"Not in his garage," she told him. "An old shed out in back. An iron pot, just like you described. That's kind of extraordinary."

He smiled. "You flatter me because now you're hungry for information."

"But how did you know?"

Two nurses knocked at the open door behind Odessa, walking right into the room. "Okay, Mr. Solomon."

Odessa's heart dropped. She stepped to the side to allow them through. "You have a visitor?" one said.

"My accountant," he said. "She handles my vast fortune."

The older nurse smiled at Odessa. "How wonderful."

Odessa stood by anxiously as they helped him out of the chair and back into the wheeled bed.

The younger nurse said, "Do you have any stock tips for us? If you could invest in one thing, what's guaranteed to accrue over time?"

Once he settled into the pillows, he said, "Human stupidity."

The nurses chuckled. Odessa was jumping out of her skin. She had so much to ask him.

"He's going for another scan," the older nurse told her. "It's going to be a while."

"Is everything all right?" Odessa asked.

The nurses were mum. Patient confidentiality. They looked to Solomon.

"I had a bad test," he said. "And these ladies will use any excuse to get me naked. How was my house?"

"Your house was fine. Fine." The room of tapes: How could she bring it up with the nurses here? "I took Dennis."

"Who? Oh—the fish. Right. You steal anything else? Found anything of interest?"

The nurses unplugged him from the monitors, releasing the brakes on the bed wheels.

What if something happened to him? What if it was now or never?

"I checked crime scene photos from my incident," Odessa said. "They photographed the entire house, as you know."

The nurses pretended not to listen, but "crime scene photos" got their antennae up.

Solomon said, "Now, how'd you get those?"

"In one of the pictures, it looks like another pot—a cauldron—in the basement behind a water heater. In Peters's house, the one his family lived in. Hidden down there. I couldn't see what was inside. The photographer probably thought it was a trash can or something."

Solomon asked, "What was inside the one you did see? On Long Island?"

It was awkward saying this with the two nurses in the room. "Bones. Trash. Beads, hair. Is it some kind of shrine?"

"What kind of bones? What size?"

"I don't know. I'm no forensic anthropologist."

"But you know a human bone when you see it. Was it a child's size? Or adult? It makes all the difference."

The nurses had him ready now, but were almost hesitant to leave, fully tuned in to the conversation now. "Sorry," said the younger nurse, to both Odessa and Solomon. "But we have to go." They started wheeling him through the door.

Odessa said, "Both—I think. They were human bones. Some big, some small."

"So, there, now—where would you get human bones?" asked Solomon as they wheeled him out the door and away into the hall.

At home that night, her half-eaten noodle bowl was growing cold next to her laptop.

Linus was at his desk by the window, headphones on, writing a brief, wearing the mint-green cable-knit pullover he favored on cold nights. A bit of Frank Ocean trickled out from the padding over his ears. Odessa didn't know how he could write with music in his head. She would be singing along with the lyrics, getting nothing done.

Linus was keeping an eye on her, glancing over now and then, watching her reflection in the night-darkened window. She could feel it. It was comforting, it was loving. It warmed her that he cared. But she also felt strange, having someone so worried about her. Was he waiting for her to fall apart, or was he looking at his girlfriend and wondering what it was like for her to kill? Or, worse, wondering if she had killed Walt Leppo by mistake. She was the person he shared a bed with.

Odessa wondered how she came across. She found herself double-checking her demeanor frequently: *Do I seem sane?* And now—never more than tonight, after the things she had learned earlier in the day.

"You going to finish that?" he asked.

"Oh, I'll heat it up later. It's good."

Linus smiled at her. "You were staring into space."

"I know. I'm fine."

"Would you be happier watching something?"

"I'm good," she said. "Just catching up on some news."

He smiled and replaced his headphones over his ears. Odessa returned to her laptop, paging through search results for news stories about grave robbing in New Jersey and Long Island—opened up in a private browsing window, because she worried how it would look showing up in her search history.

She clicked and read articles about disturbed and defaced grave sites, most of the stories from local papers in the patch.com network. Graves desecrated. Headstones kicked over. Tiffany glass stolen. She narrowed her search to incidents from the previous five years.

One story jumped out. Actually, it was a series of stories, a scandal at the time, one Odessa vaguely remembered seeing on her news feed. "Miracle Baby Remains Stolen from Grave." That was one of the less gratuitous headlines. The story went back a few years, a bittersweet article about a suburban Jersey toddler nicknamed "Baby Mia." She had been born with a degenerative brain disease and wasn't projected to survive more than a few hours. Against all odds, she had lived a month or more past her second birthday. But the health care cost of keeping her alive was prohibitive, and a feature article about the "miracle" girl became an online phenomenon. Baby Mia became a social media hashtag. Placards featuring a photograph of the girl wearing a pink elastic headband around her bandaged head appeared in store windows throughout New Jersey, from Asbury Park to Trenton, even crossing the river into parts of Philadelphia. A special SMS code was set up, a six-digit shortcut allowing direct donations of $10 to her health care fund. Six Flags Great Adventure and Storybook Land hosted fundraiser nights, and she dropped the puck at a New Jersey Devils playoff home game, becoming a local celebrity. The Devils held a pregame moment of silence for their adopted mascot after she finally succumbed to the disease.

Six months later, her burial plot in a graveyard in Allenhurst was discovered to have been excavated, her coffin stolen. The shocking story made network morning shows, and her bereaved parents suffered a second time. While the crime was never officially solved, Odessa found a subsequent story about a narcotics ring being broken up, which mentioned a link to recent grave desecrations, citing Baby Mia's and the theft of the corpse of a man who died in 1977 from a Long Island cemetery.

Odessa scanned other accounts of corpses being stolen and mausoleums broken into. A surprising number of cases. *Grave robbing? In New Jersey? News at eleven.* She finally pulled herself out of the internet wormhole, trying to make sense of what she had learned.

Why would someone desecrate a child's grave? Her first thought was a religious cult, a strain of voodoo. Narcotics rings often venerated certain dark saints or superstitious occult deities for "protection" from arrest. Santeria was the best known.

But what did this have to do with rampage killings? She X'd out of her browser more confused than ever. None of it made sense to her...and yet she was left with a chill deep in her core. It meant *something*. But what?

Odessa sipped at her seltzer, tinged with lime. Dennis the fish swam about in fresh water in the clean bowl in the center of the table. His delicate-looking fins appeared faded, the maroon of his body looking more orange. She wondered how close the fish had come to death, waiting for its owner to return home. She remembered Agent Solomon being wheeled away, close to the end himself. Dennis appeared to be looking at Odessa, swimming in place a moment before resuming his circling.

Odessa made a decision and got up.

She had a letter to write.

To Hugo Blackwood, Esq.

My name is Odessa Hardwicke. I am a special agent with the FBI working out of the New Jersey Field Office, currently on special assignment.

A fellow agent, Earl Solomon, suggested that I write to you to request your assistance on a pressing investigatory matter. This is an unusual and unorthodox act on the part of an FBI agent, but Mr. Solomon insists, and presently the investigation is at a standstill.

I am writing you concerning two separate and seemingly unrelated rampage killings recently in the news, one in Montclair, New Jersey, the other in Little Brook, Long Island.

Any assistance would be greatly appreciated.

O dessa sat on a subway seat near the center door, the handwritten note sealed inside a six-by-nine manila envelope as instructed, addressed to "Hugo Blackwood." She had folded it once, only once. The envelope lay facedown on her lap. The subway car rolled under the Hudson River, carrying late-arriving morning commuters from New Jersey into Lower Manhattan.

Odessa felt alternately purposeful and foolish, undertaking this strange errand. If it was a sign of desperation on her part, at least it was a private gesture, one she could disavow if necessary, with no harm done.

She exited the subway into a downpour, one the weather app on her phone had anticipated. She opened her umbrella, tucking the envelope inside her jacket to keep it dry. The rain blew in at a slight angle, battering the black nylon shield over her head, kicking up from the sidewalk to soak her ankles and the cuffs of her pants. She had a clear path, as the rain had frightened pedestrians off the streets, or at least forestalled their midmorning coffee runs or electronic cigarette breaks. As the wind lifted the rain onto her knees and upper legs, she considered waiting out the cloudburst herself, but decided she needed to get this over with. There was a dreamlike quality to her actions; she would not be released from this trance until her objective was completed. She hurried through the blowing rain toward Stone Street.

She had researched it that morning, after Linus left for the law office. Stone Street was a narrow cobblestone way dating back to 1658, the first Manhattan street paved with stone back when the island was a Dutch farming and trading colony known as New Amsterdam. (The street was then known as High Street.) Wall Street was at that time an actual wooden wall, a protective barrier at the northern edge of the settlement. There followed a centuries-long, inexorable descent into neglect. As recently as the 1970s, Stone Street had been a seedy back alley; in the 1980s it declined further into a graffiti-scarred garbage pit.

Construction then divided the street into two sections. The eastern half, only two blocks long, flanked by restored lofts and warehouses dating from the mid-1800s—after the Great Fire of 1835 destroyed most of what remained of New Amsterdam—had since been restored as a pedestrian-only thoroughfare, renamed the South Street Seaport Historic District. With granite paving, bluestone sidewalks, and streetlights resembling old gas lamps, it had been revitalized as a dining destination with outdoor tables in warmer months. International flags strung building-to-building fluttered over perhaps the most European-seeming street on the entire island.

The western half remained open to one-way traffic, but scaffolding-covered buildings and construction areas squeezed the road to a forbidding passageway. There were no pedestrians in sight, only a delivery truck at the far end of the street, its hazard lights flashing. Odessa passed 11 Stone Street and continued ahead, the next marked building numbered 19. She doubled back, scouring granite doorways for address numbers, with no luck. She grew frustrated and was on the verge of giving up—angry at herself for following the instructions of an obviously confused elderly man—when she peered skyward into the falling rain and noticed two building numbers on raised stone tiles, tucked beneath the ledge separating the street level from the second floor.

Two buildings grew together, the stone seam between them barely visible in the knitted brick. The exterior walls above were decorated with greened copper fleur-de-lis motifs.

There, before her now, was the black cast-iron mailbox. Somehow she had walked past it three times already without seeing it. Its face was smooth from age, not from polish. The box was slick with rainwater, the slot barely discernible due to a quirk of shadow.

Odessa looked around, the mail slot's discovery feeling like an illicit act. She withdrew the envelope from inside her jacket, pausing a moment to look at the addressee's name in her handwriting. *Mr. Hugo Blackwood.* A few stray raindrops spattered the thick manila paper, streaking the ink. She quickly fed the letter inside the slot. The envelope disappeared without a sound.

She looked around again, feeling suspicious, even watched. This felt like a dead drop, something out of a spy novel. The narrow street was dark, a sheer cavern full of pouring rain falling past the windows in the former dry goods warehouses.

No one appeared, nothing happened.

She walked away, the fine hairs raised on the back of her neck. She came to a pub a few doors up on the opposite side of the street and collapsed her umbrella, ducking inside. She took a seat at a two-top near the window and ordered a latte. She watched the onyx slab, difficult to see from that angle, distorted through the slanting rain. A few people hurried past it under umbrellas or folded newspapers, but none stopped. The stone wedge appeared to be part of the façade of the conjoined buildings, with nothing behind it. No visible way to retrieve the letter.

None of this made sense.

She waited. The latte was good, its creamy warmth easing the chill of the rain and the circumstances, the caffeine settling nicely into her nervous system. As she sat there, she realized suddenly that she felt better. Or rather: She realized how shitty she had been feeling the past few days. Delivering the letter—hell, even just having committed her thoughts to paper, and sealing them inside an envelope of precise size and color, and then depositing it in an anonymous seam in an ancient street on an island city of one and a half million—had achieved what would otherwise have taken months or years of therapy.

Maybe, she thought, this was what Earl Solomon was suggesting. Maybe this was a thought experiment to get her through this ordeal. Maybe "Hugo Blackwood" was a state of mind.

By the time she arrived back at the subway station, the rain had abated. A train came right away, and she rode back home to New Jersey thinking about the things she used to think about. Getting groceries. Catching up on laundry. The little things. There was comfort in this.

She ran to Walgreens for a few items—coffee creamer, toothpaste—and walked the rest of the way back to the apartment. Her dark mood had not been lifted, but it had been leavened. She stood her umbrella against the wall in the hallway next to the door and entered her home, hanging her nearly dry jacket on the knob of the closet door.

A man was sitting on her sofa.

"You called upon me," said Hugo Blackwood. "Here I am."

He had the darkest eyes and hair, fair to alabaster skin. He was thin, borderline gaunt, yet elegant in a mysterious way: Odessa thought of her image of male characters from eighteenth- and nineteenth-century literature.

He wore an impeccably tailored black suit—simple but flawlessly cut and assembled—with a black shirt, black vest, no necktie. He was in his forties or perhaps his well-preserved fifties. Hard to say. He held one of Odessa's teacups in his hands and looked at her inquiringly.

"I read the letter," Hugo Blackwood said, a purring British accent. "I was, in fact, expecting it a little sooner..."

Odessa's first thought was: *Get a weapon.* For the

first time since it had been taken away from her, she wished she had her Glock. She had left her keys in her jacket pocket. The door to the hallway was behind her. She could be out of here in three seconds if necessary.

"I'm an FBI agent" were the first words that sputtered out of her mouth. A warning and a threat—just one she'd never dreamed she might have to use in her own home.

"I know," he said quite simply.

Her breath came fast. "Who are you?"

"You know who I am."

She stared. "No."

"You wrote to me," he said. "So I let myself in."

When no words would come out, she just shook her head.

"I'm making us some tea," he said. "I do hope you don't mind..."

Odessa gripped the edge of the wall. "There is no way you made it back here before me."

His eyebrows arched. He indicated the sofa he was sitting upon, proof that he had indeed entered the apartment before she had.

"How did you get here so fast?"

"You are going to have that many questions?" he said.

"How did you find me?"

"Well, your name was in the letter."

"What is that...mailbox? What is this? Who put you up to this?"

"You did. The mailbox is more of a mail slot. It remains fairly efficient even in these times."

These times? As she went back and forth with him, she edged closer to her kitchen. That was where the knives were.

"Can we talk about the issues you set forth in your summoning?" he asked.

"Summoning?" Dessa said.

"You called me," he said. "I presume the matter is of immediate importance to you."

"No," she said, indignantly. "No, we can't..."

Her kettle. It was hot and still faintly steaming. He had gained entrance to her apartment and had time to boil water...all in the time it took her to drink a latte, ride the PATH back, and stop in at Walgreens?

He noticed that she was flummoxed by the boiled water. "I brought my own tea bag, I may add. Mariage Frères, Milky Blue," he said, sipping his brew. "Why don't you make a cup and sit down, steady your nerves."

That straightened her up. Her nerves did not need steadying. Her questions needed answers.

"I am fine as I am, thank you," she said.

"The elements of the cases you describe present themselves to me as symptoms," he said. "And these things occur in threes."

"Solomon said that," Odessa said.

"Earl, yes. I imagine he would." He smiled. "The facts in evidence are unremarkable on their merits. But these incidences are curious in the abstract. Especially occurring separately within such a short period of time."

"How do you know Earl Solomon?" she said.

Blackwood took in a breath, evidently inconvenienced by the question. "How did I come to know him?"

"How long have you known him? Who are you two together? What the hell is going on here?"

"Must we? You sent me a—"

"Yes, a letter," said Odessa. "I drop a letter in a blank slot near Wall Street in Manhattan and my apartment gets broken into by a British man who won't answer my questions."

"Earl Solomon should have prepared you better. How is dear Earl?"

"Dying. Had a stroke. He is in his late eighties and should have been retired decades ago. I go to him, he sends me to you, and I need to know what kind of scam you two are running."

Blackwood took another sip of his tea. "Apparently he didn't tell you much about me."

"No, sir, he did not. Left that part right out."

"I see. I assumed you would have some idea of what to expect."

"Left. That. Part. Right. *Out.*"

"Just gave you the address, did he?"

"Well, he's not well. I did mention that, right? He's dying?"

Blackwood shook his head once.

She waited. "That's it? Not curious how he's doing? No sympathy or concern, Mr. Blackwood? That is your name, correct? Hugo Blackwood?"

"That is my name, Miss Hardwicke, yes."

Nothing more. She was already aggravated and unnerved, but this strange man's casual callousness really got under her skin. "He's in the hospital."

"Unfortunate," said Hugo Blackwood. "For both of us."

Odessa smiled through her shock. "So you two are close, then."

"He has assisted me many times. I have a most favorable opinion of his work ethic and professional performance."

"He has assisted *you* many times?" said Odessa. "Who do you work for?"

"For? No one."

"British Special Branch? Security services?"

"Oh no. Not them."

Odessa tried a reset. She opened her FBI credentials and walked over to Blackwood, leaning over the coffee table between them. "Here's my identification. Okay?" She closed the booklet and pulled it back. "Now show me yours."

He said, "I don't have any."

"No identification?"

He smiled, perhaps at her doggedness. "Should we talk about the cauldrons?"

Something about the way he said "cauldrons," his voice like that of a man out of his own time, chilled her. "Fine," she said. She sat in a chair angled toward him. "Tell me about the cauldrons."

"How much do you know about Palo?" Hugo Blackwood asked.

"Palo?" said Odessa.

"I see," said Hugo Blackwood. "The cauldrons are a major element of Palo Mayombe, a dark religion that arose out of the Spanish slave trade in the sixteenth century. The cauldron is arranged with certain religious articles, as well as totemic personal items from the issuer of, or the object of, the spell to be invoked."

"A spell," said Odessa.

"Spell. Wish. Curse. An invocation by any other name. For this invocation to be successful in its intention and achieve full force and power, very often the practitioner, usually a priestess, will incorporate articles of death in the Palo ritual. Such as dead animals or birds. Human bones."

With every word, Odessa was profiling him. A professor of religion? An expert on cults?

"I understand what you are saying," said Odessa. "And I have witnessed these things you speak about. What I don't understand is, are you saying that these killers were followers of Palo...or victims of some sort of curse?"

"It is not so simple as that. What I have been describing to you is a religion—a practice unfamiliar to you, and unusual to this part of the world, but a religion with many thousands of adherents and practitioners who are neither murderers nor murder victims themselves. Palo Mayombe, in and of itself, is a system of faith and worship, and as such is blameless."

"Okay..." Odessa shook her head. "So what are we talking about, then?"

"There may be darker forces at work here. Palo is a dynamic faith, one in touch with deep undercurrents of nature that are largely unexplored. Any system—any church—may be corrupted. The invocation ceremony may have been appropriated by some other entity for its own means."

Now his logic was starting to sound squishy. "Entity?"

Hugo Blackwood sighed and sipped his tea. "There are only so many. Each religion has a name for them, but there is a basic taxonomy—no more than thirty or thirty-five kinds, really."

His perfectly reasonable expression outlasted hers. The only reason she didn't laugh was that this nonsense intrigued her. This man intrigued her. His relationship—or lack thereof—with Earl Solomon intrigued her.

"Now I think I will brew some more tea," she said and moved into the kitchen, pulling down a branded Starbucks mug celebrating the city of Newark (she had purchased it ironically) and popping in an herbal tea bag, filling it with sink water.

"Most of these entities go back to Mesopotamian times," Blackwood said. "And their sole reason for being is to harm, erode, or destroy whatever is good in the world…"

She slid the mug into the microwave and pressed the 30 SECONDS button.

"Please don't do that," he said.

She looked back at him. "Do what?"

"What you are doing."

She realized he meant the microwave—as opposed to boiling water in the kettle on the stove, as he had. "It's fast," she said.

He emitted an unhappy exhale, not quite a sigh, not exactly a grunt, but with elements of both. "So is a beheading."

The microwave beeped and she pulled out the hot water, stirring it. "You have to let it steep," he said.

"Ha," she said, returning to her chair. "Nobody has that much time."

She noticed he was still looking at her as though she had committed an atrocity. "Do you eat the tea bag when you are done?" she asked.

"The tea bag itself is a modern convenience. A shortcut from pouring water over loose tea, brewing the beverage, and straining out the leaves. You are circumventing even that process, sacrificing the pleasure of taste for immediacy."

She nodded, sipping the tea, perversely enjoying his contempt. "It's good." She sat back.

"These entities," said Blackwood. "They respond to many names, favor certain rituals."

"Favor?" said Odessa. "What do you mean?"

"The same entity can appear in Palo or in a Catholic exorcism," said Blackwood, "under a different name. They cherish role-playing. Lies. Pretense. Emotion. Just as you would tune in or out of a radio station. So they get attuned to whatever they feel like at that particular time..."

"Are you a professor of religion or something?"

"Or something," he answered.

"You've dealt with situations, cases, like this before."

"Many times, too many times, in too many places. It never really ends, you see? They're the Yin and...you could say I am the Yang."

"You sound like a fortune cookie—how do you know the things you know?"

"Experience. You appear to be a novice agent."

"Hardly," she said, offended. "I'm relatively new to the Bureau."

"Solomon was a novice once." Blackwood glanced around her apartment as though he were reading her résumé. "One has to start somewhere, I suppose, in acquiring clients."

"Acquiring—*clients?*" she said, not understanding him.

"At your Bureau. You are an agent."

"I'm a special agent, it's a designation. I'm not a...a representative."

"An agent is a liaison, as I understand it. An envoy, an instrument. A representative, yes, of the Bureau of Investigation."

She was almost amused. "How has Agent Solomon never explained this to you? We are not facilitators. We don't have clients. Our clients are the American people, as a nation."

"You are an agent of an investigatory body. I believe we are speaking about the same thing."

"No, we are not. I am a law enforcement officer, an agent of the federal government. Duly sworn. You are...I still don't know what you are."

"I am Hugo Blackwood. I was trained as a barrister, if that is what you mean. That was quite a long time ago."

"A lawyer," she said. "Me too. And how did you get in here, by the way?" She was getting weirded out again.

"Oh, the door," he said.

"The door has two locks."

"Indeed, it does. I opened both."

Odessa sat with that a moment. "A well-mannered burglar is still a burglar."

"I assure you, I am not here to burgle. Perhaps we can get back to the matter at hand. I believe you may be of some assistance to me."

"Yes, let's get back to the matter at hand...but I am not offering my assistance to you. I wrote you at the suggestion of Agent Solomon, who thought you might be able to assist me in figuring out what is going on."

"It is very important to you not to appear submissive or subservient in any way, isn't it."

Odessa crossed her arms, looking at this man curiously, still unable to get a handle on him. Smart retorts flew through her mind, but Hugo Blackwood appeared to be making an observation, not an insult.

She got to her feet again. "I want to show you something."

Odessa opened the news articles on grave robbing she had saved as pdf files on her MacBook. When she set it down in front of him, Hugo Blackwood sat back and shook his head. He declined even to touch the laptop. "You operate the machine," he said.

"You not an Apple guy?" she asked.

He squinted at the type as though this were his first time encountering text on an LCD screen. He scanned the "Baby Mia" stories, then the article about the man who died in 1977.

"Would you...where did the first document go?" he said, frustrated.

"Okay," she said, spinning the MacBook back toward herself, bringing up the article, spinning it back. "Luddite much?"

"Luddite?" He glanced at her. "If you are referring to the early-nineteenth-century protest by textile workers who smashed their looms in fear of being replaced by lesser-paid, lesser-skilled workers, then no. I would gladly welcome obsolescence. If you refer to the modern misconception of that protest, implying an aversion to technological advancement in general, then yes."

"Thus the paper letter in the precise envelope

dropped in a slot in a slab of stone in Manhattan. You know you can get text messages on your phone, right?"

She smiled when he ignored her comment, reading through the article again. "The information contained in this news item is actually quite promising. This 'Baby Mia,' she of the degenerative brain disease. Her remains may be viewed by some as magical or charmed due to how long she lived past her life expectancy. This article doesn't give her date of birth, but the photograph of the headstone does, and if you subtract it from the date of her death, she lived for exactly seven hundred and seventy-seven days. A numerologist would consider that sum quite fortunate indeed."

"Seven-seven-seven?" said Odessa, impressed by the speed of his arithmetic.

Hugo Blackwood stood, his tea unfinished, ready to leave. His height surprised her, yet he was trim in a way most men of modern diets are not. *Vegetarian*, she thought. "We must speak with the resurrectionists."

"The who?"

"The men who exhumed this child's remains, likely for a fee. The article references some arrests. You need to facilitate an interview for me with one or both of the men."

"Facilitate?" she said. "Hold on. I don't 'facilitate'

anything. If anything, if you have a question about the criminal investigation, we should talk to the detectives who worked the case. Especially if we have information that could potentially further implicate the suspect."

"I see," he said. "Is that what you did when you sent me your letter?"

Odessa stood, too. She was tired of being called out by this strange man who had broken into her apartment. "Agent Solomon suggested that I contact you."

"And you were susceptible to suggestion for two reasons," Blackwood said. "You wanted answers to questions you had. And it is personal for you. So you took the extraordinary step of corresponding with me. How can I make you understand? If this were merely a criminal investigation, you would not require my services. This is more than a criminal investigation. And you know it."

Persuasive yet still troubling. "It sounds like, legally, I should step back now and leave you to whatever it is you do. Is that what Agent Solomon did for you?" She pressed him further. "So you would help him with his investigations."

"Wrong, I'm afraid. He assisted me."

"I have a hard time picturing you and Solomon working together on anything."

"Quite right—he also hunted me down. For a

long time." Blackwood smiled ever-so-faintly. "Unsuccessfully, I may add. You see? Some of my most rewarding partnerships started with people intent on killing me. Shall we?"

She hesitated, needing to come clean. "There's something you should know. I'm on a kind of administrative probation from the FBI. A suspension. Pending an investigation into the resolution of the first rampage killing I wrote you about. I'm on the outs with the Bureau right now. Probably won't be an FBI agent much longer."

Blackwood was unfazed. "You showed me your credentials."

"Yes."

"I'm sure that will be sufficient."

The elevator doors opened on a second pair of doors in the service basement of the Lexington Regal Hotel in Murray Hill. Odessa pushed through into a narrow hallway made narrower by housekeeping carts lined along the right-side wall. She walked in front of Hugo Blackwood, heading toward the sound of industrial churning and a man's voice rapping in falsetto Spanish.

A left turn took her into the artificially warm laundry room. Four huge laundry machines sloshed and spun side by side across from four front-loading dryers, combining to perform a symphony of cyclonic droning. A woman of South American heritage wearing a brown Lexington Regal vest oversaw a chop-socky folding machine serving thin white hotel towels, which she stacked in an open-sided canvas cart. A man with his back to them rocked rhythmically to the music playing through his thick headphones before the audience of industrial washing machines.

He must have sensed their approach, because he turned, lowering his headphones to hang around his neck. "Help you?" he said.

"Mauro Esquivel?" said Odessa.

"Yes, that's me," he said.

She showed him her FBI credentials. "We'd like to ask you a couple of questions."

The woman in the hotel vest said, "Okay, bye," and switched off the towel-folding machine, walking right out of the room.

Mauro looked at Odessa and Blackwood apprehensively. "What kind of questions?"

Odessa said, "You're not in any trouble. We want to ask you about something that went down in the past."

The lights flickered. Mauro walked to a light switch timer and reset it for three minutes. Then he turned his head such that he eyed them almost from a profile. "How'd you find me here?"

"Your parole officer. She's very pleased with your progress."

"She better be," he said. "Bustin' my ass here."

He looked at Blackwood strangely, as if getting a weird vibe from the gaunt man in the expensive suit. Odessa identified with that sentiment.

"I can save you some time," said Mauro. "You trying to play me into giving up some people, rolling
over for you, I can't do it. Just take me in now, pull
my parole. It's not worth my life, my kid's life, my
family back in Argentina. Forget it."

Odessa shook her head. "We're not here about
the narcotics rap. Not really."

"If this is about papers, I am a citizen, I was born
here."

"Again," said Odessa, "we're really not here to
hassle you."

Mauro chuckled. "Right. What is it then? And
who's Slender Man?"

Odessa answered, "I don't actually know."

Hugo Blackwood said, "We want to know about
the grave you robbed."

Mauro went white. He stammered. "Look, that
was a mistake, I got snared up in something bad,
and that was a while ago."

"So it wasn't your idea to dig up the dead girl's
coffin?" said Blackwood.

Mauro recoiled as though he had just been made
to touch or taste something disgusting.

"I'm not talking about that. It was a mistake,
okay? That's not who I am."

Odessa said, "You said you have a child yourself."

Mauro nodded fast. "It's the wrong thing to do, I
know that. Right from wrong—I know."

169

Blackwood stepped toward him. "But this was deeper than that."

Mauro did not deny it. He looked at Blackwood with dread, preferring to direct his words to Odessa. "I'm sorry about that, and I did my time...and why you gotta hassle me about this at my job, yo?"

Odessa read in his reaction that this went beyond fear of the FBI. He was genuinely scared even to be speaking about this.

"We need to know why you did it," she said. "Who you did it for. This conversation stays here." She indicated the basement room.

Mauro shook his head, offering his wrists instead, as though for handcuffs. "Take me in, FBI. Let's go. Arrest me."

"You'd rather go back to jail than tell us about it?"

"Take me in!" he said, very agitated.

Odessa turned to Blackwood. She couldn't take Mauro in, obviously. The point was to get him to talk anyway. But they had touched a deep nerve in him. It looked like a dead end.

Blackwood did not return her look. His eyes remained on Mauro—while Mauro worked hard not to return his gaze.

Then she heard some rustling and thought that the woman had come back into the room to get something. Odessa tracked the noise to a large canvas bin of hotel bedsheets waiting to be laundered. The wheeled bin was larger than the housekeeping carts, and easily held many, many dozens of sheet sets and comforters. Large enough for a person of any size to be underneath the laundry.

And that was what it sounded like. Someone— something—stirring beneath the sheets. She thought she detected movement.

Mauro heard it, too. He was staring at the bin, listening to the rustling of something buried deep within the sheets. He backed away a few steps, until he was standing almost next to Odessa.

But Hugo Blackwood never looked over at the laundry bin. His eyes never left Mauro's face, Odessa realized. Blackwood acted as though he was completely unaware of any noise coming from the laundry.

"Shit, man…" Mauro swallowed and wiped his mouth. He was freaking out. "Okay, listen. I'll tell you, but you need to protect me."

Odessa looked at Blackwood. There was no change of expression on his face.

She turned back to Mauro, while also keeping her distance from the laundry bin. "Talk," she said, going with the moment.

"I did what I did, I don't make no excuses," he said. "It wasn't about anything but money. It was small-time, I don't want to hurt no one. But then...then it became about hurting people. By then I was in too deep to bounce off. I was doomed, man. Doomed." Odessa noticed that, despite his reluctance to talk, judging by the depth of his self-analysis, he had obviously been thinking about this for quite some time. "When you think you're already damned, all bets are off, right? It's just a matter of time. Some of the guys I knew, they were into Palo. It made sense. Like a protective aura. Worked out for me, 'cause I got out of jams I should never've gotten away from. It helped me get ahead. Then I...I met someone who said I could go even further. Supernatural powers. They wanted a grave dug up. They said the body was a saint's. A little girl with magical healing powers. So I did the deed. Me and another dude, we got high and did it. And that was that—but it wasn't. There was a ceremony using the bones and shit. It was too intense for me, you know? Too...what do you call it? When you play with religion, but you play too hard?"

"Sacrilegious?" she said. "Blasphemous?"

He nodded. "I took off. I just split. It all came crashing down on me. Since that night, it felt like someone put a curse on me, a mark. My good-luck run was over. I messed with the wrong stuff."

"Who was it?" asked Odessa. "Who came to you with the idea for digging up Baby Mia's grave?"

"Nah. See, I can't do that, I won't. I'm out now. I want to stay out. I got to stay out. You walk in here saying, *We just want to know this and that.* No, you don't just want that. You want me to put my neck on the line..."

"We'll protect you," Odessa said. "I can vouch for that."

"No one can," Mauro said. "I talk, I'm dead."

He shook his head firmly. The room lights went out.

Mauro headed for the timer.

Then he heard the rustling again.

In the laundry bin—more forceful this time. Like something about to rise out.

Odessa heard it. Mauro became incredibly agitated again.

Blackwood stood still, no expression.

Mauro wanted to leave, but he was unable.

The sheets moved again.

Mauro said, "You ain't no cop." He regarded Blackwood with a mixture of hatred and terror. To Odessa, he said, "What'd you bring on me?"

Blackwood said, "Tell us where to go next, and we can all leave."

"*Evil*," whispered Mauro, shaking his head at Blackwood. He hissed more words in Spanish, which Odessa did not understand.

Blackwood said, in a low, even voice, "A girl of

two years, Mauro. Gone to her final rest. Until you disturbed her."

Mauro shot one final look back at the bin of linens, and in a trembling voice told them everything they wanted to know.

Outside, Odessa stopped Blackwood away from the doormen at the hotel entrance.

"What was that?" she said, unable to hold her tongue any longer. "What happened in there?"

"Would you please use your mobile telephone again to summon our conveyance?" Blackwood said.

Odessa stood her ground. "Just tell me how you made that noise in the laundry bin. Is it a trick, like ventriloquism or something? Throwing your voice? You did something back there..."

Blackwood said, "Mr. Esquivel thought I did."

"He thought the ghost corpse of a two-year-old girl was going to rise out of the dirty laundry."

Blackwood looked at her with one eyebrow slightly raised. "Would you activate your telephone now? We must be in Newark before the hour grows too late."

The botanica was a few blocks east of Newark Penn Station, a small storefront sandwiched between a shuttered, formerly twenty-four-hour mattress chain store and a takeout-only taqueria with a prominently displayed NO BAÑO sign.

Odessa stopped Blackwood outside near a burnt-out public phone before he could walk in.

"We need a plan," she said. "A story."

"What do you mean?" he said.

"Walking in here," said Odessa. "We are obviously outsiders. This is a store of Latin religious items. We look like tourists from Fort Lee. We need a story. We have to blend in—"

"No," Blackwood said. "We don't."

He grasped the door handle and opened it with a total lack of concern. An old woman with a deeply weathered face and gray hair tied in a bun sat in a folding chair just inside the doorway. She looked

175

up from the prayer she was mouthing, her large brown eyes watching them pass. Odessa smiled, but her smile was not returned.

The store was narrow, deep. Behind a counter to the left, a woman greeted them genially.

"Hello, hello! Welcome. How are you?"

She was a tall black woman, wearing an apron over a dress, which was odd, and a soft white cotton headwrap. She had a big smile, looking up from some beadwork she was doing.

"Fine, thank you," said Odessa when Blackwood said nothing.

"Please take a look around, I can answer any questions."

"Thank you," said Odessa, noticing small, pearl-like piercings over each knuckle on the woman's hands. Apparently, the woman behind the counter was used to taking money from spiritually curious tourists. Odessa had never been inside one of these botanicas, and she drifted away from Blackwood to examine the wares.

The right-side wall was lined with shelves of labeled merchandise, including spiritual candles in many colors, set in tall jars of decorated glass with long wax wicks. Plastic jars contained different spices, herbs, grains, roots, all clearly labeled. Other shelves held books, pamphlets, affirmations, stones, prayer cards. In the most fragrant corner of the shop were the spiritual and magical oils, soaps, resins, and incense.

A smaller shelf was reserved for passion oils and lucky love spells. Also: various eye-catching vagina- and penis-shaped candles. Nearer to eye level, candles and bath spells promised healing, "jinx breaking," hex removal, application of the "evil eye," potions for love and sexual attraction, and money drawing. Next to candles offering good luck and fortune were others designed to resolve legal problems and court issues. Red wax candles in the form of praying figures were labeled ANCESTOR OFFERINGS.

Odessa moved back near the front, fascinated. One-stop shopping for all your mystical needs. Here was a table altar of "La Madama," apparently the spirit of female slaves, depicted as a darkly black woman posed holding a broom, wearing a head-dress with an open bowl balanced on top for offer-ings, next to a bouquet of marigolds. This display was not for sale, but was instead a devotional sta-tion. The table surface held two silk-lined dishes containing bits of bread, mints, coins, wilted rose petals, and neatly knotted dollar bills. A hand-lettered sign admonished customers:

Leave your offering.
Get a blessing.
Do not touch anything here.

Odessa heard voices and realized Blackwood had engaged the counter woman at the rear of the store. Odessa moved toward them quickly.

Blackwood said, "We are looking for the owner of this botanica."

The counter woman said, "I told you, the owner is not available. I can help you with anything you see here."

"What is in the back room here?" he asked.

She kept smiling. "That is a private office, and where we do readings."

"We would like a reading, then," said Blackwood. "My associate, Miss Hardwicke, would like a spiritual consultation."

"Consultations and divinations are by appointment only."

"Is there someone ahead of us?"

"No..." said the counter woman.

"I see your prices on the wall behind the counter." Blackwood pulled a wad of cash from his trouser pocket and peeled two fifties off the top. "Here you are."

Odessa said, "Mr. Blackwood, may I speak with you a minute?"

The woman received the bills and looked past Odessa to the front of the store. She spoke what sounded like a derivation of Creole. The old woman rose slowly from her folding chair and closed and locked the front door, flipping a sign that read, PRIVATE READING, PLEASE COME BACK IN 15 MINUTES.

Odessa said to Blackwood, "I don't want a reading."

"Come, come," he said, eager to get into the back room.

The old woman shuffled past Odessa, smelling of ash. She waved Odessa on with an arthritic hand, her robe swishing along the floor.

Odessa wasn't sure what Blackwood was up to, but she was certain she didn't like being the unwitting subject. She stepped through the door next to a selection of amulets, talismans, and charms.

The back room looked half storeroom, half break room. The counter woman whisked away a soda cup and fast-food bag from the reading table. If Blackwood was expecting to find the shop's owner back here, he was disappointed.

"Please sit," she said, indicating a preferred chair.

Odessa looked at Blackwood. She assumed they could leave now.

He pulled out the chair for her.

Rather than question him, she chose to trust that he had a plan. With a sharp look at him, one that she hoped conveyed this trust, she sat, Blackwood sliding the chair in beneath her.

The old woman sat across the table. Blackwood

and the counter woman remained standing, like seconds in a duel. The old woman unboxed a deck of Tarot cards, shuffling them gently with her stiff hands and clumsy fingers. She spoke, and the counter woman translated her words for Odessa.

"Please relax and clear your thoughts."

Yeah, right, thought Odessa. She made a show of dropping her shoulders and exhaling.

She smiled at the old woman, awaiting the performance.

The old woman dealt four oversize cards facedown onto the table. She turned them over in order, one at a time, not speaking until the fourth card had been revealed.

"You are in a secure, healthy relationship with the man in your life," the counter woman translated. "He is a good man, and devoted. He has genuine feelings for you. You are his one true love."

Odessa nodded. So she was starting with the soft touch.

"But he is not yours."

Not her one true love? Odessa smiled sharply. "Isn't that kind of a bold statement?" she said.

The counter woman did not translate Odessa's comment for the old woman, whose crooked, wrinkled fingers pawed gently at the cards' faces. "He will be financially secure. Successful in his

180

field. He will take a trip soon. A new man will come into your life."

Now she was coming in with the destabilizing statement, meant to stir up Odessa's emotions, get her engaged and vulnerable. Fat chance. Odessa glanced at Blackwood to see if he was enjoying the show...and also to make clear to him that she was not.

Another four cards went down. The old woman spent a few moments considering them. Her gaze darkened.

"This is a time of great transition for you. Great danger: Something evil has crossed your path."

Odessa did her best to hide her reaction. She was certain these charlatans profiled their marks, tailoring prophecies to their customers' reactions. She didn't want to give them the satisfaction of knowing she had responded to their generic prediction.

"This is not the first time you have become the focus of a great darkness. You are not an attractor of darkness, however." She puzzled over the cards here. "You are more of a...a conduit. A go-between." The counter woman was having some difficulty translating the term. "An agent."

Again she glanced at Blackwood, hearing an echo of his earlier words. She wondered what was going on here.

The counter woman translated: "You are the seventh daughter of a seventh daughter."

"I'm a...what?" Odessa did the math quickly. "I'm one of six. I have five siblings." Odessa wanted to say more, but thought that maybe this woman's game was to trick her into divulging personal information. She clammed up.

"You are the seventh," said the old woman.

"Okay," said Odessa, annoyed. "Anything else?" She wanted to be done with this.

The old woman laid another card down, this time faceup. "You have a slight backup in your intestines."

Odessa could have done without hearing that. "That's great, that's quite enough. Thank you."

Odessa started to stand, but the old woman spoke sharply to the counter woman, the two of them having a conversation.

The counter woman said, "She asks if you want to know about your father."

Odessa felt a cool shiver run through her body, and hated herself for it. The last thing she wanted was to let this old swindler into her emotional state. "My father is deceased."

Words from the old woman, translated: "He loved you."

"Okay, this is..." Odessa didn't say, *Silly.* "This is highly inappropriate. Offensive."

"He left you a note," the counter woman continued. "Addressed to you. A goodbye. But they destroyed it. They were afraid it would get them into trouble."

Odessa reacted to the emotions welling up inside her with anger. Her father had died in prison. "How do you claim to know this?"

The old woman turned over another card. This one showed four knives.

"Enough," said Odessa, bolting out of the chair. She felt sick, and she felt taken advantage of. She reached for her purse. "His turn," she said, pointing at Blackwood. "My associate, Mr. Blackwood, would like a reading now."

Blackwood looked at her, reading her distress. He had to know she was angry with him, but not why. Or perhaps he realized that he had, inadvertently, wounded her.

Blackwood slowly took her seat across from the old woman.

Odessa saw a strange look on the old woman's face, regarding Blackwood. Another back-and-forth with the counter woman.

"She does not wish to perform another reading."

Odessa's good manners—instilled in her by her father, among others—disappeared in the face of this spiritual coercion. She put her money down on the table. "You will do for him the same as you did for me."

She heard her voice shaking, but she didn't care.

The counter woman said, "Mother is tired, she needs to rest."

"Do it," said Odessa.

The counter woman looked at the old woman, who looked across at Blackwood. Reluctantly, she shuffled the Tarot deck, more deliberately this time.

Blackwood sat preternaturally still, his hands in his lap. Odessa's anger subsided just enough for her to become aware of an eerie energy in the room now, like an invisible dome over the table. For a moment, she regretted her action, fearing she had forced an encounter that should not have occurred.

The old woman looked at Blackwood with reluctant eyes, as though viewing him from deep within herself. The deck sat ready before her, but she was reluctant to turn over the top card. She shook her head, looking at the counter woman, refusing to go any further.

The counter woman looked concerned. "Mother?" she said, as though confused by the old woman's reluctance.

After a painfully long and tense moment, Blackwood reached across the table and picked the first card off the top. Without looking at it himself, he showed it to her.

The old woman tried to speak. She opened her

mouth but no words came out. She simply covered her eyes and turned away, weakened, slouching.

Blackwood stood from the table. "My apologies," he said, though neither woman heard his words. The counter woman held her headdress with one hand, herself now spooked by the British gentleman's presence. He nodded to them and left the room.

Odessa was still catching her breath. The old woman was sitting upright, looking around the room as though having woken from a deep sleep. Odessa felt responsible—reading Blackwood's fortune was her smart idea—and was relieved to see her coming back around. Odessa wanted to get out of there, but before she did, she reached for the top card off the deck, needing to see what it showed.

It was the image of a Magi, holding a wand or perhaps a baton, his hat brim curved in the shape of the symbol for infinity.

Back near the burnt-out pay phone, Odessa grabbed Blackwood's arm to stop him. Shocked at how thin he felt inside his suit sleeve, she pulled her hand back fast.

"What are you? Some kind of mesmerist?"

"All I did was turn over the card she herself dealt."

"What was that card?" Odessa asked. "The Magi. What does that mean?"

"I believe the Magi symbolizes immanence."

"Okay. I'm not going to pretend I know what *immanence* means."

"It means the quality of being immanent, or inherent."

"But what would it mean to *her*?"

"Hard to say." Blackwood's gaze was unflinching. "Some religious faiths and metaphysical theories hold that the spiritual world permeates the mundane. Whereas transcendence implies a divine presence existing on a plane outside and beyond the everyday world, immanence expresses a quality of the otherworldly extant in the world around us."

Odessa said, "She saw that in you?"

"She saw that in a card, selected at random. 'As above, so below.'"

Odessa was sick and tired of his haughty manner. "Playing these kinds of games with people is an ugly trait. It's sadistic. That old lady was terrified of you for some reason."

"I believe it was you who insisted I sit for her."

"I didn't want a psychic reading in the first place," she told him. "And by the way—you don't know me. I don't know you. How dare you sit me down for something like that without consulting me first?"

"I didn't think it would matter to an obvious skeptic."

"It's rude. And I'll be damned if I know what it got us, except some old card reader having a dizzy spell. What does it matter? I asked you for help figuring out what happened to Walt Leppo and the two rampage shooters."

"The owner of this botanica may be able to answer some of those questions. Now she is on notice that there is someone looking for her."

Odessa took a breath. It had been an alarming day, and she regretted ever dropping that envelope in the mail slot. "So it seems you are some kind of confidence man or hypnotist. You somehow got inside the head of an elderly FBI agent, and that's okay. But I am not going to let you inside mine."

Odessa turned and walked off toward Market Street, which would take her back to her home. She expected Hugo Blackwood to call after her or try to catch up, and she was all fired up to rebuff him. But she turned the corner without a word from him, and when she finally looked back two blocks farther on, he was not following her.

The only pang she felt was for all the unanswered questions about him...but she could live with that. For the moment, she believed that she was free of Hugo Blackwood.

1962. The Mississippi Delta.

Agent Earl Solomon sat alone at the serving counter of a black-owned roadhouse named Pigmeat's. His hat sat on the counter to his left, next to the first-draft report he was writing long-hand, in pencil, on a pad of yellow legal paper with only a few sheets left. He set down his short pencil and broke off another hunk of bread, swiping it through thick, hot soup, softening the crust, tasting of salted pork and carrots.

It was midafternoon, between lunch and dinner. Solomon had the kitchen's full attention. There was no server working at that hour, just the paper-hatted cook and the newspaper-reading owner. The counter was metal, cool to the touch. The stools didn't swivel. A jukebox and a cigarette machine sat near the door.

"Klansmen arrived," said the owner, scanning his newspaper through thick eyeglasses at the booth nearest the door.

Solomon turned toward him. "It says that in the paper?"

"White people's paper." The owner folded it up. "Them voting drive whites need protection now from they own kind."

The cook shook his head at the end of the counter. "Bunch of damn fools."

Solomon looked at him. "Who, the voting rights people?"

"They's just kids. Heads full of ideas. They don't know or care what it's doing to people 'round here. Coming down in here, stirring things up."

Solomon picked up his spoon. "You stir this soup, don't you?"

The cook let out a laugh like a single bark. "Can't tell you city boys nothing. You don't have to live here."

Solomon said, "Can a city boy get a slice of that fried pie?"

"If the city boy got city money, he can."

Solomon smiled and returned to his writing. Then he remembered that the Ku Klux Klan was in town and his smile went away.

The roadhouse door opened. Solomon didn't think anything of it until many seconds passed and no words were spoken. Solomon turned to look at the door, expecting to see a white-sheet-wearing Grand Wizard. It was a white man, trim and very pale, wearing a dark suit like an undertaker. European, maybe. Silk. The roadhouse wasn't strictly segregated, but Solomon could feel the owner's and the chef's distrust of the man standing inside the door. For his part, however, the man himself seemed unaware.

Solomon returned to his writing. He sensed movement, hearing a whisper of silk, but there were many empty stools at the counter and open booths along the wall. So when the man sat on the stool to Solomon's immediate right, almost shoulder-to-shoulder, Solomon turned again, setting down his pencil, steeling for a fight.

"Can I help you with something, friend?" Solomon said.

"Perhaps," he said in a cultured British accent, so out of place anywhere in America but especially deep in the Delta. Penetrating eyes. "You are Agent Earl Solomon?"

Solomon nodded, surprised to hear his name come out of this man's mouth. "I am. And you are?"

"Very pleased to meet you. I have never been to this region of the continent before. Rather humid. But not entirely unpleasant."

"Rather," said Solomon. "You a journalist?"

"No, certainly not. I am a barrister by trade, though I haven't practiced law in quite some time.

No, I am here in no particular professional capacity. I heard that you are in charge of the murder investigation here."

"Not in charge. Just here to help."

"You misunderstand me. I mean that you are the highest-ranking law enforcement representative here. The Federal Bureau of Investigation. Caused quite a stir among local enforcement authorities, judging by what I've heard. An interesting situation, you investigating the lynching murder of a white man."

"Interesting is one word for it," said Solomon.

Before Solomon could ask his name again, the cook slid a plate of fried pie in front of him. It was a fruit-filled turnover, fried and sprinkled with confectioners' sugar. The cook side-eyed the white man and asked Solomon, "This guy okay?"

Solomon shrugged and turned to his European seatmate. "Interested in some pie?"

"What is it?" asked the British man.

The cook said, "Crab Lantern. Ain't crab apples, though. Macintosh."

The Brit said, "Can you prepare it with meat inside?"

"Pigmeat?" said the cook.

"That's pork," explained Solomon.

"On second thought," he said, "perhaps just a

cup of boiled water." He removed a small paper envelope from his jacket pocket, a packet of tea.

The cook walked around the back wall into the adjoining kitchen. Solomon smiled at the man on the stool next to him, ready to dismiss him. "Unless there's anything else, I have a report to write, as you can see."

"I am here because I was told you were asking for me," said the man. "My name is Hugo Blackwood."

Solomon turned around, and this time he looked him up and down with fresh eyes. *"You're* Hugo Blackwood?" he said.

"What were you expecting?"

"I don't know," said Solomon. "It wasn't me asking for you. It was a young boy...he's very sick. Strangely sick. Lives near here, his name is Vernon Jamus. You know him?"

Hugo Blackwood said, "I do not."

"Well, he—apparently—knows you? Or knows of you. Is there any reason why a six-year-old boy would ask to see you?"

"A boy? No. No reason whatsoever. But I believe I'm well acquainted with the very thing that makes him summon me."

Solomon had lost all interest in his fried pie. "Well, I can think of one way to find out." He slid his yellow pad and his pencil into a leather folder.

"We'll go pay him a visit, maybe get to the bottom of this. I should warn you...the boy is psychologically sick. I've never seen anything like it."

"I agree, we should go to see the boy," said Hugo Blackwood. "But first I would very much like to see the corpse of the hanged man."

"The...?" Solomon shook his head. "Why would you want to see that?"

"I might be able to help you with your work here."

Solomon was confused. "You said you were not here in any professional capacity—"

"That's correct."

"Then...why are you here?"

"My curse is that I go where I am needed. And right now, it seems I am very much needed here in Gibbston, Mississippi."

The county hospital, half an hour's drive south, was segregated. Solomon, in a borrowed Bureau car, drove past the COLORED ENTRANCE side door, parking under a carport overhang in the main entrance. A signpost inside the entrance read, WAITING ROOM FOR WHITES ONLY—BY ORDER POLICE DEPT.

An old white man sat at a table with a telephone on it inside the foyer. He had only one arm, the cuff of the right-side sleeve of his oxford shirt tucked into the waistband of his pants next to his suspenders clip. He looked to Hugo Blackwood. "Help you?"

Solomon showed the man his FBI badge. "Would you mind directing us to the morgue?"

"Negroes are on the other side of the hospital."

"The white morgue," said Solomon.

"What for?"

"To see a dead body. The hanged man from Gibbston. Hack Cawsby."

The old man looked back and forth between Hugo Blackwood and Solomon. It seemed that having a white man there made it all right. "Side stairs, all the way down."

"Thank you kindly," said Solomon, putting a little topspin on his parting congeniality. As they turned the corner, Solomon looked back and saw the gatekeeper dialing his rotary telephone, no doubt calling up Sheriff Ingalls in Gibbston.

Solomon had to wave his badge again to gain entry into the morgue. The gowned attendant knew exactly which drawer table to pull open. The smell was sickening. "You here to release the body to the funeral home?"

Solomon shook his head, covering his nose, gasping for breath.

The attendant grimaced such that his mustache rode up high to cover his nostrils. "Do me a favor and tell them to hurry it up, will you?"

He pulled back the sheet and stepped out of the room.

Solomon buried his nose and mouth in his jacket elbow. Blackwood played like he was unaffected.

The flesh of the man's neck had separated and was further blackened from decomposition. The man's eyes were closed, his face elongated in agony from his final moments. His wrists were abraded like his throat from the wire restraints.

But Blackwood didn't appear to be interested in the man's wounds.

"Would you mind helping me roll him over?"

Solomon found a pair of stiff latex gloves and pulled them on, offering Blackwood a pair.

"Is this really necessary?"

"It is."

Solomon winced at the thought of moving the cold, fetid corpse. "What are you looking for?"

Blackwood did not answer at first. Of course, corpses do not roll. Solomon had to take the shoulders and Blackwood the feet, and they rotated the body, releasing even more odor.

Solomon backed away, his throat bucking. Blackwood examined the corpse's hairline, his gloved hand smoothing back the dead man's thick blond hair. Strands of it came off onto his yellow gloves, along with flakes of scalp.

"What is it?" asked Solomon, between shallow breaths.

Blackwood straightened, his mouth set flat. "Nothing. Help me right him."

Solomon did, then shoved the drawer closed. The stench lingered.

"How are you able to tolerate this smell?" asked Solomon.

"There are much worse things to tolerate," said Blackwood, distracted. "Now I need to see the site of the hanging."

They drove there with all four car windows down. Solomon told him about finding the small footprint in the soft forest floor beneath the burnt leaves. He asked Blackwood again about the boy. "A very peculiar situation" was all Blackwood would say.

They raced the sunset there, and lost. There was a blue glow in the sky, but that wouldn't help them once they were inside the trees. Solomon found a flashlight in the glove box and led the way. He wasn't sure he would be able to find the site, right up until the moment he stepped into the small clearing.

He showed Blackwood the low branch and described the murder scene without aid of photographs. He kicked aside the forest debris to reveal the faint footprint, but Blackwood was less interested than Solomon expected.

"May I?" he asked, taking the flashlight. He examined the trunk of the hanging tree, its ridged black bark. Standing with his back to the trunk, he shone the flashlight up into the high branches of the surrounding trees, then began inspecting their trunks.

On one, he discovered a carving that in daylight would not have been readily visible. It was slight and small, a curious, crude design consisting of a large circle overlapping with a small circle and a line originating from the overlap, pointing northeast.

Blackwood shone the flashlight beam in the general direction of the odd line.

"What is it?" asked Solomon. "Like a hobo marker or something?"

"Something like that," said Blackwood, walking ten or more yards to another thick trunk. "A marker indicates, warns, or suggests paths for the hungry and the desolate. So in that sense, this thing is similar..."

Another small symbol was rendered there, this one more elaborate, with curving, connecting lines and what appeared to be one half of a star. It could have been a character in a strange, primitive language, a hieroglyph or a pictograph. To Solomon's eye, it looked like a sort of signature, as though dashed off by a spirit of the wood.

This symbol lacked a directional line, at least as far as Solomon could tell, but Blackwood turned the flashlight beam to blaze an illuminated trail to the next tree, and the next, each one with a faint carving... taking them deeper into the woods.

"Where are we going?" asked Solomon.

Blackwood stopped a moment, standing still, as though listening. *"We are here."*

He played the light around a small clearing. Two wooden posts jutted from the ground, supports to a long-ago-destroyed sign. Blackwood cleared fallen leaves off eroded stone markers with words and dates carved into them. Only remnants remained. Partial names and partial dates, ending in the mid-1800s.

Solomon realized what it was. "This is a slave graveyard."

Blackwood wielded the flashlight as Solomon stepped off burial stones set every ten to fifteen feet. This had been either a remote section of a slave owner's property, or else an unofficial burying ground.

"My goodness," said Solomon, imagining the pain of this place from just one century previous. "What a find," he said. Then he remembered how they found it. "What does it mean?"

Blackwood examined the earth. "The graves are undisturbed."

"Of course they—what?" Solomon closed the gap between them. "Why would they be disturbed?"

"I don't know."

"Tell me about the markings in the trees."

"They are called sigils. Occult markings."

"What do you mean, 'occult'?" Solomon was getting spooked, standing in a forgotten graveyard in the middle of the woods, talking about black magic.

"I don't know the translation," said Blackwood. "But it is notable enough that they exist here."

"Sure is," said Solomon, having had enough of this. "Let's get back."

They retraced their steps to the hanging tree. Solomon was still trying to make sense of it all. "Are you thinking the hanging has something to do with the...the..."

"Sigils," said Blackwood.

"Sigils," said Solomon. "Or is it the graveyard? Or—the boy?"

"Yes, all three," said Blackwood, playing the flashlight beam around the hanging site.

Solomon stepped in and relieved him of the flashlight. He didn't want him to find anything else here.

Solomon said, "Since you're not being very forthcoming, let me tell you a little bit about myself. I don't like the world *occult*, for one... and I don't really like spending time in graveyards after dark. I don't believe in any of it, but I don't believe it's something to fun around with, either. I need to know what this is, and I need to know who you are."

"Yes," said Blackwood, looking into the woods past Solomon. "But first, we should ascertain who this is coming our way."

Solomon turned fast. He saw flames in the trees, torchlights. Half a dozen of them—more—coming through the woods.

Solomon felt for his gun through his jacket flap, his Colt Detective Special reassuringly holstered on his hip. "And this is just what we needed here tonight."

The torches slowed, voices talking back and forth. They had seen the flashlight beam.

"How good are you in a fight?" asked Solomon.

Blackwood said, "A fight?"

"A fistfight. You any good?"

Blackwood said, "I've never participated in a fist-fight."

"Perfect," said Solomon. The only thing to do was get ahead of this. He aimed the flashlight at the oncoming torches, switching it on and off as a signal. "This is the FBI!" he called out. "You are entering a crime scene area!" When the flashlight was off, the woods were as black as sleep.

The torchbearers stepped through the last layer of tree trunks, revealing themselves. White pointed hooded masks, wrinkled white robes, blood-drop cross insignia on their breasts. Ten Klansmen. Ten hillbilly white nationalist terrorists arriving at the scene of a white man's hanging to find a black man and a very, very white man.

"FBI," said Solomon again, shining the light on his badge. He let the beam fall upon Blackwood so these Klansmen knew he wasn't alone.

Their eyes were barely visible through the cutout holes in their hoods by flickering torchlight.

Solomon said, "You ought to be careful with those torches. You don't want to set the whole woods on fire."

Or maybe they did. Maybe they had come to burn the hanging tree.

"What kind of badge is that, boy?" said one of the Klansmen.

Solomon smiled through his anger and said, "The kind they hand out with a loaded gun."

"A white man was hanged here," said the Klansman.

"I'm here to find out who did it," said Solomon.

"So're we!" said another Klansman, jabbing the night air with his torch.

"You're mistaken," said Solomon. "And I'm through talking to men in masks." He ran the beam over their hoods, prompting a few of them to block the light with their robed arms. "Show your faces. Face me like men."

The Klansmen looked at each other. Clearly, that wasn't going to happen.

A gust of night wind set the high branches to waving and made their torch flames flicker and flatten. "How about you show us your gun."

Solomon knew that if he pulled his weapon, it was guaranteed he'd have to use it. The Colt had a six-round cylinder. Six rounds weren't enough for ten men.

Solomon said, "How about we talk to Sheriff Ingalls about this."

The lead Klansman turned his head this way and that, as though looking for him. "Which tree he behind?"

The other Klansmen laughed. They were becoming emboldened. Solomon knew even one gunshot from his Colt meant reams of paperwork and the possibility of this becoming a national incident, a black FBI agent shooting at hooded Klansmen.

"You sure are a brave bunch," said Solomon, "afraid to show your faces."

Another swift gust of wind whistled through the

trees. This was going to be an incident, that was plain. Now all Solomon had to worry about was not ending up on the wrong end of the hanging branch.

Hugo Blackwood, about whom Solomon had almost forgotten, stepped up just behind Solomon's flashlight arm. "Agent Solomon, do you trust me?" he whispered.

"No, I don't," Solomon whispered back. But he was out of options. "Why?"

"Allow me to hold the electric torch for you."

Solomon did not want to relinquish his only source of light. "It's called a flashlight. Why do you want to hold this?"

"I think you can use some help."

"Okay," Solomon said, after a moment. He needed both hands for whatever was coming. Solomon handed Blackwood the flashlight.

"What are you talking about there?" asked the lead Klansman, moving up a few steps.

Blackwood said quietly to Solomon, "Now, when I switch off this electric torch, be prepared to run."

Solomon said, "When you...what?"

The other Klansmen stepped forward, following their leader. "What're you doing there?" he said.

Blackwood said, "And...now."

Click. The flashlight went dark. For a moment, the torches lit the trees with orange, dancing light.

"Elil," uttered Blackwood—in a harsh whisper.

A sudden and thorough gust of wind ripped through the clearing. The torch flames whipped back and went out. Blackness fell like a guillotine blade in the disorienting wind.

The Klansmen shouted in alarm.

Solomon felt a hand on his forearm, pulling him. He ran alongside Blackwood, headlong through the darkness, turning quickly this way and that, brushing past—but never once striking—trunks and low branches.

Their steps seemed hushed—muffled—as if they were barely touching the ground, Blackwood guiding him firmly past and above all obstacles, gliding through the dense tree cover like mercury.

He was aware of frantic yelling behind him, the Klansmen either chasing them or simply fleeing the woods themselves. At once, Solomon saw pale moonlight. He emerged from the tree cover onto grass that looked silver, and rough gravel beyond.

There they stopped, Solomon struggling to catch his breath. "How did you do that—?"

Solomon felt something come into his hand. The flashlight.

Then the harried voices of the Klansmen, shouting to each other—*Over here...it's this way...I can't see shit!*—as robed bodies began stumbling out of the woods. The fear in their voices was palpable, and enjoyable.

Solomon hit them with the flashlight beam, and they shouted in fear, covering their eyes. A few of them were on their knees, gasping for breath, the run through the trees having ripped their hoods away, their white robes slashed and shredded, and speckled with blood from branch wounds.

Solomon turned the light beam away from them, leaving them temporarily blinded.

"Evening, gents!" he said, and found the keys to his car in his pocket. He peeled out on the hard gravel.

As Solomon drove, he found himself laughing out loud. It was glee at the humiliation of those Klansmen, but it was also an expression of relief from his own fear. Damn those clumsy hillbillies for the terror they could strike in good people's hearts.

"I don't know how you did that, but that was incredible!" Solomon slapped the steering wheel with his hand, then hit the horn a couple of times in celebration. "How do you see so well in the darkness?"

"A talent, I guess," said Blackwood, shrugging slightly, staring out at the road ahead of them.

His sober reaction brought Solomon back down

to earth. The end triumph couldn't overshadow all the strange things Blackwood had shown him.

"What does it all mean?" asked Solomon.

"I am not sure," said Blackwood. "Something is happening here. Those masked men arrived at this town like dark spirits invoked. This is a flashpoint here, in this place called the Delta. And you, Agent Solomon, are at the nexus."

"Me?" said Solomon. "What do you mean, me? How?"

Blackwood looked out the window, whose glass the dark night had rendered reflective. He took a moment to answer, and when he did, he did so in a low whisper.

"You will decide the outcome," Blackwood said. He turned to see Solomon. "I am ready to see the boy now."

You're doing what?"

Linus laid two carefully folded dress shirts next to his shaving kit in his luggage. "I have to go to Omaha for a few days. We need depositions from half a dozen people at this insurance company...and the partners asked me specifically."

Odessa stood in the doorway to their bedroom, watching him pack. "You are going on a trip," she said, echoing the words of the strange old woman in the back room of the botanica.

He buffed some dust off the top of a pair of shiny black loafers with the underside of his shirtsleeve. "I don't know how this fell to me, but I'm ready for it. The travel office already emailed my tickets and accommodations. Business class."

"That's great," she said, her mind still reeling.

"It is great," he said. A bit of silence followed, Linus probably taking note that she seemed a little out of it. He crossed to her. "How are you doing?"

"Um…good." She hadn't told him anything about Hugo Blackwood. Or the botanica reading. Or the thing in the hotel sheets. She wouldn't know where to begin.

Linus rubbed her upper arms, waiting for her to focus on him. "Come with me," he said.

She sputtered. "Omaha? Nebraska?"

"I hear it's actually pretty great. And I'll be wall-to-wall with depositions, but you can see the town, and we can do dinner. Maybe squeeze an extra day out of it."

"Right," she said.

"This is the perfect opportunity to get away. This will be good for you. In fact, this is exactly what you need right now."

Odessa was nodding, because he was right. But it wasn't that simple. "I know."

"Room service breakfast…?" he said, hoping to entice her. "Hotel spa for you…? We can work out in the gym…?"

He was endearingly persuasive about it. And she should go, she knew that. But the old woman's words…

"You're going on a trip?" Odessa said again, trying to get her head around it. *A coincidence?*

Linus touched her chin, as though focusing her attention on him. "Come with me," he said.

Odessa smiled, won over by the sentiment, by his

tenderness. But she knew that if she went, she'd be standing by the window of the hotel in a bathrobe with her mind back in Newark on Walt Leppo and grave robbers and a peculiar British man.

She backed away. "I'd love to..."

"But what?"

"I don't think it would look good if I ducked work right now. If they need me for an interview about the shooting...and find out I'm on vacation in Nebraska..."

"It's a work trip with your significant other."

Significant other. She liked the sound of that. But now it made her think about other things the old woman had said.

You are his one true love. But he is not yours.

Bullshit. Offensive bullshit, at that. She couldn't let that old crone inside her head.

He will take a trip soon. A new man will come into your life.

This is how they get you, she realized. Paradoxes and general pronunciations—one size fits all: *You are truly private—no one knows the real you—but once you trust someone...it's forever!* Planting a seed underneath your insecurity, fertilizing it with doubt or praise, and then letting it spread like a thorny weed.

She went up to Linus and kissed him, hard. "I wish I could go," she told him. Because she did.

Linus gripped her, another kiss. "Vacation sex is the best," he said.

Odessa nodded, her lips still pressed against his. "How about staycation sex?"

Linus shoved his half-packed suitcase off the bed and they tumbled into it.

She was out of the shower and wearing a towel when she picked up her ringing phone and saw that it was her mother. Due to either resignation or simply a weak moment, she answered.

"Hi, Mom."

"Oh, you answered! How are you? Where are you? Are you okay...?"

It went on like that for a few minutes, Odessa catching her up and reassuring her at the same time. There followed a recitation of her mother's luncheon the previous day, what she ate and what her friend Miriam—whom Odessa had never heard of before—ate and what was discussed.

"And how is Linus?"

Linus was a curiosity to Odessa's mother. Not because she was at all racist, but to her, interracial dating was a young person's province, like streaming music and Postmates. Odessa made the mistake of mentioning he was going to Omaha.

"He's leaving *you* there *alone*?"

Odessa assured her she was fine.

"What's going to happen to you?" her mother asked. "The FBI, your career?"

Odessa sighed. "I think that's over."

"Oh no. But did you ... you didn't ... "

Her mother's concern always made her furious. Made her feel like a failed child. Her mother knew where all her buttons were. She had, in fact, installed them there.

"Look—it's not about right or wrong, it's about how can I go on with this hanging over my head like a flashing neon sign," said Odessa. "I don't know what's next." Then quickly: "But it will be fine."

"Your law degree," said her mother, hopefully.

"Yes. My law degree."

"Always something to fall back on. Just like your father."

The corners of Odessa's mouth fell at the mention of her father. That her mother still revered him was a source of fascination for Odessa ... and also a source of pity.

"Mom, you were the youngest of seven, right?"

"Well, yes, of course." She rattled off her six siblings' names in birth order. "What makes you ask that?"

"No reason, but—"

"I always wanted seven of my own," her mother interjected. "I suppose because that's what I grew up with. And I was the baby, like you, so I wanted to emulate that. Funny now."

"You had six children, Mom. That's pretty good."

"I know. Six is enough," her mother said and then chuckled.

Odessa felt a pang of relief, marking the old soothsayer wrong on that one.

"Although there was a...a stillbirth," said her mother.

Odessa shook her head, wet hair swinging over her ears. "A...*what?*"

"She was...it was my very first pregnancy. Ended in a neonatal death."

"But...wait, was it...was she...born alive or dead?"

A pause on her mother's end. "She died in my arms, Odessa. She didn't live but an hour."

Odessa had her free hand against the wall, leaning against it, dizzy. Stunned. "So then I am actually...the seventh daughter...of a seventh daughter?"

"Well—I guess, technically speaking. But why do you say it like that?"

"Why haven't we talked about this before?" asked Odessa. *How could I not know this?*

"Because it isn't very pleasant for me to speak about, Odessa," said her mother, an uncharacteristic curt note in her voice.

"I'm sorry." Odessa realized she was dredging up painful memories without thinking about her mother's side of this. *The seventh daughter of a seventh daughter.* What the hell did this mean?

"Mom, I never...I can't know what it was like to go through that. I didn't really know. Sorry."

She found herself with a newfound appreciation for her mother's strength. It almost forgave—and went a long way toward explaining—the decades of weakness that followed.

"Odessa," said her mother, "where are these questions coming from?"

An old soothsayer. "Nowhere, Mom. Just...soul searching."

"Odessa...are you thinking about starting a family?"

"*What?* God, no..."

"Are you pregnant?"

Jesus. "No, Mom. Nope. None of the above."

"You know your sister is expecting her third..."

Odessa lived through another two minutes of denials and trying to get off the phone, until finally the line was dead and she was staring at her screen display, deep in thought.

She replayed the Tarot reading. All the things that woman said. Still, Odessa found ways to knock down some of her statements, her predictions. She was still fighting the reading, denying it.

The counter woman wearing the headdress, translating:

She asks if you want to know about your father.

And then the old woman's eyes rolling back when confronted by Hugo Blackwood, almost fainting.

Odessa walked into the kitchen. The teacup was on her kitchen counter, still unwashed.

The cup from which Hugo Blackwood had drunk. The one he had held.

Odessa endured the glances, the eyes following her in the hallway, as she moved through the New Jersey Field Office in Claremont Tower. Only something like this could have made her return there. Her friend Laurena was waiting for her in a secure conference room.

They hugged. Laurena studied her face, and Odessa knew she was scrutinizing her complexion as an indicator of health. "You look good."

"Thanks," said Odessa. There was water—a fancy mason jar and two glasses. She poured herself one. Hand trembling.

"I'd be a blotchy, dried-out mess. I miss you. What do your lawyers say?"

Odessa shrugged. "What can they say? What can anyone say?" She sipped the water.

"I can say, it's all bullshit. You're a good agent,

Dessa. I don't know what happened that night, but I know you didn't lose your shit."

"Thanks."

"There's rumors...I don't believe them, but I'm telling you because I'd want to know...rumors about you and Leppo."

Odessa felt a wave of sickness and anger. "Fuck."

"I said that. I said, 'Fuck that.' People looking for explanations, for reasons. How one agent shoots another. They can't get their male heads around the fact that maybe their buddy Leppo lost his shit. Maybe it was the man who went off the reservation. Wouldn't that be a novel idea."

"He was going to kill the girl. It sounds terrible because it *is* terrible. I can't explain it—maybe nobody can. But he had the knife and he was going to cut her throat. And people think we were sleeping together?"

"It's tribal, male versus female. That's how they think. Forget it."

"His poor wife," said Odessa, thinking about Leppo's widow, and not for the first time.

"She's in rough shape. But of course."

But she couldn't help thinking of Walt Leppo's wife hearing rumors about her husband, who was a straight arrow, getting shot over some sordid romantic fling. It didn't even make sense, really...but she hoped Leppo's wife was spared that.

Odessa remembered the paper bag in her hand. "Will you do me another huge favor?"

"*Anything*," said Laurena. But then, remembering what she'd done for her before, getting Odessa the crime scene photos from the Peters house, she pulled back. "Wait. What favor is it now?"

Odessa handed her the lunch bag. Laurena held it, not opening the top fold.

"Oh shit," she said. "What is this?"

"A teacup. I want you to run a full biometric analysis, including DNA casework and latent prints."

Laurena stared at Odessa, her face slowly breaking into a smile. "You realize what you're asking me?"

"I do."

"This breaks, like, every protocol we have."

"I know."

"People have gotten fired for using the FBI lab for personal grievances."

"I'm the only one getting fired here," said Odessa. "I'll take full blame."

"You're sure this isn't about you and Linus? Some domestic incident? Maybe he had a girl over to the house or something? Is there lipstick on the rim?"

Odessa shook her head. "No lipstick. This is not about Linus."

"Okay...then what is it about, exactly?"

216

"It's about my case. But not exactly."

"Explain."

"I wish I could."

"Oh shit." Laurena turned in a full circle, a pirou-ette of protest. "Dessa."

"Would I ask if it weren't really *that* important?"

"This is crazy, girl. This is getting out of hand. All of it. I'm worried about you."

"Yeah," said Odessa. "Tell me about it."

Laurena waited for more. "That's all you're gonna say?"

"One more thing. The cup needs to be processed here. Not Quantico. I need the results to stay in-house."

Laurena let out an exasperated sigh. "Anything else?"

"And the results need to come to me exclusively. Any database hits, I want to know. But just for me. Understand?"

"Dessa. Girl. Are you sure you're okay? You don't seem okay."

Odessa touched her temples. "I will be," she said, willing it to happen. "I will be."

Odessa returned to NewYork-Presbyterian Queens Hospital in Flushing, riding the elevator up to the patient care unit. She found Earl Solomon's room, and Earl Solomon in it. He sat against a stack of four pillows in his hospital bed, covered by a blanket over the sheet, though she found the room warm.

The sight of his bedsheet took her back to questioning Mauro Esquivel in the basement of the Lexington Regal Hotel with Hugo Blackwood. That focused her mind.

There was another man in the room, though again, not a family member. He was heavy, with thick, friendly jowls, wearing a generously tailored suit, his scalp bald to a fold of flesh at the back of his neck.

"Hello," Odessa said, "am I interrupting?"

"Come in, Agent Hardwicke," said Solomon, his voice a bit raspier than the last time she'd spoken with him. He welcomed her in with a pale-palmed hand. "It's almost happy hour."

She smiled, relieved to see him in good humor, if physically more weakened. A thin tube across his face fed oxygen through his nose.

"Hello," she said, shaking the other man's hand.

"This is Mr. Lusk," said Solomon. "He's a lawyer."

"Pleased to meet you, Agent Hardwicke."

Odessa released his hand and turned to Solomon. His eyes were still yellowed, the skin of his neck looking looser, like he was losing weight quickly. "How were those tests...?"

"Oh, that. I guess they'll get around to telling me one of these days."

She couldn't tell if he was putting up a good front or if this was his natural disposition.

"But you're okay? How are you doing?"

"Getting there."

Odessa nodded, unsure what to say. *Getting there.* But he wasn't specific about just where that was.

"Good, good," she said, hating pleasantries and small talk at a time like this.

"What brings you back here?" asked Solomon.

"Well, I wanted to check in on you, and, um...I don't mean to be rude, but can we speak privately for a moment?"

She smiled awkwardly at Mr. Lusk, who stood

there with his hands in his pockets listening. He looked at Solomon as though to say, *Not a problem.*

Solomon said, "It's fine, you can speak openly in front of Lusk, here. He's a lawyer."

"Um...okay." She smiled again at Mr. Lusk, hoping he would take it upon himself to step outside for a bit. But the corpulent man simply smiled back.

Fine, then. She wouldn't feel self-conscious. If Mr. Lusk wanted to stay, he was going to hear quite a tale.

"I mailed, if that's the right word, a letter at the address you suggested," she said, turning back to Solomon. "Hugo Blackwood appeared soon thereafter—very quickly, in fact—at my home."

"Yes," said Solomon, as though he were aware of this already, which was not possible. "Go on."

"He, um, well, I guess he agreed to help me, or try. And we pursued some leads—one lead—and...yup." She wanted to be blunt, but despite her determination she found it difficult to be completely open with the lawyer in the room. She knew she would sound ridiculous. "And then we parted ways. How do you know him exactly? He said you two go way back."

"We do. What was it...'62? Summer of '62."

Solomon was looking to Mr. Lusk to confirm, for some reason.

"Wow," said Odessa. "Was he a child...?"

"No," said Solomon.

"And he is...what is he, actually?" said Odessa. "His job?"

"His job is being who he says he is, I think." Solomon shook his head as though they were discussing the weather. "There's no explaining him."

"Tell me about it," she said, unable to express her thoughts at the moment. "He has an interesting perspective on the Bureau."

"He does, doesn't he? I don't think he fully understands. He thinks we are agents like real estate agents or sports agents. Representatives. At least, that's his patter."

"Patter?"

"I don't know if everything he says is straight ahead, or sometimes tongue in cheek. He's easier to be around if you don't take everything he says to heart."

"Is that right?" she said, still burning at his treatment of her.

"He gives more than he takes, I'll put it that way. It's worth putting up with the Hobson act for what he gets you."

Odessa nodded but did not quite understand. "The Hobson act?" She thought Solomon was referring to some obscure federal law.

"Hobson, yup. Ever see the movie *Arthur*?"

"Uh, no, I don't...wait. Russell Brand?"

"Nope. Short guy, so funny. Funniest drunk since W. C. Fields."

"I'm very lost here," she said.

Mr. Lusk said, helpfully, "Dudley Moore."

Solomon pointed to Mr. Lusk. "That's him. Not him, though. Not his character. He was a rich kid who grew up into a wealthy man, but he had the same butler since he was a boy. Funny British manservant, old guy, straight face, cut him down to size every single time. Blackwood is a little like that, except he's only older inside. Hard to like, at times, but good to know. That pretty well sums him up."

Odessa nodded, needing to get this conversation back on track, pivoting to Solomon's house. "Anything else you want me to take care of at your residence while you're here?"

"Can't think of anything. Just the damn fish."

"The fish is fine."

"Well, I wasn't all that worried, to be honest," said Solomon.

She chuckled too long. "By the way, while I was there, I was looking for a net for Dennis, to take the fish out of the bowl of dirty water? And I found one in the small closet off the kitchen."

"Good."

"Yes." She nodded, working her way up to this. "But while I was in there, I noticed the back wall—"

Solomon smoothed out the blanket beside his hips. "Have you listened to any of them yet?"

"Any of...of the tapes?"

"Well, yes. Sounds like you found my hidden room."

"I really didn't mean...I'm not normally a snooper. But that 'room' represents about a third of the house..."

"Did you listen?"

Odessa shook her head, surprised he was so unperturbed at her trespassing on his inner chamber. "No."

"You should. When you're ready."

"When I'm...ready? For what?"

Solomon nodded, then coughed suddenly, turning away from her to reach for a Styrofoam cup of water with a short straw sticking out.

Mr. Lusk grinned at her in the moments Solomon was turned away from them. He motioned to his own elbow, then nodded to Solomon. Odessa, confused, looked at Solomon's arm where intravenous fluids entered his circulatory system. Then she understood: Mr. Lusk was hinting that Solomon was sedated, which might explain his oblique questions and answers.

Solomon turned back before Odessa could look to Mr. Lusk for more information.

"The tapes started arriving at my house back in '62," said Solomon. "After every case, sometimes a week later, sometimes more, a bundle of seven-inch Mylar recording tapes would be delivered by US Mail. Blackwood transcribes each case, sometimes four or five reels per. Not sure why he does it. I think he likes the technology, for one...in his mind reel-to-reel is cutting edge. I asked him early on, about his reasons, but he Hobson'd me. Anyway. I had the bright idea of sending one to an audio lab once—independent, not the Bureau, I didn't want that can of worms opened—just to see what they could tell me. Voice analysis, whatever. I was curious. The technician said the tape was recorded at a very high frequency and then transferred to a lower one. I don't know what it means. But it was something he'd never encountered. Long story short, he couldn't tell me jack about it. It was like filing the serial number off a gun...Maybe nowadays they can do things digitally, but...I guess I'm trying to save you some effort."

"All those tapes," said Odessa. "That's a lot of cases. What kind of cases?"

"Listen first," said Solomon. "Then we'll talk."

She shook her head, because what she was about to say sounded crazy. "Are they occult cases?"

"It's okay," said Solomon, summoning a smile. "I was like you, once upon a time."

"Like me?"

"That's why I saved all the damn tapes," said Solomon. "It wasn't like he asked me to. I wanted a record. I wanted some backup, in case things ever went sideways on me and I had to defend myself."

Odessa was rubbing her temples again. Was there some sort of hypnosis going on, or contagious insanity? "Can we go back to 'occult cases'? Because that's just not something the FBI investigates."

"True enough, Agent—it's not our job. It's not anyone's job. It's not a job at all. Except for *him*." Solomon held up his hand, stopping her next question before she could ask it. "Speaking of whom. Now that you've encountered him." Solomon turned his head fully toward her, not just his eyes. His demeanor changed, became more solemn. "It's been more than a year since I've laid eyes upon Mr. Blackwood. I was hoping he might come by here, pay me a visit, you know? One last time."

Odessa swallowed softly. *One last time?* Did this mean Solomon's condition was terminal? She couldn't bring herself to ask.

She said, "I don't want to disappoint you...but we separated on kind of bad terms. I won't be seeing him again."

Solomon's eyebrows rose a bit, tiredly. "You will,"

he said. "And when you do...tell him." He smoothed out the blanket again. "It's kind of funny, I guess. To come to the end, to have lived a life of, you could say, proud independence, only to find...you got no one. That's a thing I'm facing now."

Odessa's heart dropped. She reached out to him, touching his shoulder. "You're not alone," she said.

"It's mainly my own fault," he said, trying to smile. "Outliving everyone else..."

"No family...?" said Odessa.

"None. And no trusted friends. And the hospital here—or my health insurer, I'm not sure—needs me to update my health care proxy." He looked at Mr. Lusk, who nodded his second opinion. "It's a formality. You won't have to make any difficult decisions, I marked down how I want everything to go."

"Oh," she said. "Me?"

"It's a lot to ask, I know. We don't know one another very well at all..."

She felt a panicky feeling rising in her chest and wasn't sure why. She fought it.

"You can read the form," he said. "You're a lawyer. It's all spelled out."

Mr. Lusk produced a three-page contract. "Palliative care for dignity and quality of life, but no extending treatment beyond that. At no time will you be required to make a life-or-death call, as it were."

Mr. Lusk had a fountain pen, too. Odessa felt herself nodding. "Of course," she said.

She read through the form quickly. Standard medical legalese. She signed.

"And, if you would," said Mr. Lusk, swapping out another set of pages, "power of attorney. Standard formality."

This one she skimmed, then signed her name to it.

Mr. Lusk smiled and slipped the contracts back into his leather portfolio, which he tucked under his arm.

"Odessa," said Solomon. He held out his hand to her. She took it: cold and rough. "This is a special thing you've done for me. Thank you."

There was emotion behind his voice. He was grateful to her, and maybe there was something more.

"Happy to help, really I am." She gave his hand a light squeeze. "I'm really glad we met."

"Aren't you sweet. Do me a favor and give your parents my regards, they raised a special one."

Odessa let out a soft laugh. "I'll do that."

She made to pull away, but he gripped her hand a while longer.

"We in the Bureau, we answer a higher calling. Something sacred."

"Yes," she said, smiling. She patted the back of his hand. "And you did it longer than anyone, it seems."

Solomon closed his eyes, smiled, and nodded. "Not better, but sure longer." With a chuckle, he released her hand, his head settling back against the top pillow. "I got to close my eyes a bit now," he said.

"Rest," she said, feeling a surge of respect for the man.

With a friendly nod to Mr. Lusk, she backed out of the door.

Odessa waited at the elevator, suffused with a lingering warm feeling of connection with Agent Earl Solomon, and at the same time a mournful ache for his apparent loneliness at the end of his days. She watched the floor numbers light up in sequence as the elevator rose to receive her. The only good thing about hospitals was leaving them.

Another person appeared at her side. She looked over with a courtesy grin and saw that it was Mr. Lusk, his chubby fingers tapping softly on his leather portfolio.

"Going down?" he said with a smile.

"Yes," she said. He seemed pleasant enough, but also like he had something on his mind.

"Difficult," he said, nodding with meaning.

"It is," she answered. "He's a good man."

The doors opened. Mr. Lusk waved his arm the-atrically for Odessa to enter, joining two other rid-ers already inside the elevator car. They turned to face the closing doors.

"How long have you been Agent Solomon's lawyer?" she asked.

"Oh, I am not Agent Solomon's lawyer," he said, again with a smile. "I'm just doing a bit of pro bono work for him as a courtesy." His fingers drummed the portfolio again. "No, I represent Hugo Black-wood."

Odessa turned to him. He stood smiling at the doors as they descended. "You're Blackwood's lawyer?"

He nodded.

"Then why can't you get him to visit Solomon?"

"Me? Oh no. Mr. Blackwood does as he pleases. I don't have any luck persuading him to do anything. I am simply his representative."

The doors opened, and they walked together to the exit. Odessa said, "I don't suppose you want to tell me what Mr. Blackwood's business is, or how he affords personal counsel..."

Mr. Lusk smiled and shook his head. "Mr. Black-wood has asked me to take you to him. He wants to show you something."

"Show me what?"

"I don't know the answer to that."

"He wants you to take me?"

They stepped out onto the street. "I have a car with me," he said.

At the curb, parked in a clearly marked yellow NO PARKING NO LOADING zone, was a Rolls-Royce, vintage but not antique, black with faint gunpowder-gray styling.

Odessa stopped. "That's your car?"

"That is Mr. Blackwood's car. A Rolls-Royce Phantom."

Odessa smiled and shook her head. "Here's what bothers me most," she said, as though Mr. Lusk cared. "The presumption that I would do what he wants. Get in his car and go to him and be shown whatever it is he wants to show me."

Mr. Lusk nodded, smiling pleasantly. "I feel exactly the same way."

"Like I don't have anything better to do," she said.

Mr. Lusk smiled and half shrugged. "Completely in agreement." He opened the door for her.

"What could he want to show me anyway?"

"There is one simple and straightforward way to find out."

Again he swept his arm forward theatrically toward the interior of the vehicle. Odessa saw that it was weirdly roomy inside, and well appointed: burgundy leather seats with dark stitching, a bar to one side that appeared to feature only bottled water, tinted windows. There was no one else inside.

"He's not here?"

"I am to take you to him."

Odessa looked around at the street: the people walking past, glancing at the fancy vehicle; cars rolling by; buildings high above. It almost felt as if she were leaving this everyday world for another one.

She remembered Solomon's words from their first meeting, which had made little sense to her at the time, but kept coming back around in her memory. *Everything is an invocation. Little moments of holy summoning.*

"You know what?" she said. "Why not?"

She entered the vehicle, and with a formal nod Mr. Lusk closed the door behind her.

The Phantom rolled out of the city, heading north. Odessa had accepted Blackwood's strange invitation with the assumption that the destination was close by.

Three and a half hours later, the Phantom pulled off the highway in the city of Providence, Rhode Island.

"Almost there," sang Mr. Lusk, his porky hands gripping the ivory-colored steering wheel in the front seat.

Underneath the elevated highway, they turned near the industrial waterfront, rolling along a decaying part of the city replete with crumbling brick factories and strip clubs. Mr. Lusk pulled the Phantom up outside a tattoo parlor with a hand-lettered sign over the door reading ANGEL'S.

"You're kidding me," she said.

Mr. Lusk lifted his bulk out of the driver's-side door and came around to open hers. Odessa stood out on the sidewalk smelling the salt air, looking up and down the vacant block beneath the highway. The front window was mostly blacked out.

"Seriously," she said.

Mr. Lusk walked ahead of her to the door. He pressed a buzzer and waited. The door was pushed open by a large, well-inked man with a flared brown mustache.

"Come in, come in," he said, his voice deep and Mexican-accented. Odessa and Mr. Lusk entered, and the tall man closed and locked the door behind them. The walls were decorated with tattoo designs—nothing hip, all low-rent—everything from Warner Bros. cartoon characters to pissing Calvin to tramp stamps to a single, perfect rose. Variations on MOTHER. Every branch of the armed forces, cartoon renderings of naked women and men, and multiple alphabets in various forms of Gothic script. Also for sale were knives and Zippo lighters, in displays near the front counter.

"I am Joachim, the proprietor." Joachim stood six feet, six inches, dressed in a black T-shirt and black jeans under a full-length brown duster. He shook Odessa's hand, his palm dwarfing hers. "Here he is," he said to Mr. Lusk, shaking his hand as well. "I expected you half an hour ago."

Mr. Lusk said, "We were delayed leaving the city," apparently meaning her visit with Agent Solomon.

"No matter," said Joachim.

Odessa scanned the ink sleeving his arms. Symbols and sunsets and religious iconography: as careful and complete a mosaic as she had ever seen on any surface. *Guernica* on flesh.

"You here for a tattoo?" said Joachim.

Odessa shook her head, checking with Mr. Lusk.

Joachim chuckled. "I'm kidding. But if you ever want one, you come to me."

Odessa nodded, still reading his skin. One face on his forearm caught her eye, looking familiar. Was it...?

Joachim saw her looking at it. "You like this one? Pretty good likeness, no?"

Odessa looked back and forth between the tattoo and Mr. Lusk. The attorney smiled pleasantly, nodding. Yes—it was Mr. Lusk's face.

"Really captures his spirit, I think."

She scanned the other faces, wondering who and why and what...

"Check out my newest one, here."

Joachim stepped to the counter, turning on a bright lamp and flexing the arm to focus on his midsection. He lifted his T-shirt up to his pecs, revealing more inked flesh, much of it radiating off a large cross in the muscled center of his chest, sunlight or divine light shining from behind it. A small bandage covered a patch of skin on his left side near the bottom of his rib cage. He peeled back the adhesive, revealing red, swollen flesh around a raw impression roughly the size of an extra-large egg.

It was a woman's face.

It was Odessa's face.

She stepped back. She looked up at him, smiling down at her.

"Not a bad likeness," he said.

Odessa was speechless. He covered up the new ink and lowered his shirt on the living mural.

"Come on in back," said Joachim. "He's waiting for you."

"How did you...?" She was too mystified even to finish the sentence. *Get a picture of my face?*

"Right back here," he said, staring ahead of her.

Joachim led them through the back office and another door, down a narrow hallway to a locked door leading into an adjacent factory.

Stepping inside, she felt the wide-open, high-ceilinged space more than she saw it. It was dusty and dark. The floor was grimy, the sound of her shoes upon it carrying wide into the room.

Hugo Blackwood walked out of the shadows, wearing the same dark suit, or an exact replica, that he had worn before. "You're late," he said.

Odessa was still shaken, speechless.

Blackwood nodded to Joachim, who stepped back to the wall near the door, pressing a small switch.

Lights clanked on along the high ceiling, light raining down, dust motes swirling lazily. Parts of the ceiling had crumbled away, exposing the next empty floor, high above.

In the center of the room, arranged in a diamond, were four clear polymer cylinders, running floor-to-ceiling. Each one was eight to ten feet in diameter, and easily twenty-five feet in height.

A circle of coarse sea salt surrounded each cylinder.

Small, black-feathered creatures—they were roosters—stepped around the inside of the cylinders, pecking at the bare feet of hunched-over, aged beings, their flesh the glistening pineapple yellow of human body fat.

Each had the wrinkled body of a three-hundred-year-old man. Eyeless, earless—seemingly featureless—but when the nearest being, tormented by the roosters, twisted around, Odessa saw its entire face flap open and reveal a mouth, yawning in hunger.

Much like a lamprey, the mouth was made of concentric circles of vibrating flesh, lined up with cartilaginous protrusions, not properly teeth, but barbed nubs.

Odessa grasped the fabric on the back of Blackwood's jacket, steadying herself. Blackwood said, "They are called the Hollow Ones. The emptiness—the ever-hungry. Mesopotamian lore has them born last of the *Udug Hul*—the foul spirits. Don't come close to the sea salt circle, you don't want to touch it."

Another of them hissed and gnashed its teeth, shrinking away from a rooster at its ankle.

"Foul entities," said Blackwood. "You see them revealed here in visible form. But there are many entities surrounding us, at all times. I have seen, in the course of certain investigations, forensics experts enter a crime scene and use a special ultraviolet lamp..."

"A Luma Lamp," said Odessa.

"Yes, to reveal how a clean room truly looks—that which is invisible to the naked eye. Well, that's the way these things are visible to me. All around us. All the time. These particular ones: larvae, who jump from human body to human body like young adults stealing cars and taking them on a...what is it?"

Joachim said, "A joyride."

Distressingly, all three entities followed Odessa around the room with their gazes, turning their eyeless heads in unison.

"Yes, a joyride. A Hollow One only inhabits a

human host for a limited amount of time. They are creatures of chaos. They thrive on it. They enjoy when their host body is killed. That is how they are forcibly ejected from the body, ending the ride. You have to understand that the moment of death, of being murdered, is to them an immensely pleasurable experience, which is why they go on killing sprees. The hosts experience these occupations as blackout moments. Such as your fellow agent, Leppo."

The thought of Walt Leppo was the only thing that could bring her voice back into her throat. "Walt?" she whispered.

Blackwood walked toward the cylinders, Odessa releasing his jacket. "They are compulsion—addicts to heightened emotion: The moment of death, of ejection, is a sensation such that they seek to repeat it again and again."

"Dying?" said Odessa.

Blackwood nodded. "Oftentimes, if for whatever reason the death wasn't satisfying enough, they will leap directly from one corpse into another nearby human, in the hope of intensifying the experience. They gain access most easily to the emotionally conflicted and the mentally unstable...though they can take advantage of any situation with the element of surprise. They are wily, cunning creatures who will exploit any opportunity."

She watched them turning in circles, plagued by the roosters. Odessa said, "I don't know if I can believe what I'm seeing."

"Hollow Ones are mortally afraid of only one thing, and that is roosters—black capons—virgin capons. Interestingly, they love to eat boiled eggs. We have to keep them separated at all times. Together, they could achieve great destructive power, a mass casualty event."

Odessa saw now that the fourth cylinder, the one farthest away from her, was empty. "Where's the...?"

"Ah, yes. Over the years, I have caught and captured three. The fourth receptacle awaits the last of them. The last of the last—born at the end. The hungriest."

Odessa watched the creatures jerk away from the small roosters, screeching. "And you think the fourth one is...?"

"Is free, raising havoc—yes. Rode the disgraced governor's aide in the airplane trip over the island of Manhattan, crashing and slaying his own family. Rode the town supervisor in the office massacre on Long Island."

Odessa realized now, having not put it together before: "Both political figures."

"Yes, I thought of that. The Hollow Ones' only weakness, other than their fear of the black capons, is their random nature. They embrace the thrill of death and all its chaos without any regard for the circumstances, careening from one tragic catastrophe to another. But if they were focused somehow...say, directed to inhabit persons in positions of power...you could imagine what would happen..."

Odessa shook her head. "How did you catch them?"

"Different situations, different eras. Their inconsistency of behavior has served them well in that regard. But now the fourth—the elusive fourth—appears to have established itself, of all places, in the New York–New Jersey region."

Joachim wandered over to the cylinders, standing inside the implied diamond. He knocked on one of the hard, clear polymer containers, startling the Hollow One trapped inside. It immediately attacked, pressing its concentric-circled mouth against the Plexiglas. A fat, pale tongue rotated hungrily, slowly, streaking saliva all over it.

Blackwood said, "Joachim watches over them here—their jailer, you might say. If they ever get free, it would be, well—something mankind has not experienced for a while."

"Then...why keep them here?" said Odessa. "Why keep them alive?"

"They are elemental beings," said Blackwood, as

though that should have been obvious. "They cannot be destroyed. Only caged. The closer they are to each other, the calmer they stay. They sense each other...they sense you..."

She saw one of the Hollow Ones squeal with its face-wide mouth and felt sick to her stomach. "This is one hundred percent, completely insane."

Blackwood said, "We have to focus on why here, and why now? Who might have unleashed the fourth, or harnessed its energy in some way? What is their goal?"

She was still catching up mentally. "I saw nothing like these things leaving Walt Leppo's body. It was waves of heat, almost. I smelled—"

"Burnt solder. I know. I've smelled it. As I said, these are their visible forms. Similar to water expressed in solid, liquid, or gaseous state. There is only one way to tell if a person is inhabited by a Hollow One. Their telltale mark is a sigil on the base of the neck, just inside the hairline. It is a raised-vein mark in the shape of a compass. It goes without saying that it is very difficult, if not impossible, to examine the hairline of someone possessed by a rampaging larva."

"That goes without saying," she muttered. She touched her temples, her go-to move now. Why did she get into that Rolls-Royce?

"My guess," said Blackwood, in a manner that

made clear it was not a guess at all, "is that a misguided ceremony attracted the fourth one. Palo most likely—in the last few years there has been a streak of grave robberies in New Jersey, widely documented in the news."

"Is there any way we can go back to before I walked in here and just…forget the whole thing?"

Blackwood looked at her as though uncertain if she was serious or not. "You wanted answers. You wanted to know what happened to the agent you shot dead. Why he would attack that girl suddenly." Blackwood stepped in front of her, making sure he had her full attention.

"It wanted you to shoot. It wanted to be killed— to be blasted out of that body. And it wanted *you* to do it…"

"Why me?" said Odessa.

"Through no fault of your own. It probably sensed your affection for that man," said Blackwood. "His—and your—suffering would have added an extra flavor to the thrill."

She realized that, in his own strange way, he was trying to absolve her of shooting Walt Leppo. But every answer begat another question. "Then why didn't one of these mouthy monster things…I don't know, jump into me?"

"I think it would've. Perhaps a moment of hesitation was sufficient for others to enter the room.

Also, as pleasurable as the sensation of being thrown is, I think it loses its jolt if it is performed too many times in succession."

Odessa looked at him. Was he relating it to an orgasm? That was a question she did not want to ask.

Blackwood said, "I need to find and capture the fourth before it can realize its objective. They crave chaos above all, and the ultimate chaos would come from inhabiting a human being of great power and prestige."

Odessa said, "You want me to help you catch one of those things."

"It is not a matter of want," he said. "It is a matter of great necessity. We need to trace back everyone that went in and out of your crime scene in the half hour after your partner was shot."

Again, he was delicate enough not to make her the active shooter in the sentence.

"Half an hour?" Odessa said. "Why the time limit?"

"The fourth one had already jumped bodies. Its time in the open would have been reduced to that, or less."

She couldn't believe that she was even considering this. "I need to know things. If you want my help, I need to know who you are... who all these people are. And how you know these things..."

"All in time."

"The time is now," she said.

Blackwood tipped his head slightly to one side. "Yes, of course," he said, to her surprise. "You need to know everything there is to know about the Hollow Ones. Starting with how these elemental beings were released into this world…"

"And who did it," said Odessa.

"Oh, that one is easy," said Blackwood. "I'm afraid it was me."

1582. Mortlake, Greater London.

In the days following the séance inside John Dee's library, strange occurrences began happening in and around barrister Hugo Blackwood's home.

The plantings shriveled and died, leaves crumbling like rust, as though all the water in the soil had been turned into bad iron. Holes appeared in the turf as though dug by small animals, except that the soil was piled as though something had dug its way out of the underground, rather than in.

Scratching on the wall. Shrieks in the night, waking him, baying cries from the direction of the Thames. Blackwood had a dream where a shadow on the wall assumed form, dropping down onto the floor of his bedchamber, slithering onto his bed next to him, feeling cold and wet. He woke without breath, falling to the floor until, at once, his throat opened with a great, groaning gasp, and he breathed.

A haze had settled over the entire parish. But

most troubling to Hugo Blackwood was the behavior of his dutiful wife, Orleanna, a raven-haired, doe-eyed beauty. After a day of acting distant and appearing unnerved, she had taken to her bed in sickness. On the advice of her physician, he hired a nurse to tend to her while he was away at court. After two days, the nurse refused to treat Orleanna any longer, but would not explain why, leaving shaken. Blackwood, when he visited his wife's bedside, found only a woman in confused distress, beseeching his help. So sudden, the light gone from her eyes, her chest heaving to draw breath. Tormented and feverish, she spoke to people who weren't there.

"Can nothing be done?" he said, sponging at her brow with a cold compress. "My love, my love."

Orleanna was the muse behind all of Hugo Blackwood's successes, the fire in the furnace of his ambition. She was the daughter of one of his mentors and grew up in a home of learning and study. Intelligent and also savvy, Orleanna was the more ambitious of the two of them; she desired for her husband success in every form. He still marveled, daily, that he had won her affection; and every day since their wedding, he endeavored to reward her support.

She glowed as though lit from within, and Blackwood was a doting husband. Were it not for Orleanna's attractive nature, the way she drew people to her, Blackwood would have been perfectly happy never attending or hosting another social event. Indeed, it was her influence that made him seek out a compelling and charismatic personality such as John Dee. Orleanna Blackwood possessed, in the parlance of the day, "the intellect of a man," to the point that Blackwood sometimes would remind her, in social settings, to mind her role; privately, their far-ranging discussions sometimes ran into the late hours, fired by candlelight and a draught or two of wine. Extraordinary figures such as Dee delighted her, and whereas other wives were content—nay, encouraged—to mix only among those of their fair gender, Orleanna thrived in the acquaintance of learned men. This made Blackwood selfish; she made him possessive, though not to a fault. It is human nature to want to possess beauty, to celebrate purity, to safeguard uniqueness.

Dee himself had once told her that she was born in the wrong era, that she was a woman who existed "centuries before her time." Privately, Orleanna dismissed Dee's compliment as mere polite chatter, but Blackwood knew she had drawn deep satisfaction from his evocation of her.

And now seeing her suffer so was the greatest burden Hugo Blackwood could bear. That night at

John Dee's library, the sinister séance, haunted him, and he feared he had somehow brought harm to his home, his hearth, his love. He had little memory of the events of that night—though he had racked his brain to recall them, to the point of despair—but only of returning home just before dawn, and Orleanna waking in their bed, and in her somnolent state asking for a kiss...

He remembered she recoiled from his taste, the flavor of solder lingering in his mouth. She said she woke the next morning with the burnt taste still upon her palate, the source of which he could not explain.

Talbot, the spiritualist, called upon Hugo Blackwood one evening, appearing at the door wearing his monk's skullcap, his eyes furtive and inquiring.

"A manbeast," he said, relating his wild story to Blackwood in the kitchen over tea. "The face of a wolf and the arms of a bear."

"Talbot," said Blackwood, seeking to calm him.

"I've seen it. Out of the corner of my eye, always—but there. In the shadow. Behind a tree. In the next room."

"You have a fever," said Blackwood.

Talbot gripped Blackwood's hand and brought it to his forehead. "Cool as river stone."

The shadow—it had crawled next to him—wet—cold.

248

"Mind fever," said Blackwood, taking back his hand.

"And the odors," said Talbot. "The dampness. Over all."

"Edward," said Blackwood. "I thought you were...more of an enthusiast with regard to the spirits..."

"A charlatan?" said Talbot.

"That sounds harsh," admitted Blackwood. "But I thought you were more of a performer. The scrying. Your trances."

Talbot stared deeply into his shallow cup of tea. "Have you any port?"

"None, I'm afraid. Orleanna hasn't been to market. She's unwell—"

"The wormwood we drank that night. I feel I remain under its spell. I can't trust my own eyes...my own thoughts..."

Blackwood nodded, relieved that Talbot had given air to his own fears. "A shadow has been cast."

Talbot sipped at his tea, and, finding it foul, threw it cup and all into Blackwood's sink, where it smashed. "Rotted," Talbot muttered. "Everything..."

Blackwood sniffed his own brew. Indeed, it was foul. Even the tea leaves had turned.

"*Hugo!*" cried Orleanna, her voice muffled through the walls.

Talbot looked frightened.

"My wife," said Blackwood, leaving him, moving through two closed doors to the bedroom. "The noise must have alarmed her."

Orleanna sat up in their bed, looking horrified.

Blackwood explained, "Talbot's here, my love, he dropped a teacup..."

She wasn't listening to him. He saw that her call to him had nothing to do with the crash.

She was staring at the wall upon which she had hung a tapestry not three months before.

A pleasing cross-pattern in colors of burgundy, gold, and jade, purchased from a shop in London on a balmy, carefree summer day, a furnishing for their bedchamber.

Blackwood looked at the hanging. He saw nothing remarkable.

"No—behind it, Hugo," she said, her face and mouth twisted as though she was about to scream.

Blackwood went to her, touching her face, imploring her to look at him. But her eyes would not leave the tapestry.

"Shall I...shall I take it down?"

She stared, unanswering. Mesmerized.

"Down it comes," he said at once, determined now. He crossed to the wall and gripped the woolen textile. But before he removed it from its mounting rod, the weaving collapsed as though of its own weight, falling heavily to the floor in a heap.

Blackwood jumped back. The wall behind was unmarked, and unremarkable.

"There, you see—?"

He turned around but Orleanna was lying back upon her pillow again, eyes closed.

"Darling," he said, feeling her cheeks, patting her hand. She breathed deeply, suddenly and completely asleep. Blackwood stepped back from the bed, a spike of terror in his chest.

He returned to the kitchen to find Talbot pacing nervously. "What is it?" Talbot asked.

Blackwood gripped the man's shoulders. "We must go to Dee."

The white-gowned occult philosopher swept through his grand hall with, for him, a quick and eager step.

"On the contrary, a great and profound success!" John Dee said, refuting their concerns. "We have finally pierced the veil of the mystical."

He led them toward his esteemed library, but Talbot leapt ahead, blocking the door. "Not here," he said. "Anywhere but in here."

"Edward," said John Dee, with the disappointed look of a parent at a weak child. "Come now, spheromancer. Don't tell me you lack the courage of your convictions."

Talbot shook his head, eyes averted. "I saw

things," he said. "I felt things. You must smash that orbuculum."

To Blackwood, Dee said, "To arrive at the precipice only to lose one's nerve. Come."

He led them instead to his observatory, its glass ceiling inviting the night into the room.

Blackwood was impatient; he needed to return to Orleanna. He hated leaving her alone and untended.

Blackwood said, "Perhaps you have succeeded in some way, Master Dee, and should be commended for it. But what if...I say, if...you have touched a realm across a divide that you were not meant to breach?"

Dee shook his head, his silken white beard swaying. "No such thing." He stepped away before turning back to look at Blackwood and Talbot. "You are like agents of doubt sent forth from this earthly plane to cloud my mind, to beg me off this great revelation. Guardians of the old world, my own co-conspirators, turned against me. The final obstacle I must obliterate before the transcendence. This is to be my moment of doubt, is it?"

"Mage," said Talbot, "have you not witnessed strange portents here, auguring darkness?"

"Wonderful marvels," said Dee. "I have seen spiritual splendors. We have done it, Talbot! We have synthesized the magical and the scientific. We have invoked and conjured an Enochian angel to guide and instruct us. This will return me to my rightful place in the queen's court. First, we will witness it. Second, reveal it to the world. And third, understand it."

The brilliant sorcerer's wide-eyed boasting deeply troubled Blackwood. "Understanding it is third, is it?" he said.

"Marshaling it is fourth." Dee looked upon his barrister contemptuously. "Do not concern yourself with matters of the spiritual world, barrister. Your world of laws and writs is but a soft candle to the thunderbolt about to strike. I have opened a seam into the mystical world."

"Or," said Blackwood, for a moment glimpsing a megalomaniac inside the philosopher's robes. "Or have you opened a seam into this world from the mystical? How do you know if you have penetrated another realm... or merely allowed another realm to penetrate ours?"

Dee looked at Blackwood a long moment. Blackwood saw that his words injected a bit of doubt into Dee's bravado... before Dee quickly expelled it. "The riddles of lawyers," he said. "I am surprised the invocation succeeded in the presence of one so... unworthy."

"Wormwood," said Talbot, apparently hosting a separate conversation. "It has bittered our souls..."

Dee sat in a brocaded chair with silver arms, like a wizard usurping a king's throne. "It was always to be this way," he said. "Alone shall I navigate into the realm of the mystical. The journey, and the rewards, shall be mine."

Talbot walked toward him. "You can have it, mage."

"Leave, then. Leave me to await the angel as it assumes human form."

Blackwood shook his head at this impertinence, his gaze running along the books of celestial spheres and astral planes, next to tomes of astronomy and cosmology. Had the old wizard conflated the two, the mystical and the scientific, but instead of arriving at a unifying theory, lost his way?

Blackwood looked skyward for a moment, not knowing which way to turn. As he did, he spotted a glowing white form peering down at them from a gabled roof—or perhaps hovering behind it. A human figure in a white bed dress, levitating, black-eyed.

With one last leering look, the apparition slid, soundless, behind the peaked roof, and vanished.

With a shout and audible gasp, Hugo Blackwood fled the observatory, racing through Dee's wide hallways to the door, out into the chilly, damp night. Almost falling on a patch of muddy turf, Blackwood turned the corner, eyes skyward, searching the roof and all its peaks, seeking out—and simultaneously terrified of finding—the leering apparition.

Forgetting Talbot, even forgetting Dee, Hugo Blackwood took to his horse and raced back to his home.

He burst inside the front door, moving to the bedroom. Orleanna lay in bed as before, only now—and strangely—the tapestry was pulled over the bedclothes.

"My love," said Blackwood, tears bursting from his eyes upon seeing her, having convinced himself on the harsh ride back that it had been Orleanna he had seen floating over John Dee's residence, the ghost of her dead body seeking him out for one last farewell.

He gripped her head to his chest, feeling it damp with fever. He wept a bit, then suddenly stopped, fearing for his sanity. What did it mean that he had hallucinated her image? Had their scrying unwittingly unleashed a plague of mind fever?

Blackwood lowered his face into hers, leaving a light kiss upon her lips. In that moment, he wished to fall ill like her. He wished them to be united always.

He startled as he straightened, finding his wife's doe eyes open but distant, unseeing. Vacant.

Mr. Lusk let them off near the intersection of 72nd Street and Central Park West. Odessa followed Blackwood, entering an unmarked side door. A narrow service corridor led to another door, through which she found herself standing at a bank of old, ornate elevators.

"Wait a minute," she said. "Are we in the Dakota?"

The Dakota was famously the oldest luxury apartment building in Manhattan, and among the most exclusive. Elevator doors opened and they boarded alone.

When the doors closed, Odessa said, "This is where John Lennon lived when he was shot."

Blackwood watched the arrow count off floors on the dial. "Oh, yes—the singer. I remember him..."

"The singer?" Was he playing dumb?

"I believe his wife sought me out once. An interesting sort. She wanted to know if this building was haunted."

"Was it?"

"It still is."

The doors opened, and Blackwood walked to an unlocked door almost twice Odessa's height. The entrance foyer was floored with smooth, dark marble, the walls papered a velvet claret with an inlaid William Morris pattern. Blackwood strode straight through into the next room, a wide parlor with street-facing windows looking out on Central Park. The ceilings were towering, easily fourteen feet high, the ash moldings meticulously ornate. A cyclopean stone fireplace stood opposite the windows; an elaborate carved panel flowed from the mantelpiece and into the walls. The figures—they looked like antiquities—were naked, writhing bodies, both male and female intermingled with what seemed to be clouds of flames.

The patterned floor was mahogany. There was barely any furniture, nothing comfortable to sit upon, a parlor without chairs. Other than a long, heavy table, its surface entirely covered—indeed buried—by unrolled, unfolded maps of ancient cities, countries, and ocean routes, the room was made of books.

Not only were the walls lined with bookshelves and filing cabinets, but the entire floor was a maze of piles of books, arranged in different forms and sizes: some of them as high as six feet or so, some of them arranged in an almost pyramidal base.

"This is your home," said Odessa, a question hidden in the form of a statement.

"This is my Manhattan home," said Blackwood.

He stepped through a door into a long hallway. She counted four more doors ahead, on either side. She had been inside many New York apartments; none were arranged off a common hallway, none were this spacious.

"How long have you lived here?" she asked.

"The building was constructed in the 1880s."

She believed him, eyeing the detail of the European trim along the chair rail running the length of the hallway. "Right, so how long have you lived here?"

He fished a key out of his jacket pocket, inserting it into a door lock. "This was the only building this far north and west on the island then. The city has grown up around it. The park, too. The city of London has always seemed fully formed, but from here I have watched a metropolis get up on its feet rather like a new fawn. The building was constructed with electric lights already installed, powered by its own dynamo. I rather like electricity. The building went...I believe the term is *co-op*...some years ago. Do you know what that means?"

"Sure," she said.

"I do not."

This mystery evidently did not trouble him, as the key turned in the lock and he swung open the door. Another wide room, a library. The shelves bulged with aged book spines and unbound manuscripts of old, flaking paper, as well as folios and parchment scrolls. These were rare books indeed, most with Latin or French titles, like *Ethici philosophi cosmographia*...*Mysteriorum liber primus*...*A Booke of Supplications and Invocations*...*De Heptarchia Mystica Collectaneorum*...

The room smelled milky, of vanilla and almond, from the breakdown of chemical compounds in the old paper. "There is no way you've read all these," she said, tired of asking him questions, always feeling off-balance.

He did not rise to her challenge. "My library travels with me," he said.

"Travels? Where?"

"I have other residences."

"Okay...how do you travel anywhere without a passport?"

"Mmm, yes, that, " he said, conceding the point. "It is more trying every year."

He opened yet another door, this one opening into what would in any normally grand residence have been perhaps a formal dining room. But here, arranged upon a long mahogany serving table and on shelves and inside locked glass cabinets on the walls, were...?

"What are these?"

"Instruments," he said.

The religious articles jumped out at her first. Silver and bronze, some jeweled, crosses and what seemed like astrolabes and compasses. Goblets and candleholders. Powders in corked glass vials and accessories such as gloves and scarves that looked like vestments.

"These look like weapons," she said.

Daggers and chisels and drills. Metal picks and short swords. There were wooden cases filled with tools for either medieval surgery or torture.

Another broad shelf held amulets fashioned from metal and from cloth. Stone figurines and carved totems. A handful of skulls. "Or trophies?" she said.

"They are work tools," said Blackwood. "Please touch nothing."

He had rolled out a black leather kit and began selecting items from his collection, inserting them into the worn pouches. He selected a dagger, a weird cross, a tube containing a pinkish potion that could only be called an elixir.

"You amassed all this over time," Odessa guessed. "Acquired or stolen?"

Blackwood said, "I have built this collection for no other reason than necessity."

Odessa wasn't nervous anymore. She was beyond intimidation. "How old are you?" she asked.

He hesitated in packing his kit, a sign of impatience. "How old do I look?"

Odessa shrugged, walking along the table behind him. "Thirty-five."

"Then I am thirty-five," he said.

She passed a collection of writing instruments in an old glass jar. "How long have you been thirty-five years old?"

"Ah," he said. "Now you are asking the right questions. But I hesitate to give you the answer."

"Why is that?" she said.

"Most of the time—when I answer, the most irritating sound comes out," he said. "A *guffaw*, I believe you call it, and I don't much care to hear it again…"

"Try me," she said.

After a long pause, Blackwood said, "Four hundred and fifty years."

Odessa, of course, guffawed. Blackwood sighed.

"Coming up on half a millennium," she said. "Quite an accomplishment."

"Not really."

"How is that possible?"

"Too open-ended," he said, working with his

261

back to her, unlacing a soft calfskin pouch, sniffing at the powder within.

"How did it happen?" she said. "How does a man—a human—live so long?"

"I think it should be obvious," he said. "I was cursed."

"Cursed," she said. "By whom?"

"Not by a whom."

"By a what, then?"

"It was the result of a transgression. A transgression against nature. It was just a folly, or so I thought. A séance…an invocation. But a line was breached. The sacred was met by the profane. And I was doomed to this existence."

A lot to take in. Odessa said, "You were a barrister…?"

"Outside London. I was respected but unremarkable."

"Did you have a family?"

"I was married."

"How did a married barrister get involved in—"

"I had a retainer, a friend…an amazing man, actually. Someone I looked up to. Someone with many connections in the royal court, someone I thought could help me improve my professional standing. But also someone charismatic and fairly brilliant. I guess you could say I fell under his sway. I was little more than a bystander, I didn't understand the depths he was exploring, nor the heights. I was fascinated, curious—but a dilettante. A layman. An amateur who had no place at his side. You must understand, though, this was 1580s London. I was a city barrister. And this man—his name was John Dee—opened my eyes to a speculative world of magic and mystery. Though the truth is, I blundered into his ministrations. The fact is, I'll never know why he allowed my presence in the first place."

Odessa continued slowly around the table of ancient instruments. "And...? What happened?"

"The world went out of balance. We—he—invited entrance into our plane of existence."

"From...?"

"An astral plane. He was convinced he could contact an angel. But that is not what happened."

"What did happen?"

Blackwood sighed, though with his back to her, Odessa could not tell if it was from impatience over this line of questioning...or regret for what had occurred.

He turned and stacked a few books on top of each other.

"Imagine, if you will, layers of reality—many astral planes existing on top of and beneath each other. These planes mostly stay separate, save for the occasional aberration or the dream world..."

"Dreams are an astral plane?" she asked.

"Entirely so," answered Blackwood. "And we can live or die in them if properly trained..."

He pulled out a book from the center of the newly formed pile.

"Now," he said, "through a complex process, these planes can be visited, or one can summon entities to visit our own. We did just that...The world, as I said, went out of balance...and I was thrown into, well, righting it. Not my choice, mind you."

"Righting it?"

"A gateway was opened into our world. A seam exposed. A thruway that I do not know how to close."

"And do you...?"

"I have to push back at what comes through. Every time. I have to right my original wrong."

"So you are a...a guardian of sorts?"

"A penitent. A zookeeper. A negotiator. And, on occasion, an exterminator. DON'T TOUCH THAT!"

The sudden force of his voice, always so calm and soothing, achieving volume and depth she had not imagined possible, sent terror up her spine. She had been looking at a sphere of fine crystal, perfect but for an interior crack like gossamer thread, almost like the neural network inside a single diaphanous brain cell. Her hands were by her sides.

"I wasn't going to!" she snapped back at him. "And you can stop treating me like a child."

Blackwood started to disassemble the small book pile, no apology forthcoming. The sphere sat upon a small stand resembling an upside-down crown. Now she was curious.

"What is it?"

"An orbuculum."

"What I mean is... what is it to *you*?"

Blackwood's eyes were low-lidded, lacking his usual air of curiosity. He was in a foul mood suddenly.

He said, "You mentioned that you succeeded in tracing ownership of the botanica."

Odessa nodded. Unexpectedly, his angry reaction rendered him more human in her eyes. Instead of feeling like she had offended him, she felt that she had broken through his persona, which had perhaps settled in him over four and a half centuries of living.

Odessa said, "What happened to your wife?"

Blackwood's expression did not change, at all, which conveyed meaning in and of itself. She wondered what she looked like to his 450-year-old eyes.

"Hmm," he murmured finally, as though arriving at a judgment. "You are perceptive. It is frankly tiring. To be honest, I prefer dealing with persons of lesser intelligence."

That wasn't a compliment. She didn't know what it was.

"So sorry," she said, in a way that let him know that she was not—not at all.

"The owner of the botanica?" Blackwood said, prodding her. He rolled up the leather kit full of implements and vials.

Odessa nodded. "I traced the tax records back through two shell corporations, to an address in Englewood." She nodded at the kit sticking out of his jacket pocket. "What are you going to do if we find her?"

Blackwood slid the compact collection of spirit-hunting tools deeper into his jacket pocket. Then he turned to the door they'd entered through.

"We will find her," he said as he exited. "Hopefully before she finds us."

The house was unviewable from the street, due to an eight-foot solid gate and tree-lined fence. A keypad with an attached camera stood at the side of the short driveway.

Odessa said, "Are you going over, or am I?"

Blackwood looked at her, saying nothing.

"Thought so," she said. She found the sturdiest-looking pine and climbed it, offsetting her weight by pushing her feet against the wall. She got to the top, which was a few inches wide, not sharp, and surveyed the property. It was a low-slung contemporary, unusual for the neighborhood, with a widely angled roof and a paired front door. No car in the driveway. No sign of movement inside the front windows.

She lowered herself down, landing softly upright on the grass. The gate latch pulled mechanically from the inside, and she swung it back just wide enough to admit Hugo Blackwood. He eyed the quiet house.

"You do know that I don't have a gun," she told him.

He nodded.

"And you don't have a gun," she continued. "You don't even have a phone to call nine-one-one. I'm not sure your little kit there is going to be enough if something bad goes down. Just so you know, I will be calling the local police if we get into an issue."

If Blackwood was listening, he did not answer, starting up the curling driveway to the double doors. Odessa moved to the doorbell but Blackwood stopped her. She noticed he had a small chapbook in his hand.

"What?" she said.

Using the tiny print as a guide, he recited a few lines in Latin, quietly. An incantation. He tucked the book back inside his jacket.

"That was...?"

"A spell of protection. Before we cross this threshold."

Normally she would have laughed. But everything she had seen and heard had disabused her of the luxury of skepticism, at least for the moment.

"I'm going to ring the doorbell," she said, an act of incantation itself.

The bell rang inside, a series of musical notes, faintly echoing. Odessa did not expect it to be answered.

She saw movement inside, obscured by the opaque door glass. The anticipation of a confrontation spiked the adrenaline in her system, hitting her like a shiver. The door opened.

It was a man in his mid-thirties. Hispanic, maybe Cuban. Barefoot in bulky sweatpants and a half-zipped linen hoodie.

He blinked, looking from face to face. "Who are you?" he said.

Odessa saw no one behind him. His hands were empty. "Is Juanita here?"

The man squinted as though confused. The sun had a disorienting effect on him. "What do you want?"

"We are looking for Juanita. Would you get her for us please?"

He said, "She didn't send you?"

Odessa opened her credentials, showing him her FBI badge. "Juanita," she said.

The man read the large blue letters but was unfazed. "She gone. Not here."

He started to close the door. Odessa got her foot against it before he could shut them out. Something about his face.

"I know you," she said.

He shook his head.

Odessa found the printout of the arrest report in her handbag. She unfolded it and showed it to him. "You're the other grave robber." Checking the article. "Yoan Martine."

Martine did not deny it. Nor did he try to run. He looked at Odessa and said, "I don't get it."

"We're coming in," she said.

Martine did not resist. She pushed the door open and entered ahead of Blackwood. Martine stepped backward as though their entering was no big deal.

The house was dirty. Furniture and rugs had been shoved to the sides. Trash piled up. Odessa could see through back windows to a pool full of black-green water. Some pool furniture floated in it.

Two large animal cages were set against the wall to the left, empty but for heavy-duty rope toys. Odessa said, "Where are the dogs?"

"Run off. I let them free."

"You let them free?"

"I didn't like the way they look at me."

"Were they pit bulls?" she asked.

Martine nodded.

Over the smell of trash and food gone bad hung a fragrant odor. Not incense. Nothing supernatural. It was weed.

Martine's eyes were bloodshot. He was high, all right. And not just from marijuana.

"She gone, man," he said, feeling his way down into a sitting position on the arm of a sofa whose cushions were covered with smaller furniture: a side table, matching lamps. He scratched his forearm. "Juanita, she's gaga—crazy. Talking all kinds of shit."

Blackwood stood in the center of the room. Odessa questioned Martine. "When was the last time you saw her?"

"We done bad things, but...we had protection. *Bakalu.* The ancient spirits..."

Odessa looked at Blackwood. "Spirits of ancestors," he said, translating.

"She promise money, she promise power, she promise sex. It was all there. And then it wasn't there."

Blackwood said, "Juanita. She was *kindiambazo?*"

Martine's face soured as though the word itself caused him pain. "*Mayombero,*" he said.

Blackwood translated: "Sorceress, practitioner of Palo Mayombe." To Martine, he said, "Tell me about the working."

Martine shook his head. "Don't want to, man. She was the *palero*. She tell us, Get this, get that. Like a shopping list."

"Such as?"

Again, Martine reacted as though hearing the question caused him actual pain.

Blackwood prompted him. "Human bones."

"*Fula.*"

"That is gunpowder," he said to Odessa.

"*Azogue.*"

"Quicksilver," said Blackwood. "Mercury."

"Blood. Animal hair. Sticks, herbs, feathers. Stones. Sulfur. She did the work. She set the *nganga.*"

"The sacred iron cauldron," Blackwood explained. "How many did she prepare?"

"She had one she would do for the rites. She do the Palo here, outside." He pointed at the backyard with the fetid swimming pool. "For protection."

Blackwood said, "And then?"

"Then she say she was told to make more. Smaller ones. Three others."

Odessa said, "Did you go to Montclair? To Little Brook, Long Island?"

Martine scratched his forearm again, now digging at it. Almost trying to distract himself from painful memories with actual physical pain. "She was the mediator. She was the guider of souls, *nkisi*, spirits. Until...she became like an instrument herself. Now it talked through her. *Kinyumba.*"

Odessa looked to Blackwood. "Bad spirit," he said. "A fiend. A specter."

"She change," Martine went on. "Everything change. She wanted strength. She wanted power from the ancestors. But something else come through." Martine looked around as though hearing voices. "It's like, you leave a door open...and a raccoon walk in. Wild spirits."

Odessa saw now that Martine wasn't just high, he was half mad.

"She's not Juanita no more. Juanita never coming back. And now I see things. Strange emissions. I hear them. *Nfuri.* The wraiths."

Martine jumped up from the arm of the sofa. He had filed his fingernails to sharp points, and his forearm scratching had drawn blood. He walked toward Blackwood, stopping a few feet away.

"*Mpangui,*" he said. He looked at Blackwood, and also all around him, as though Blackwood were radiating energy. "Cleanse me. You can eat this curse. *Limpieza. Limpieza.*"

Blackwood shook his head. "No, Martine."

"I see you," Martine said, emotion rising. "Free me, *mpangui*. Rid me of this curse."

Blackwood shook his head sadly. He said, "Martine, I am afraid there is nothing I or anyone else can do for you."

Back outside in the driveway, Odessa could hear Yoan Martine inside, still talking, his voice occasionally rising to a yell. "What did he want?"

"*Limpieza.* A cleansing to remove malefic influences."

"Could you do such a thing?" she asked.

"Such a thing is possible," he said. "But not for Martine. Including mercury in the spellcasting is a wish for madness in one's enemy. I can't help but think it backfired on them. She was using Palo as an aggressive magic."

Odessa said, "It fried his brain."

"I could no more cleanse an insane person of their psychological mania. He is mad. He is lost."

Odessa kept one eye on the double doors, expecting him to come out after them. "As are we," she said. "Lost. Shouldn't we have checked the house?"

"No one else is there," said Blackwood, with a finality she did not question.

Something smashed inside the house. Odessa wanted to get going. She started toward the high gate.

"Sounds like she crossed a line in one of those rituals," said Odessa. "Like your John Dee."

Blackwood said, "Everything is linked. There are no little things, no random coincidences."

"But why Peters in Montclair? And Colina on Long Island?"

Blackwood said, "The design of the world is complex, and the Hollow Ones are its thirteenth floor."

"So no leads. Without Juanita, we are at a dead end."

"No such thing," said Blackwood. "The world will give us a sign. We only have to be ready to see it."

Odessa shut the gate behind them. The Rolls-Royce Phantom rolled to the curb, Mr. Lusk at the wheel. They climbed into the back. Odessa felt better when the door was closed and she was farther away from Martine's corrosive psychic energy.

"While we wait for the world to give us a sign," said Odessa, "I need to eat something."

"As you wish," said Blackwood, distracted.

"Where to?" asked Mr. Lusk.

"We'll find something on the way to Flushing, Queens."

Mr. Lusk looked at Blackwood, waiting for the order.

Blackwood said, "On the other side of Manhattan? Why? What for?"

"For Earl Solomon," she said. To Mr. Lusk, she said, "New York-Presbyterian Queens Hospital."

"No, no," said Blackwood.

"Why not?" said Odessa. "We have time. Solomon asked to see you."

"We have no time for needless errands," said Blackwood. "I understand that food is a necessity, but—"

"Needless errands?" said Odessa. "Earl Solomon is a dying man. He asked to see you. Don't you want to say goodbye?"

"Goodbye?" said Blackwood. "What is goodbye?"

"You've known him forty-five years."

"And?" said Blackwood.

Odessa felt a rage welling up inside her. "He's dying. Okay, so you say you've lived for centuries. What are you, like a vampire who's forgotten what it's like to be mortal?"

Blackwood sat back in his seat, looking at her, interlacing his fingers on his lap. "What do you imagine my and Agent Solomon's relationship is?"

"Forty-five years!" she said again.

"You're very angry," he said.

"Of course I am! You're very cold!"

Blackwood cocked his head a few degrees, seeing her from a slightly different angle. "This isn't about me at all, Agent Hardwicke. You want this. You want to see us together. This is about your own curiosity."

She fumbled her words a bit, because there was

some uncomfortable truth in his. "This is about saying goodbye."

Blackwood smiled. He said, "Take her where she wants to go, Mr. Lusk." And then he tipped his head back and closed his eyes.

1962. The Mississippi Delta.

The sun was low over the cotton fields when Solomon rolled up outside the field path leading to the sharecropper's house occupied by the Jamuses. Blackwood walked alongside him toward the low structure, a pair of crows lifting off from the laundry line off the rear corner of the house with a panicky *CAW-CAW*. The heat of the day hadn't abated yet, Solomon billowing his damp shirt under his jacket.

"How old?" asked Blackwood.

"Six," said Solomon.

Solomon's shoe squeaked upon the board before the front entrance. He knocked on the door, Blackwood standing behind and to his left.

A young girl answered, wearing the same blue cotton dress he had seen her in before. "Hello again, miss," he said. "Agent Solomon, do you remember me?"

"I thought you were Pastor Theodore," she said.

"May I come in again?"

She looked behind her, uncertainly. There was no one there.

"Do you want to get your mother?" he asked.

The little girl shook her head. She stepped back from the door. Solomon entered, standing on the dirt floor.

"Maybe an older brother?" he said. Solomon wanted to be acknowledged by someone of age before moving farther into the house to see the sick boy, Vernon.

She went away down the hall, along where the wooden flooring started.

Solomon waited, smelling buttermilk. A radio or a turntable somewhere in the house played marching music. Flies flew at a nearby window, *buzztap-buzztap-buzztap*, again and again.

Solomon checked Blackwood. He was looking up at the unfinished ceiling. Solomon looked up himself but didn't see anything remarkable. The British man must have been simply clearing his thoughts.

Coleman, the twenty-year-old, came out of the back, slowly but not shyly. Deliberateness was part of his manner.

"Cole, it's Agent Solomon."

"Yessir."

"Here to see Vernon. I brought along a specialist."

Cole looked at Hugo Blackwood. He did not ask what kind of specialist Blackwood was. Nor did he appear to be very optimistic.

"He's been quiet," said Cole.

"Everything all right, Cole?" asked Solomon.

"No, sir," said Cole, turning without further explanation, walking ahead of them to the rear pantry. He stepped inside there rather than the closed door next to it, pulling on a chain to illuminate a bare bulb, and removing a key from a high shelf. He handed it to Solomon rather than unlocking the door himself.

"Thank you," said Solomon, but the young man was already walking away.

Solomon listened at the door, expecting to hear the boy call Blackwood's name again. There was no sound. Solomon inserted the key, turning it, pulling the door open.

Inside was the same bed with the same thin, bare mattress stained with blood.

But no young boy. The chains lay on the floor, manacles open.

Solomon, alarm rising, hurried back down the hallway of loose floorboards, calling Cole's name. The young man stood near the front entrance.

"Who took him?" asked Solomon.

Cole shook his head, confused. "Took him?"

"Vernon. He's gone."

Cole started past Solomon, needing to see for himself. Solomon saw the young girl sitting in a metal folding chair inside an adjoining room, watching him, scared.

Blackwood gripped Solomon's elbow suddenly, pushing him toward the front door. Solomon allowed himself to be maneuvered outside.

"What?" said Solomon.

Blackwood said, "I think I know where he is."

Solomon's senses were on high alert as he followed Blackwood back into the dreaded woods. There was just enough light through the overhead canopy to allow them safely through the trees and the grabbing branches without use of the flashlight gripped in his left hand.

Blackwood strode ahead with an uncanny sense of direction, having only visited here once. They arrived at the hanging tree, but Blackwood's pace never slowed. He continued toward the first marked trunk he had seen, moving symbol-to-symbol toward the forgotten slave burial ground. Through the trees ahead, harsh orange light through fitful shadows. A campfire, thought Solomon, the young agent rationalizing everything he encountered with some real-world explanation.

As they came upon the clearing, Solomon's mind was unable to take in everything at once. The images appeared to him in sequence, like a series of smaller explosions culminating in a total demolition.

A ring of fire burned in the scrub grass, five feet in diameter, black smoke rising into the night.

Inside the fire ring knelt the boy, Vernon, all of six years old, before the row of grave markers, wearing only a pair of dirty cotton pants. He held his arms high, hands open, as though summoning something from the sky.

But what appeared came from below, a fine haze rising from the grassy floor like an evaporating mist, suffused with light. Out of the headstones arose a different vapor, thicker, violet-hued, forming roughly human shapes. With the imagination of a man seized by terror, Solomon made out the upper torsos, heads, and outstretched arms of rising, gaseous specters.

Beyond the graves, standing at the far edge of the tree line, stood a figure in a hooded white robe, sleeves drooping from its outstretched hands in the shape of open, moaning mouths. Shadows thrown by the flame gave the illusion of more figures moving behind it, a league of black-robed officiants performing ministrations over the burial site...but there was only one.

Solomon froze at the sight of this ungodly rite. His mind had no accounting for it. The distress rang like alarm bells in his head.

The robed figure was immediately aware of their intrusion. Its unseen head turned toward Blackwood, and suddenly it withdrew into the trees, obscured by the frenetic shadows.

Blackwood ran after it. Solomon could hear nothing, not even his own voice as he called after Blackwood, not knowing what to do. Blackwood rushed past the circle of flame, the low mist swirling at his legs as though grabbing after him. He hurried between two violet apparitions, their hazy forms rippling in his wake as they seemed to turn and reach out to him.

Blackwood entered the tree line where the robed figure had disappeared, and vanished himself.

Before Solomon's eyes, everything in the slave graveyard started to collapse. The flames dipped as though controlled by a dial. The ground mist faded like smoke. And the gaseous grave figures— the half-risen spirits of long-dead Negro slaves— died a second death, limbs and torsos dissipating, their pained faces the last to go.

The boy, Vernon, turned slowly, head first, his small, skinny body following. He was emaciated, his small ribs plain against his midsection, arms and legs thin. His eyes were silver moons with a small black dot in the center, eyes more animal than human. His lips were curled back to reveal his teeth, though not in the form of a smile.

At once, a gust of wind came up and grabbed the black smoke off the dying flames, whipping it toward Solomon. He covered his eyes as the oily emission washed over him, choking the oxygen where he stood. It lasted no more than a second, and was gone. But when Solomon opened his eyes, Vernon was standing before him, having crossed a distance of ten yards with the speed of one step.

The boy leapt at him, ferally, one hand on Solomon's throat, the other scratching at his eyes. Solomon tried to grasp the boy's frail body, but whether from sweat or moisture or some more diabolical balm he was slippery to the touch. With a cry, Solomon fell backward to the ground.

The boy was more wild than strong, his hand scraping Solomon's eyes so that he could barely see. Solomon tried to forearm him off, but Vernon's little clawlike hands would not release. The boy found Solomon's windpipe and gave it a wrenching squeeze. The boy's face was close to Solomon's head, his breathing coming out in a rapid, seething hiss.

Solomon still held the flashlight and he struck the boy twice in the side to no effect. He felt the boy's small fingers dig into the flesh around his orbital bones. Solomon couldn't get any breath. The only true advantage he had was the boy's slight weight. Solomon wedged his arm between the boy's chest and his own, and with a great heave threw the boy clear of him, gripping his choked throat to make sure Vernon hadn't taken a chunk of skin with him.

Solomon got to his feet. The boy was up and running at him, and Solomon swung the flashlight, catching the crazed child on the side of the jaw. It sent him spinning down into the dirt, but he popped right back up, baring his teeth again . . . only now a few of them were gone.

Solomon put out his free hand, warning Vernon, "Stay back!" He reached for his gun, but just as he got it clear of his holster, the boy flung himself at him again, rabidly, Solomon's gun discharging once into the ground as it was knocked from his hand.

Vernon clung to him tight, having gotten under Solomon's arms. He felt a wet sensation at his throat and realized the boy was trying to bite him with his jagged, broken teeth. Solomon let out a scream, feeling the feverish heat of the boy and re-alizing he was fighting not a child but a *thing*—a possessed *thing*.

With two hands he worked the handle of the flashlight beneath the thing's throat and pushed back, keeping his gnashing teeth from the arteries in Solomon's neck. The thing snarled and snapped its jaw but Solomon could not push it off him. He felt something rough at his back and found that he had backpedaled against a tree. This close, the thing's eyes looked almost glowing, their madness boring into him, powered by demonic strength and, at the same time, an element of terror.

At once, the thing's expression changed to surprise. Its head bucked backward and its grip on Solomon's back lessened. Its head lowered and Solomon saw Hugo Blackwood revealed behind it, his hand holding something to the back of the thing's neck.

Solomon threw the fiendish child off him with a yell. He slapped at his throat and face, exploring for bites or mortal wounds, but his hands came away unbloodied.

The thing lay on the ground some feet away, half on its side, twitching. Blackwood looked down at it, too. Solomon now saw the thing Blackwood had been holding, a thin silver handle sticking out of the base of the thing's neck.

The thing's slender hands reached for the implement impaling it, but never touched it. The twitching stopped. The thing lay still.

Solomon, however, could still feel its small-handed grip on his throat. "What was that?" he said. "*What was that?*"

Blackwood looked him over. "You appear unhurt."

"I SAID WHAT WAS THAT?"

Solomon heard his own voice echo into the trees

and was scared he had woken some other evil spirit.

Blackwood had turned back to look at the dead thing. "That was an invocation."

"The robed figure—?"

Blackwood shook his head.

"Got away?" said Solomon, each word like a gasp.

"I heard you scream," said Blackwood. "I had to make a choice."

Solomon was a moment processing that. He looked down at the thing. He remembered the flashlight in his hand and switched it on. The flat glass lens had cracked against the thing's jaw, but the light worked. He shone it on the thing's bare back, the silver-handled implement shining in the beam. "You killed it."

Blackwood crouched next to the body. As Solomon watched in horror, Blackwood placed one hand on the back of the boy's head, and the other on the silver handle. He pulled the blade out of the boy's neck.

It was slick with blood, but there had been no bleeding. No spilled blood. The implement was a dagger with a fine, thin blade, almost the shape of a screwdriver or ice pick.

Solomon turned around and doubled over, vomiting violently. He continued until he was through retching. He felt no better.

He turned around again. Blackwood was cleaning off the blade with a soft cotton cloth. "May I have your electric torch?" he asked.

Solomon handed over the flashlight. Blackwood trained it on the back of the boy's skull at the base, using his free hand to ruffle the hair.

Solomon saw the sigil in the boy's flesh, looking like an old-fashioned letter seal pressed into hot wax, but formed by raised veins beneath the skin. He couldn't make out the exact design, bisected as it had been by the wound from Blackwood's dagger.

Blackwood handed him back the flashlight. Solomon waved it over the clearing, over the graves where the spirits of dead slaves had arisen in a violet mist.

Again, he said, "What was that?"

Blackwood rolled the boy over onto his back, and Solomon remembered that it wasn't a boy anymore. Its face was contorted and evil, now locked in an agonal expression of terror.

"What is it?" said Solomon.

Blackwood answered him only indirectly. "Possessed," he said.

Solomon remembered his gun then. He wanted it in case this thing woke up again. He found it quickly with the flashlight, the muzzle still warm from the gunshot fired in error.

"It's murder," said Solomon. "You killed a boy."

He turned back. Blackwood had produced a leather kit, unrolling it open upon the ground. Solomon saw that its interior pouches contained glass vials with powders and liquids, bits of plant matter, metal crosses. Blackwood returned the dagger to one pouch.

"He was no longer a boy," said Blackwood. "He was well gone. I couldn't save him. But I can release him now. I can grant him rest."

Blackwood uncorked one of the vials of powder. He took care to lay the boy's body out straight, arms by its sides, hands open, palms up. He closed its eyes.

Solomon said, "What the hell are you doing?"

It looked like some funeral rite. Blackwood poured the powder into his hand and arranged five generous pinches of the substance on the ground around the boy's corpse, like points of a star. He pulled a vial of milky liquid from his kit and then stood at the boy's feet. He spoke Latin, quietly but forcefully, an incantation. Solomon grew nervous and backed away. Using an eyedropper, Blackwood squeezed drips of the milky substance onto the powder, igniting five flames of pure white.

Blackwood extended his arm over the boy's body, palm open and downturned, still chanting, the volume of his voice rising and falling. Blackwood's hand trembled and his intonation became more insistent.

Solomon backed away farther, nearly tripping over the root of a tree.

Shadows moved over the boy's face, his chest, his legs. Squirming, writhing. It looked like they were tugging at his flesh, a play of shadow...but how?

Something unexplainable was happening to the boy, outside and in.

Blackwood's voice reached a crescendo, and at once he squeezed his open hand into a fist. The shadows raced away from the surface of the body to the five white flames, which surged and suddenly grew black—then were extinguished, leaving only a foul stench behind.

Blackwood dropped to one knee, momentarily sapped of strength, catching his breath. Solomon ventured forward a few steps, shining his flashlight on the boy's face.

It was the visage of a young black-skinned boy again. Normal. Human. Innocent.

Solomon barely slept that night. He took two cleansing showers in the black-run motel on the edge of town, stopping the water multiple times to make sure the noises he heard—of someone moving around inside his motel room—were only in his head.

Toweling steam off the sink mirror revealed scratches over his throat, bruising around his eyes. Without these abrasions, he could have dismissed the whole thing as a terrible dream. When he closed his eyes and tried to sleep, he saw Vernon Jamus's bright-silver irises, his jagged white teeth—but in Hugo Blackwood's face. Solomon kept his handgun—the empty cylinder filled with a fresh round—on his nightstand, well within reach.

He was relieved when the sun hit his window, and he dressed and holstered up and left the motel early. He was fiddling with the keys to the borrowed FBI sedan, and didn't see the British man in the dark suit standing by the car until he was almost at the driver's door.

"Good morning, Agent Solomon."

Solomon dropped the keys and reached for his gun. He drew it, staggering backward a few steps, putting space between him and Hugo Blackwood. "Get...get away from the car."

Blackwood did not move. "Come now, Agent."

"Hands where I can see them."

"You had a difficult night, I see."

"Stop talking—stop—and listen. You are under arrest."

Blackwood's mouth formed a tight smile, indicating a limited reservoir of patience. "Arrest?"

"For murder. The murder of Vernon Jamus."

"You saw it yourself last night, the boy was already gone—"

"Stop talking." The handcuffs were in the glove box inside the car. Dammit. "Get in the passenger seat."

Blackwood said, "Do you want me away from the car or inside the car?"

"Just get inside the car and don't make me shoot you, sir. Because I will. I have seen enough."

"You've seen hardly anything. What are you going to tell them? 'The whole truth and nothing but'?"

Solomon glowered at him. "I'm not only taking you in. I'm turning myself in, too."

"For what?"

"That's not up to me to decide. I was a witness, maybe an accessory after the fact."

"The boy was attacking you. Do you know what he would have done had I not returned?"

"No, and I don't want to know."

"He would have ripped your throat out of your neck. Either by his hands or with his teeth. I've seen it before. It is entirely unpleasant."

"The boy...he was mad, he went insane..."

"Or, and we'll never know, the demonic spirit occupying him might have jumped into you. Taking the form of a law officer is almost as good a disguise as that of a six-year-old boy."

Solomon shook his head. "There's no demonic spirit. You need to shut up."

"I did not kill a boy, as I showed you last night. The boy was no more. We were too late, the demon had swallowed him whole. I released him from its grip after death. It was the best I could do."

Solomon's gun shook a little from emotion. "That boy called for you. When I first came to this godforsaken town and visited him in that room where his scared family had chained him to a bed. He asked for you. *By name!*"

Blackwood nodded, looking at the ground. "I know."

"He summoned you!"

"Did he? Do you think he wanted me here? Or did he fear me?"

Solomon's eyes widened. "*Fear* you?"

"The boy is a pawn in all this. An innocent victim."

Solomon shook his head, needing Hugo Blackwood quiet. "Are *you* a goddamn demon?" he said. "With all those tools and potions, and the chanting. *What are you?*"

"I am a man with a difficult job to do."

Solomon nodded harshly, for no good reason. "If you're a man, then you can stand before a judge and plead your case. You put me in this thing, right beside you."

"You saw it last night—"

"*I don't know what I saw,*" insisted Solomon.

Blackwood said, "There are things that exist beyond the rule of law."

"No, there aren't. Not in this county, this state, this country. The taking of a life is murder. Call it self-defense, call it unpremeditated, that all comes out in the wash. I am no different from those behind the lynchings in town, black and white. Except that I am a sworn officer of the law. I took an oath."

"Your job, as I understand it, is to uphold the laws of the land by protecting the innocent and punishing the guilty."

"And I can't cover up a murder. No matter how strange, no matter how . . . distasteful."

"The boy was already lost," said Blackwood. "But there are other lives still at stake here. He was an innocent . . . an instrument through which a spell was being cast. He's a victim, but he is not a victim of us. Don't you want to stop whoever did that to him?"

Solomon resisted Blackwood's argument, having promised himself he would not be swayed by anything this murderer said to him.

But he thought of the boy's mother, his brothers and sisters. He thought of facing them, trying to explain what happened. Solomon fought the tears that threatened to squeeze out of his eyes.

Solomon said, pleadingly, "He was only six god-damn years old."

"I know," said Blackwood. "We have to find who-ever set him loose. He didn't shake off those chains around his wrists and ankles."

Solomon exhaled deeply, remembering the im-age of the chain lying on the storage room floor, the manacles unlocked. "Then...who did?"

Blackwood said, "Who else had access to the house and that key?"

2019. Englewood, New Jersey.

Yoan Martine went about the house smashing things until he was exhausted. He sat down on a sofa cushion he had disemboweled with a knife.

Even the *mpangui* would not help him. Yoan let him walk away. No one could cleanse him now.

What to do? He had nowhere to go. Nowhere in this world.

He was pulling at his hair when the great noise of a sudden crash outside took the air away from the room. The power was out. Yoan jumped to his feet and ran to the door.

Outside, diagonally across the bend in the street, a late-model white Infiniti had smashed head-on into a parked pickup truck with such force that it had driven the truck onto the sidewalk and cracked a telephone pole, the top two-thirds of which now lay over the Infiniti. The driver lay flat on the collapsed front seat, bloody, dead. A live wire sizzled on the street like an asp. The Infiniti had to have been traveling upward of fifty miles an hour in order to inflict that much damage, a speed unheard of in this residential area.

Nfuri.

Yoan looked around. The spirits were invisible, but still one looked for them, it was human nature. *What would the taking feel like?* he wondered.

Nothing happened at first. He retreated to the front step of the house and sat down, weeping, to await his fate. He cursed himself for the mistakes he had made—for the desecrations he had sought—for the blasphemies he had performed. Between vomit-like, throat-heaving sobs, he looked openmouthed at the sky.

*O*bediah sensed the spell of protection, recently cast at the entrance to this place. Its magic had dissipated, but a trace of the incantation remained, showing the entity it was at the right place, on the right track.

The grave robber sat on the brick step tearing at his hair. The man awaited his possession, was resigned to it. Almost—welcomed it.

This angered Obediah. The entering was violent, the takeover traumatic. The grave robber submitted with a terrible scream that faded into a groan.

Obediah took the man, stood. Walked back into the house. The destruction inside further incensed the entity, for whom destruction was its essence. It walked to a mirror, centering the grave robber's face between the cracks in the glass. It took the man's hands with their long, filed, pointed fingernails and began scraping at its face.

Grating away the flesh to reveal the tissue beneath.

Obediah searched the madman's memory for information about Blackwood. It found there the agent as well—

the very one he had passed over at the house where it took the agent's partner.

Yes, *it thought.* Blackwood's agents. His accomplices.

All Obediah knew was that it was on the right path now. Beyond that, the vehicle told it very little. Obediah regarded its revealed face, the blood and meat of this human, and twisted it into a smile.

And then it ran. Sprinting through the streets of Englewood.

Past the screams.

Running hard until the expressway came into view.

And then the overpass.

Climbing the curved safety fence. Goring itself on the top spikes.

Getting over the top.

And then falling.

Until impact.

And expulsion.

Ecstasy.

Odessa returned Linus's call from a hospital bathroom. "How's Omaha?" she asked.

"It's good, it's good. Not enough desk space in my hotel room, I'm working the desk, bureau, and bed here, but everything else is fine. Lonely, though. Where are you? I was calling."

"I'm back in Queens at the hospital where the old agent who had a stroke is," she said. "Checking on him again."

"That's good, that's nice. How's he doing?"

"I'll find out, he's not in the room again. Waiting for him to come back."

"You sound better," Linus said. "Energized. More like the old you."

Odessa did feel better, though she knew it was temporary and illusory. "Staying busy," she said. The mystery that was Hugo Blackwood had invigorated her, no question. And frustrated and annoyed her. She couldn't begin to get into it with Linus over the phone.

"You hear back from the lawyer?"

Her mood dipped a bit. "I have a few emails to catch up on."

"Just asking, just asking. It didn't feel right, leaving you."

"You're sweet," she said. She looked at the door, anxious to get back to the room before Solomon did. "I'm glad I caught you."

"Okay," he said. "Don't leave me hanging so long, keep checking in."

"Sure, Mom," she said, and heard him laugh.

"Okay," he said. "Keep smiling."

She hung up, then stood looking at Linus's picture on her phone before his contact screen faded out. After these strange escapades with Blackwood, it felt reassuring, and also discomfortingly strange, to have a straightforward human conversation. She noticed her email notification light flashing and reluctantly opened her inbox before stepping back into the hall. The one email that jumped out at her was from Laurena, her friend at the New Jersey Field Office, but sent to Odessa from her personal Gmail account. Subject line: *WTFF?!*

Odessa returned to Solomon's room. His bed was still gone, and she was relieved she hadn't missed the reunion. The corner television was on mute, a grid of six pundits performing on a news network. Blackwood stood with his back to the room, looking out the grimy window at the city below, turning as she entered.

He said, "That took a long time. I was about to leave."

"You don't do waiting very well, do you? I would think after four hundred and fifty years, you'd achieve some higher level of patience."

"Maybe if I felt this was a prudent use of my time..."

Odessa regarded this strange forever man standing in the gray light of the dirt-speckled window, challenging every expectation she held about reality. At times, he seemed a fearsome alien figure to her. Maybe it was the rush of energy from the Greek salad she had eaten, but at the moment he struck her more as a novelty than anything.

She carried her phone over to him. "Do you spend much time in Eastern Europe?" she asked.

He looked at her strangely. "Why do you ask?"

She showed him a washed-out color photograph on her phone, featuring a group of men standing near a Volkswagen with a German license tag before a rainy bridge crossing. The men wore hats and thin neckties. One sign read ALLIED CHECK POINT and featured images of American, French, and British flags. The other sign read, in three languages, YOU ARE LEAVING THE AMERICAN SECTOR.

She held it up for him to see, though Blackwood

veered back from the smartphone, as one might withdraw from a knife blade or a snarling dog.

"Checkpoint Charlie," she said. "One of the main crossing points between East Berlin and West Berlin during the Cold War. This photograph is from the FBI archives, taken in 1964."

She widened her thumb and forefinger on the touch screen, zooming in the image on the men's faces. Each man was smiling except one. She zoomed in closer, as wide as she could.

Blackwood looked at the face, then looked at her, unfazed.

"That's you," she said. She worked her phone back to the email, opening up another attached photograph. "How about Waco, Texas, 1993?"

She showed him a photo of an observation post set up at a roadblock. A group of FBI agents consulted near a man wearing a large pair of binoculars. To the left stood a familiar man wearing a dark suit.

"The Branch Davidian cult?"

She zoomed in on Blackwood's profile. The man next to him was facing away from the camera, but dark skin was visible beneath a blue ball cap.

"And could that be Agent Solomon?"

Blackwood looked at her, seeing if she was proud of herself. "A friend at the FBI," she explained. "Did you pose for many portraits back in your day?"

She brought up an Elizabethan-era painting of a man wearing a high collar and robe, standing by a high desk. "This painting was recovered from Nazi pillaging more than a decade ago, and is now in cold storage at the National Portrait Gallery in London." She held the phone near his face. "A pretty good likeness."

"Why, thank you," he said flatly.

"Here's one I did not see coming. I would never, ever have pegged you as a Disney fan. Mind truly blown." The photograph showed groups of people gathered festively around a smiling Mickey Mouse face formed out of planted flowers. She zoomed in past some primitive-looking character costumes and a young Ronald Reagan, finding Walt Disney standing behind a microphone stand. One row behind him, not five people away, stood a trim man wearing a dark suit. He wasn't smiling, but appeared to be the only one in the photograph looking at the camera.

"July seventeenth, 1955. Must have been a tough ticket."

"You are having fun, aren't you."

"Not really. Just smiling instead of screaming. These aren't Photoshopped photographs."

"I know."

"And this is just what turned up—probably by mistake. Because who else would label you in photographs, except maybe Solomon?"

"I imagine that is correct."

Odessa's phone screen timed out, going dark. She said, "I gave a teacup, the one you drank out of at my apartment, to the Bureau lab. The cup wasn't washed, never cleaned. I handle evidence all the time. How is it there were no fingerprints on the cup?"

Hugo Blackwood shrugged.

"They disappeared? Faded somehow?"

He showed her his fingertips, which contained the usual whorls and ridges. He rubbed his thumbs against them. "You tell me."

"Your name appears on a variety of property deeds worldwide. That doesn't include undigitized ledgers or many international transactions that occurred pre–Nine Eleven. It suggests vast holdings, and a substantial net worth, but one impossible to approximate. Because of aliases and does-business-as's, and old titles tangled up in renamed villages and provinces, it appears money is always moving behind you."

Blackwood nodded as though pretending to hear this for the first time.

She went back to her phone. "Here's one. Lorraine, 1914." It showed World War I soldiers standing in trenches, looking exhaustedly at the photographer. In the background, drinking from a tin cup, was the Brit in the dark suit.

"I remember that cup of tea," he said. "Wretched brew."

Odessa put away her phone, having had enough of her own games. "I'm willing to bet that a comprehensive archive of photographs and paintings would put you at or near every major world event over the past four and a half centuries. All for so-called occult investigations?"

"You would be surprised."

She looked at him standing there before her. He was just a man. And yet he was not. "You like tea," she said. "So do you eat?"

"When I am hungry," he said.

"Where do you sleep?"

"In a bed."

"How did you get so wealthy?"

"Are you familiar with the phenomenon of compound interest?"

She nodded. That part made sense. "So are you... immortal?"

"I hope not."

"You want to die."

Blackwood looked out the window.

She pressed him. "Can you be hurt? Wounded? Shouldn't a four-hundred-year-old man have scars and cuts over time?"

"I experience pain, certainly. I don't know what you mean by wounds. I am an occult detective, not a gunfighter."

"But—you cannot die."

Blackwood sighed. "How about if you tell me something about you?"

Odessa was taken aback. "Me? Compared with you? Let's see. I'm not very good at Scrabble..."

"Tell me about your father."

"My father?"

"At the botanica, the old woman who gave you the reading. She asked if you wanted to know about your father."

Odessa went cold. "And I didn't, did I."

"You didn't want *her* to tell you anything," said Blackwood. "That doesn't mean you didn't want to know."

"Why do you want to know?"

"I need to know your weaknesses," said Blackwood. "It is good to know where the seams are. Weaknesses can be exploited."

"By these Hollow Ones?"

"By any aggressive, malevolent spirit. That is how they work. That is what they feast upon."

Odessa shook her head, backing into the padded chair below the silent television. "It's not a weakness. I made it a strength."

"Did you?" said Blackwood.

She knew he was baiting her. It didn't matter. Something inside her wanted him to know what happened.

"My father was a lawyer in the small town I grew

up in. He had an office for years next door to the library in an old converted farmhouse. A real family practice, like a doctor. He always had butterscotch candy in a jar on his desk when I'd come by. He had this ancient secretary named Polly, worked there forever. I was the youngest, his last child. We were close.

"He was a real man about town, on a lot of boards, the school board, the zoning board. Part of the job, I guess. Everybody's friend and counselor. He really liked what he did, which was mostly estates, property transactions, and wills. He especially liked visiting with and spending time talking to aging clients, even taking them to lunch, befriending them. I had *To Kill a Mockingbird* images in my head, but he never got anywhere near a criminal case. Still, unlike my brothers and sisters, I was determined to go to law school, to be just like my dad...only not in a small-town setting. I wanted out of there. Take those values with me. And though I would have denied it completely then, I wanted to make him proud.

"I was in my second year of law school when I got a call from my sister saying that Dad had been arrested. I had to come home from Marquette to see him. He denied everything, and I was right by his side. An elderly client with no heirs, a friend of my father's for years, had passed away and left a sizable estate, worth half a million dollars, to an Alzheimer's charity in honor of his wife, whom he had nursed through the disease. The amount that went into the charity was little more than fifty thousand dollars, and the charity, promised ten times that, looked into it. They found that my dad had charged the man his full hourly rate for all the times he'd visited and all the lunches and phone calls. Add to that administrative fees paid out as the executor of the estate, and he collected just under four hundred thousand dollars from the man. An exorbitant fee, and I asked my dad about it, many times, and he always had an answer, he denied stealing a cent from this man that wasn't owed him...but over time it became evident that my father had defrauded this man's estate. He had violated his position as attorney and executor. And this was a good friend of his. My dad convinced himself that he had done nothing improper or illegal.

"The scandal changed everything at home. I left Marquette for half a year and helped defend him when he refused to negotiate a guilty plea. We won him a reduced sentence in the end, and I felt shitty doing it. He was disbarred, had to make full restitution to the Alzheimer's charity—which bankrupted my parents—and was sentenced to thirty months in prison."

She looked at Blackwood, who listened without

judgment, but also without any sympathy. The few people to whom she had told this story tripped over themselves to reassure her that her father's crime wasn't her fault, and that she should feel no shame because of what he did, but Blackwood simply listened.

"My mother always believed his story, and after a while that really drove a wedge between us. You and I, we went after grave robbers, right? What he did wasn't much better—stealing from a dead man. And then I wondered, is that the reason why he befriended all those old clients? How many times had he done this before? How much money meant for charities or gifts had he pocketed himself? And if he had...what had he spent the money on? I didn't want to know any of these answers. As soon as I could, I transferred to law school in Boston, working in a restaurant to pay for it. The first month or so that he was in prison, I would call him, we would talk. But I would be sitting in class and thinking about the trust he'd broken with his clients, with his family. It made me feel sick, speaking to him now. And he knew it. We were close, I was following in his shoes. He had my mother, of course. She would never turn her back on him. But I think losing me, his shadow, the daughter who came in for butterscotch candies and thought he could do no wrong...I think knowing he'd lost my respect might have hurt him most of all.

"They found him dead in his cell one morning ten months into his sentence. He had soaked one of his shirts in toilet water to add strength and hanged himself from the top bedrail while his cellmate slept. Another shock. I would never have guessed that he was even capable of that. But he had demons—the psychological kind, not the kind you seem to deal with—that I never knew about. And when his public veneer, the family lawyer, trustworthy and true...once that was gone, he couldn't bear it. Couldn't bear that people saw the greed, the glutton, the immoral thief, within.

"That's not a weakness, see? That's an education. Spoiled me for the law, that's for sure. I got my degree, but I had already decided I wanted to apply to the FBI. Law and order." She chuckled bitterly. "And now that's over with, too. What's left?"

"Maybe not," said Blackwood.

She rubbed her temples, refusing to be distracted by hope. "No," she said. "Time to pivot again. Time for yet another fresh start."

"Hello," sang a new voice, a nurse appearing at the open door. "Oh, look. You have guests."

She was talking to Earl Solomon, who lay flat on his bed, one arm stretched limply across his chest.

Odessa moved out of the way so the bed could

be wheeled back into place. Solomon's head was turned to one side, and as they set the brakes on the wheels, Odessa ducked into his line of sight. His eyes were open but unfocused.

"How's he doing?" she asked.

One nurse checked his tubes and bandages while the other stepped back near Odessa. "He's doing okay," she said, the tone of her voice indicating that he was not well. "He had a breathing scare overnight, but his lungs are clear. He thought he had some visitors, also, but he was alone." She laid her hand upon his foot beneath the sheet. "Right, Mr. Solomon?"

Solomon looked her way when his name was called, but said nothing, drily licking his lips.

The other nurse finished, and they each pumped sanitizer into their palms at the door. "He knows where the buzzer is if he needs anything."

"Thank you," said Odessa, turning back to Solomon, fearing he had declined further. He looked at her but he said nothing. "Mind if I raise you up?" she asked.

She raised the head of the bed, his face still turned toward her, away from the window and Hugo Blackwood.

"Are you too tired for a visit?" she asked. "There's someone here you wanted to see."

Solomon's eyes rolled around in his sockets, seeing no one. Slowly, he turned his head so that his face was looking at the television...then further around until he saw Blackwood.

Blackwood cocked his head, looking at him. Odessa could only see half of Solomon's expression from her side of the bed. This was the reunion the dying agent had asked her to facilitate.

Blackwood said, "Hello, Solomon."

Solomon's voice was raspy, his jaw stiff. "There you are," he said. "You son of a bitch."

Blackwood glanced past him at Odessa, then back to Solomon. "I was told that you asked to see me."

Solomon pointed at him, his hand connected by tape and tubes to the infusion pump behind his bed. "Damn right," he said. "One last look at the man who put me through hell."

The awkwardness of Solomon's confrontation made Odessa's skin crawl, but Blackwood seemed unperturbed. "We've seen a lot together," he said.

"Together." Odessa started slowly around the foot of Solomon's bed, toward Blackwood—enough so that she could see the sneer on Solomon's face.

"It was important work," said Blackwood.

Odessa moved into Solomon's line of sight. "You asked me to bring him here, remember? I thought you wanted to say goodbye."

Solomon looked at her with eyebrows raised, as though trying to remember who she was. "That's right," he said, looking back at Blackwood. "'Goodbye.' The irony is pretty sweet. I don't want to die. You do."

Odessa looked back and forth between them. This was nothing like what she had expected. Bringing Blackwood here was a mistake.

"I tried to arrest him," said Solomon, speaking to her now, about Blackwood. "A few times. Early on. Bust his ass. When I saw what he was doing." Solomon pointed at Blackwood again, so that Odessa would have no question to whom he was referring. "He's an assassin. It's evil spirits he's after. But he will go through anyone and anything to do it. He has committed murder. I've seen it. To protect others, he says. To save the world. But at the cost of a human life."

Blackwood listened without reaction.

Solomon found the angry strength to raise his head off the pillows, confronting Blackwood. "You're running from something you can't escape. And chasing something you can't catch."

The effort was too much for him, and Solomon sank back deeper into the pillows and mattress than before. He looked at the window beyond Black-wood and Odessa.

"All I wanted was to be a cop," he said. "Since I was a kid. They said, 'Black kid, you ain't never gonna be no cop.' I went to Morehouse College, and I told people, 'I want to be a detective,' and they said, 'Why you want to waste yourself on that?' And then the FBI announced they were taking black agents into the academy. I said, 'I want to be an agent of the FBI.' And I was. One of the first."

He licked his lips, his tongue pasty and parched.

"I had a silver badge, all right, but I still had a brown face. I was still out on the fringes. An outsider. They didn't know what to do with me. And he used that. He took advantage of that, exploited that. Made some sort of arrangement with the Bureau. Made me his 'boy.'"

Odessa stood frozen. Solomon's emotions were raw. She felt that most of this was due to his declining health, the stroke that affected his brain. He was so changed from when she'd first encountered him just a few days before.

Blackwood said, "You asked me to show you what was out there. You had a great curiosity for things that challenged your faith—"

"Maybe," said Solomon, his jaw trembling. "Maybe at first. But all I ever wanted...was to be a cop."

Odessa said, "You were a cop, Solomon."

Solomon looked at her. "And now you. There's a reason why he's with you. No accidents, right, Blackwood? No coincidences. Everything is connected."

In an attempt to settle him down, Odessa said, "You wouldn't have sent me to him if you didn't think he could help me."

That made Solomon blink a few times. "I didn't have a choice. You were assigned to *me*, Odessa Hardwicke. That's no accident. That's no coincidence."

Odessa looked at Blackwood. So did Solomon—but with different eyes. Solomon looked back and forth between Blackwood and Odessa. "Maybe we were partners once. We had a . . . a special job to do. The two of us. I'll give you that. But now, at the end . . . it all looks so different. What was it all for? I go off . . . and he stays. With a new partner to take my place."

Solomon meant her. "No," Odessa said. "You sent me to him for his help. In clearing my name. But I'll never get my gun back. It's only a matter of time before I'm let go."

"I'm sorry," said Solomon. "Sorry you got pulled into this. Sorry for my part in it. I'm not thinking very straight. Do you understand what I am saying? I am trying to warn you."

Odessa hated seeing Solomon like this. She put the back of her hand to her mouth, unable to think of anything to say.

Blackwood stepped forward. Solomon's hand rested on his chest, and Blackwood reached for it.

Solomon tried to pull back once he realized what was happening, but Blackwood would not let him go. He gripped Solomon's hand, the forever man looking down into the eyes of the dying man.

Blackwood said to him, "You never got over the boy in Mississippi. Your first case."

Solomon's face relaxed. "Vernon," he said. Solomon's mind seemed to clear. His eyes found Blackwood's face—really found it—for the first time that afternoon.

"You are wrong about what you accomplished in your time," said Blackwood. "You were instrumental in saving this world many times over. You have a legacy, Earl Solomon. A great and secret legacy. No one else knows the things we have seen."

Tears welled in Solomon's eyes. Odessa saw his knuckles whiten, returning Blackwood's grip with what little remained of his strength.

"You were right about one thing," said Blackwood. "I do envy you your final journey. May it be a peaceful one."

Tears shook loose, spilling down Solomon's gaunt cheeks. On deep, cleansing breaths, he said, "Thank you."

Blackwood released him. Solomon's hand lay back across his belly over the sheet. He was calm again. He was present.

His gaze found Odessa's. After a moment, he

nodded, as though reassuring her he was all right. "Just be careful," he said.

Odessa nodded, smiling out of relief rather than joy.

Solomon's gaze drifted upward almost to the ceiling, as though watching something else. Odessa thought they were losing him again, until his hand lifted up, pointing above her head.

"There," he said.

She turned slowly, indulging him...only to realize that the television was in fact behind and above her head, the sound muted.

On it, a live shot of a bank robbery in progress, a siege situation in Forest Hills, Queens. Police vehicles with lights flashing were part of a cordon half a block away from the bank's entrance. The news camera zoomed in on the door, which was held open by a woman wearing a business suit, the tail of her blouse hanging out, pointing what appeared to be a handgun in the direction of the camera, screaming something at the police.

The chyron read: ACTIVE SHOOTER IN HOSTAGE SITUATION AT QUEENS BANK: BRANCH MANAGER SUSPECTED.

Odessa was emotionally drained. It took her a moment to understand what she was seeing.

"Branch manager suspected?" she said. "Shooting up her own bank?" Blackwood was standing at her shoulder now, looking up.

"It's a Hollow."

1962. The Mississippi Delta.

S olomon parked behind some pickups with out-of-state tags from Arkansas, Missouri, Tennessee. Outside the corner gas station and auto repair shop, a white station attendant in a dark-blue jumpsuit with his sleeves rolled up leaned on one of the pumps, watching the men in suits, one black and one white, walk past. The station was open but there was no business today.

Solomon approached the ramshackle post office in the center of Gibbston. A crowd of whites, maybe thirty strong, stood on and off the sidewalk, mostly men in short sleeves with two or three women wearing light dresses and sun hats. That's where Sheriff Ingalls stood with his deputies, his thumbs in his gun belt. On the other side of the street, not far down from there, a smaller crowd of blacks stood out in front of the church, an even number of men and women, staring uneasily at their opposite number.

Organ music played from the church, but it wasn't Sunday. It was an impromptu weekday morning service. The congregation was mourning the death of Vernon Jamus.

The boy's corpse had been discovered in an old, unmarked graveyard overnight, not far from the tree where Hack Cawsby had been hanged.

Solomon glanced back at Blackwood, who had slowed a few steps behind him, an *I told you so* look, but also an accusatory one.

The boy's death had set the town on edge. And now Blackwood expected Solomon to lie for him.

Macklin, the Jackson special agent in charge, came off the sidewalk in front of the post office, cleaning his eyeglasses with the end of his necktie. "Good Christ, Solomon," he said, sliding on his spectacles and blinking. "Now what?"

"I know, sir."

"Lucky piece of work, you finding the boy's body so quick."

Solomon cleared his throat, feeling Blackwood a few feet behind him. "The graveyard and the hanging site are not far from the boy's house as the crow flies. There's paths through the sugarcane."

SAIC Macklin nodded. Solomon couldn't be sure he believed him. Macklin looked down at the black crowd outside the church. "They think it was retributive. A life for a life."

Solomon said, "Wouldn't you?"

Macklin glanced at the white crowd, nearer them. "I don't know," he said. "Killing kids is not usually how it's done."

Solomon could think of a handful of cases off the top of his head where that wasn't true, but he let it stand. The less talking he did, the better.

"No sign of foul play, I'm told," said Macklin. "The boy was sick? Wandered off?"

Solomon acutely felt the scratches under his collar, the bruises on his side and back. "Family's refusing an autopsy."

"That's not good," said Macklin. "That means the story will grow and grow. The sheriff can insist."

Solomon said, "He can but he won't. You think he wants something found? Something he'd have to go after?"

There was an exchange of words down the street, a colored man pointing at a handful of whites standing together, yelling back. Two deputies wandered over to quell it.

Macklin said, "Both sides spoiling for a fight. This goes any further, they're going to get the National Guard in here to keep the peace."

"You want peace kept?" said Solomon. "Or you want justice served?"

Macklin looked at Solomon. "I want you to talk to your people, put a lid on this grease fire."

"They aren't 'my people,'" snapped Solomon, his stress level reaching a breaking point. "I don't have control over them just because we look alike."

Macklin said, "Easy now."

Solomon wasn't having it. "Am I a Negro or am I an FBI agent? Because anybody you ask thinks I'm the opposite and can't be trusted. If I was brought down here because of some perceived advantage, being both—well, that backfired mightily."

Solomon's raised voice attracted the attention of Sheriff Ingalls, who ambled over. "There a problem over here?"

Solomon said, "You just walked over to the one place in this town where there isn't a problem."

Sheriff Ingalls frowned at Solomon's tone. "Funny you should mention that. I got a complaint about you."

Solomon said, "Oh?"

"Some fellers say you gave 'em a hard time out in the woods by the hanging site."

Solomon looked past the sheriff to the crowd, focused on the eager-looking men standing in the front with cuts and scratches on their faces. "These gentlemen here?" said Solomon, pointing them out. "Why, I didn't recognize them without their hoods on."

Sheriff Ingalls was unfazed by the remark. "Between that and finding the sharecropper boy, you been spending quite a bit of time in those old woods."

Solomon looked at Sheriff Ingalls, trying to gauge whether he was accusing him of something or just fishing. "I don't know what the complaint is. Their torches went out and they panicked in the darkness."

One of the white Klansmen said, "Hey, where you from, boy?"

"Where you boys from?" said Solomon. He turned to the sheriff. "You make a practice of allowing outside agitators to dictate what goes on in your town?"

The sheriff scowled. "These are concerned citizens. They have every right."

Solomon nodded. "Indeed, that's the letter of the law. So if a group of black folk show up, as concerned citizens, you'll show them the same courtesy and consideration, I'm sure."

Sheriff Ingalls was no longer smiling. He said, "You here, ain't you?"

SAIC Macklin stepped gently between Solomon and the sheriff before things escalated.

"Okay," he said. "We're all on the same side."

"No, we ain't," said Sheriff Ingalls. He pointed past Solomon. "And who's that you got with you now?"

Solomon turned. The sheriff was referring to

Hugo Blackwood—who was walking down the other side of the street, toward the black church.

"A concerned citizen," said Solomon, stepping off, going after Blackwood.

Solomon knelt in the last high-backed, hand-milled oak pew in the rear of the church. Pastor Theodore Eppert preached with tears rolling down his face, the collar of his violet vestment soaked deep purple. Mourners sobbed. The Jamus family, now only eighteen children, filled the first three rows.

Solomon hung his head. He was fighting his memories of the demon child who attacked him the night before. Blackwood stood behind and to the left of Solomon like a dark specter. Solomon didn't know how he was able to be here at all. His rage at the killer standing behind him burned anew.

Solomon had been raised Christian, but he hadn't prayed to God in quite some time. Now he asked God for forgiveness. He asked Him for guidance. He asked for assistance.

Pastor Eppert said, "Vernon was the best of us," and the congregation answered, *"Praise the Lord."* Pastor Eppert said, "Vernon was the most innocent of us," and the congregation answered, *"Praise the Lord."* Pastor Eppert said, "Vernon will be waiting for all of us in the Better Place," and the congregation answered, *"Praise the Lord."*

"Praise the Lord," said Solomon, a few beats too late.

After the special service, Pastor Eppert came down off the altar and had family and friends gather around him. The grief was oppressive, draining. Solomon felt like his own soul had shriveled to nothing inside him. He felt empty, worthless.

He wasn't aware of the mourners exiting the church until they were almost all gone. They were back out on the street where the opposing mobs were, and Solomon had to find the strength to join them. He stood in the empty church, leaning on the high-backed pew in front of him, looking up at the cross hanging from two cables over the altar, the simple wooden pulpit, the doors flanking the worship area, and tall candles that remained lit. He turned to exit, passing the landing of one of the paired wings of staircases leading to a rear balcony, where organ music played a somber hymn.

Solomon got to the door, looking behind him for Blackwood. He saw the odd Brit walking down the center aisle toward the altar. Solomon couldn't believe it.

"Hey!" he called out to him. "What the hell do you think you're doing?"

Solomon's voice carried loudly off the church

walls. He remembered the organist above and lowered his voice, moving quickly to stop Blackwood.

"I'm talking to you. Where are you going? Get out of here."

He grasped Blackwood's arm, turning him around.

"You've done enough," said Solomon. "Don't make this worse."

"Let me go," said Blackwood.

"I've never thought about hitting anyone in church," said Solomon. "Don't test me."

Blackwood's eyes communicated something unexpected. A warning. Not about Blackwood retaliating, but about what he might find.

"If you want to leave," said Blackwood, shaking his arm free, "then leave. But don't get in my way."

Solomon watched him approach the sanctuary, which was small and unadorned. An empty table was set against the rear wall under the hanging cross. Other than the candles and the pulpit, there was nothing here.

Solomon turned, looking at the empty pews. He wanted to leave. He wanted out. If only to show Blackwood he wasn't someone to be intimidated or coerced. He wouldn't be a party to desecration or disrespecting a house of worship.

Blackwood never did enter the sanctuary, nor

tread upon the church altar. Instead, he walked to a door to the right, leading to the sacristy.

"Don't go in there," said Solomon.

Blackwood opened the door and stepped inside.

Solomon looked at the empty church again. No one was watching them. Outside on the street, a small-town race war was brewing. Solomon was torn.

He walked to the door leading behind the altar, just to see where Blackwood had gone. Inside was an open closet of shelves for hymnals, communion plates. Solomon, hating Blackwood, moved inside.

He was beside the altar now. A doorway led out to the pulpit, where the pastor made his entrances and exits. A bowl and towel for anointing hands stood in a recessed part of the wall. Bibles and religious schoolbooks for children sat on a table with a cup of pencils, some votive candles, a box of matchsticks. Blackwood was near a window at the very rear, looking out at trees. Solomon thought it could be that those same trees led eventually to the hanging site, and the graveyard.

"Okay, this is all there is," said Solomon. "Let's go."

Blackwood pulled on a small door with a fixed wooden handle. The entire piece pulled free, not a hinged door but a flat section of wood, revealing a crawl space behind the altar. It was dark inside, no windows.

"Matches," said Blackwood.

Solomon again felt himself caught in the middle. What tipped the scales for him was Blackwood's quiet determination. He was a man on a mission. Solomon had to know what Blackwood had found.

He retrieved the box of matches and watched Blackwood strike flame. The orange nimbus of light did not reveal much until it found the wick of a blood-red candle. A moment later, the flame rose to illuminate the space.

The candle sat with others upon a wax-stained table. There were gnarled roots, cleaned of dirt, selected for their twisted shapes, resembling a natural sigil. A bowl of powder. Some dried flowers and a chart of hand-drawn symbols.

"What is this?" said Solomon.

Blackwood responded literally. "Jimsonweed and sulfur."

"No...*what is this?*"

Blackwood plucked the candle off the table, illuminating the wall where a crude face was drawn in red wax and blood, its eyes upturned, mouth open. "Hoodoo," said Blackwood.

"Voodoo?" said Solomon.

"Folk magic," said Blackwood. "It originated in West Africa, but was brought to the American South with the transatlantic slave trade. Ancestor veneration and spiritual balance. But that balance, during slavery, became in some regions translated as retribution. Hoodoo is more backwoods, less homogeneous than voodoo. Therefore, it is more open to spiritual corruption. Especially when practiced on hallowed ground."

Solomon said, "The pastor?" He remembered seeing him at the Jamus house. Talking to him, listening to him praise the character of Vernon Jamus. "No," said Solomon, less a denial than a plea.

Blackwood oriented himself. "This is the wall directly behind the altar. The dark side. A mirror reflection."

He turned and used the flickering candlelight to search the floor. He sorted through some items there, lifted a white article of clothing. It was a robe, the hem dirty with soil as from the woods.

"Oh no," said Solomon, not wanting to believe it. "A man of the cloth."

Blackwood said, "The pastor had access to the key to the boy's chains."

Blackwood passed the robe's hem over the candle flame, the fabric catching fire, crinkling, starting to burn.

"What are you doing?" said Solomon.

Blackwood draped the flaming robe over the table. The sulfur caught quickly, a blue flame rising out of the bowl, filling the space with the smell of rotting eggs.

Solomon said, "This whole church will go up."

Blackwood said, "That is the idea."

The robe was engulfed, flames dripping to the floor.

"This is arson," said Solomon, but there was nothing to fight the fire with. The smell was overpowering in the small space.

Solomon got out fast. Blackwood was behind him. Solomon was figuring out what to do. Call in the volunteer fire department first. Question Pastor Eppert, but away from the tensions outside. Arrest Hugo Blackwood. How was he going to keep this situation from exploding into violence?

He exited the sacristy, back into the main part of the church, just as the pastor, with his silver blaze in the middle of his black hair, returned inside. "What are you doing back there?" his voice boomed. "What is the meaning of this?"

Solomon pointed at the pastor accusatorily, his own voice rising to match. "Confess what you've done!"

The pastor stopped in his tracks before the altar. "I am the one people confess to," he said.

"Confess and go quietly or else I swear I will throw you to the mob out there."

Pastor Eppert looked at Hugo Blackwood stepping up beside Solomon. "Who is this man with you? Get out of my church. This is a house of worship, and you will leave immediately. Call the sheriff, Mother!"

Only then did Solomon realize that the organ music had stopped. But nothing could stop Solomon, his anger rising, walking toward this man of God.

"Vernon Jamus was the best Sunday school student, you said. He was 'the best of us,' you said."

Pastor Eppert stared back at Solomon, never before having been confronted in such a way in his own church. "And he was."

"You said you sensed evil," said Solomon. "You said you saw 'the devil's hand in this.' Well, now, so do I."

The smell of smoke and rotting eggs reached the pastor's nose. "What is that?" he said, sniffing. "My God, what have you done?"

"What have you done?" said Solomon, gripping the pastor by his collar.

But Pastor Eppert was defiant. "I tried to help him!"

Blackwood was at Solomon's side. He said, "The corruption of an innocent, of something pure. He was used as a conduit, a conductor. You needed him to serve as a circuit through which vengeance could be enacted...conducting the spirits of the slaves whose blood and sweat founded this church.

You used Vernon Jamus as an instrument in this dark rite. Just as you are being used now."

Blackwood reached out to Pastor Eppert, his hand near his face, palm open, fingers curled in a beckoning motion.

Solomon looked back and forth between the men, not understanding.

Blackwood uttered a few words in Latin, a chant, his voice dropping an octave as he did.

Pastor Eppert's eyelids fluttered. His pupils dilated and rolled back into his head. He went limp, sinking to the floor, held up only by Solomon's hands on his shirt. Solomon caught him and laid him down beside the pews.

"What in the hell...?" Solomon straightened next to Blackwood. "What did you do?"

Blackwood was looking up at the rear balcony. In most churches the organist sits with his or her back to the congregation and the organ faces the altar. This organ, with pipes of graduating height, faced the other way, obscuring the musician playing it.

The organist appeared, descending the staircase to the left. She seemed to float down the stairs, which were divided into two half-flights switching direction halfway to the bottom. Her hair was silver to her shoulders, but with a natural-looking stripe of silky black in the front: the reverse of Pastor Eppert. "Mother," as he called her, was his wife, a few years older than he was, if any. She wore a choir robe that was maroon and knee-length, of a completely different cut from the white robe found in the backward, back room altar.

The rotten egg smell permeated the church now, not the smoke so much, but ashes. Swirling around the church like glowing blackflies. The pastor's wife moved with incredible stillness, as though pulled forward by invisible hands. Her chin rested on her chest as though she were asleep.

Blackwood had removed a leather kit from his jacket pocket. Solomon was only vaguely aware that he had unfurled it on a pew.

Mother reached the rear center of the church, in the aisle between the two rearmost pews. Her arms hung limp, her feet arched, balancing perfectly on the tips of her toes as though supported by ballet shoes, not sandals.

Blackwood moved into the center of the aisle, facing her across a distance of fewer than ten feet.

He turned his head a fraction toward Solomon behind him, saying over his shoulder, "Do not look into her eyes."

Solomon looked at Mother as her chin lifted off her chest. Her eyes were open and pure white. Solomon was transfixed and could not look away. If the woman was blind, she must have adopted a mystic sixth sense, because she faced Blackwood directly. She opened her mouth to speak, but Blackwood spoke first.

"Non butto la cenere..."

I do not throw the ashes...

"Ma butto il corpo e l'anima Abdiel..."

But I throw the body and soul of Abdiel...

"Che non n'abbia più pace..."

That he may no more have peace or happiness...

As he continued his incantation, Blackwood reached into the pouch he had pulled from his leather kit. He sprinkled a fine powder before him like a farmer sowing seeds. The powder drifted toward Mother, who stood fast, as though compelled to do so by Blackwood's voice.

When the floating powder reached Mother, it formed suddenly into a misty smoke. The smoke rose in a column around Mother, rising as high as the balcony above. Mother's form remained essentially the same, but like a fine filter the smoke revealed an alter-figure, a manifestation that was purely spiritual, at least three times larger—taller and broader—than Mother.

She wore a flowing nightgown of diaphanous mist. The spirit inhabiting Mother—or so Solomon intuited, staring raptly at this enormous feminine figure dwarfing Blackwood and himself—waved her arms as though floating in a viscous fluid, her raven-black hair rippling behind her head like a dark aura. Her facial features twitched as though she were in distress or pain.

Hugo...

Her voice originated not from the giant apparition but from the air around Solomon's head. Mother was black-skinned, a woman in her forties. The haunting projection was white-skinned, a woman in her thirties or perhaps even younger: Torment obscured her face.

Blackwood paused when he heard his name. He looked up into the vast face of anguish-plagued beauty, and for moments appeared grief-stricken, stuck.

Solomon, entranced by the sight of this behemoth phantasm, reacted almost too late. Pastor Eppert—compelled by the thing that entranced him—had risen from the floor, lunging at Blackwood's back. Solomon grasped the larger man around the chest, tackling him into the pews across the aisle.

Blackwood resumed his ministrations, the incantations and more powdery smoke. Solomon, his knee on the back of the pastor, saw the swirling ashes briefly assume a form like that of a large crow before the widening eyes of the suffering spirit.

The crow of ashes sailed into the smoke-consumed apparition... and through it, blasting into a million glowing cinders, the giant spirit collapsing and dissipating like a vanishing curtain.

Mother fainted, released, falling to the floor.

Blackwood lowered his outstretched arms like the conductor at the conclusion of a mad symphony.

Solomon felt the pastor move beneath him. He let the man up cautiously, eager to look into his eyes.

Pastor Eppert looked bewildered, exactly as a man waking from a dark trance should.

"What is happening?" he said. "Who are you?"

Blackwood gathered the elements of his kit and walked to the woman in the choir robe, now stirring on the floor. He helped her to roll over and sit up.

She retched, dazed, shivering as though from a fever. Her pupils had returned, eyes reddened around the rims, lids lowered as though in pain. Black ash fell from her silver hair.

Solomon pulled the pastor out into the aisle. He saw his wife sitting at the back and staggered over to her. "Mother!" But as he reached her, an angry roar exploded behind them. Solomon ducked and turned, expecting a monster or some other hideous entity.

It was the flames ripping into the altar from behind, the blaze bursting through the wall in a cough of heat and ash, blackening and blistering the thin wall, licking at the suspended cross.

Bodies ran into the church entrance, the black townsfolk, yelling, *"Fire! Fire!"*

Sheriff Ingalls, his deputies, and SAIC Macklin followed, looking up at the blazing altar, finding Solomon and Blackwood with Pastor Eppert and his wife in their arms, dragging them out.

"What happened?" exclaimed Macklin.

Solomon could not answer. How could he put words to it?

Blackwood said, "Make sure there is no one else inside!"

The lawmen responded to that, racing toward the sacristy as the church filled with searing heat.

Blackwood and another man carried Mother out, while Solomon got Pastor Eppert's arm over his shoulder and walked him into the street.

They laid them down on the sidewalk a safe distance away, where other folk tended to them. Solomon looked up at the black smoke billowing out of the rear of the church. He found Blackwood and put his hand on the British man's chest, pushing him away from everyone, needing answers.

"What was that?" he said.

Blackwood said, "A slave demon. Possessed the woman. Exploited her and the pained souls who built this church."

"Why?"

Blackwood looked at him as though the answer was plain. "Because it could. Drawn by the legacy of suffering of this place. This is a vindictive spirit. Sorcery of death, injury, and revenge."

Solomon was going crazy. Either that or Blackwood already was. "The slave demon is a white woman?"

"That is the face it showed me. Evil comes to you in a familiar form."

Solomon looked at the whites who had moved across the street, drawn by the fire. He turned back to Blackwood.

"I need to know what this is. You burned down a church. We're going to have a riot here."

"That is what it wanted," said Blackwood. "To cause an uprising that would consume the town."

"You're damn right," said Solomon. "You want blood in the streets, just set fire to a black church."

Blackwood said, "The corrupt site had to be cleansed. Abdiel would have returned—"

"I don't give a hot damn about that, what am I gonna do right here, right now?"

Solomon stepped back from Blackwood. He looked at the street again. The black congregants held each other, most of the women weeping anew, the men becoming angry. The whites that had crossed the street stood near them, looking concerned, almost reverently so. The destruction of a church—even one that wasn't theirs—was an affront that affected them deeply.

Then Solomon saw the ten or so people who remained on the other side of the street—literally and figuratively. The unrobed, uncaring Klansmen.

Solomon remembered something Blackwood had said that night in the woods, after the Klansmen fled the hanging site in the dark.

Those masked men arrived at this town like dark spirits invoked.

Sheriff Ingalls and SAIC Macklin were out of the church now. Flames raced across the roof of the old wooden building. The deputies were clearing everyone back.

Solomon, mind racing, waited for the two lawmen to come to him.

Sheriff Ingalls said, "What happened? You were in there. Who did this?"

Solomon looked at Hugo Blackwood standing on the sidewalk, brushing ash from his shoulders.

Sheriff Ingalls said, "Answer me, goddammit! These people are going to riot."

"Answer him, Agent," said Macklin sharply.

Solomon stepped up to the two men, his back to the Klansmen across the street, making it clear that he was talking about them. "I saw who set the fire," said Solomon. "It was two of those concerned citizens over there."

The sheriff looked at the men, then back at Solomon, unhappily.

Solomon said to him, "If word of that gets out, you'll get your riot, by God. You'll see this whole town in flames. You need to do what you should have done before, and that is get those Klansmen out of this town. Or else I tell these church people what happened."

SAIC Macklin said, "Solomon, you'll do no such thing—"

"I will tell them what I saw." He stared down the sheriff. "Your choice. Your town. Your way."

Sheriff Ingalls looked at Macklin as though blaming him, then scowled deeply at Solomon, jabbing his thumbs deeply into his gun belt. "You son of a bitch," he said. Then he started across the street to hassle the Ku Klux Klan.

Leaving Solomon looking at his superior, Macklin.

Macklin said, "You telling him the whole truth and nothing but, Agent?"

"Yes, sir," said Solomon, before starting back to Hugo Blackwood. "As far as you know."

1582. Mortlake, Greater London.

Hugo Blackwood had not slept or eaten in days. Orleanna lay in a catatonic state in their bedchamber. She had been visited by three doctors and a priest, each departing deeply dismayed, unable to offer either a diagnosis or a cure. Her malady was somewhere in the netherworld between a disease of the body and a disease of the spirit. Neither discipline could diagnose the cause of her sickness, nor recommend a cure. She existed in a realm of suffering beyond the reach of medicine and religion—the very schism Dee had endeavored to reconcile.

As did Blackwood. He was at his wit's end, unable to understand what accursed illness had ensnared his love, only that he had played some unknowing role in its divination. And this knowledge haunted him, darkening every thought, cursing every moment. He wasn't ready to mourn her, and had already decided that her demise would lead inexorably to his own.

The scream—an ungodly shriek of pain and panic—brought him running from the kitchen to her bedside. Orleanna lay still, her flesh pallid and clammy, eyes distant—but untroubled. She was not the source of the outcry.

Another screech made him shiver, tearing at his heart, originating outside. He threw open the window shutters on the early night and saw, just steps away, a silver-furred wolf with a mink thrashing in its mouth. Two other oily-furred minks gnashed at the wolf's legs. An extraordinary portrait of cruelty in nature, one from which Blackwood would normally have hastily retreated. But the fighting went on, the minks' cries so shrill, the wolf's manner so savage, the confrontation resounded in his head. Blackwood became crazed.

He left the bedchamber, finding an ornamental spear and charging outside to confront the animals. He went at the wolf with the forged steel tip of the spear, howling at the wretched minks. The wolf bared its bloody teeth at Blackwood, the mink falling from its jaw, dead. The other minks shrank away from the wolf, racing away.

Blackwood faced the bright-eyed wolf. He was enraged at nature, and meant to go at the beast, jabbing the spear at the animal's head as it pawed at the ground with a low, guttural growl, wanting to pounce. Blackwood felt the confrontation coming to a head, until the growling stopped, and the wolf's eyes widened, and its gums lowered over its sharp teeth. It almost seemed to be looking past Blackwood, into the air behind him.

The animal was scared. Its tail lowered and it backed off, forsaking the dead mink, turning and bounding away.

Blackwood lowered his weapon. Had the wolf seen Blackwood's murderous intent, his killer instinct having curdled its blood? Suddenly sense came flooding back into Blackwood. Shaken, he turned away from the dead mink and returned to his domicile.

He splashed water onto his face in the kitchen, cooling his composure, his thoughts. He prepared a bowl of water to take to his Orleanna. Arriving, he realized he had left the window open to the night. When he saw the bedclothes thrown back, the bed empty, he dropped the bowl of water at his feet. She was gone.

He went to the window, seeing only the bloody mink in the mossy ground. To the side, just a glimpse, a white-clothed figure rising in the distant night, out of sight.

He leaned out as far as he could but saw no more of it. He did not trust his eyes but could not think where else his wife could have gone. And then he remembered the wolf's cowed expression: Perhaps it had been intimidated by the sight not of him, but of her, rising from the open window into the sky.

Half out of his mind, Hugo Blackwood rushed to the door, pausing only to take up the spear again. He raced to his stable, riding to John Dee's house in a fugue. The sliver moon barely lit the way. He was courting madness; he cared nothing for himself anymore.

He pounded on the door, prepared to smash a window to gain entrance. The lock was thrown inside, the door pushed open a few inches. Edward Talbot peered out, his face shadowed by candlelight.

"Go away, Blackwood," he said. "Begone."

"Is she here?" said Blackwood, gripping the door, pulling it from Talbot's hand, wedging the ashwood handle of the spear inside the opening.

"She has been here many times," said the scryer. Quite a turnabout from the scared, haunted man who'd visited Blackwood's kitchen a few days before.

Blackwood shoved inside past Talbot, sending the older man sprawling, his candle extinguishing upon impact with the stone floor.

Blackwood raced through the wide halls of the dark manse shouting Dee's name, pole weapon in hand. He turned the corner and slowed, seeing the doors to the great library open.

An eerie green light, the soft, sweet green of parrot feathers, shone out of the doors with enough vibrancy to illuminate the hallway. Blackwood heard a voice speaking in a bizarre language he recognized but did not understand: the Enochian language John Dee had spoken at the initial séance in that very library.

Blackwood started toward the library, but a pair of hands grabbed at him from behind. Talbot restrained him, pulling him back.

"Don't interrupt the communion—"

Blackwood elbowed Talbot off him, driving him back against the wall with the shaft of his spear up against his throat. Talbot's skullcap slid off his head, revealing the butchered sides of the forger's head, the ears Talbot had lost as punishment for his earlier crimes.

The earless scryer looked like any of the heretics and convicts Blackwood would see in shackles in the Old Bailey, on their way to Newgate dungeon. Blackwood threw him aside, turning back to the open doors, entering Dee's notorious and celebrated library.

The green glow and its weird energy made him throw his arm up to shade his eyes. He saw the philosopher John Dee, his customary white gown and snow-white beard bathed in green, standing across from the spectral image of Orleanna Blackwood, her nightdress and raven-black hair rippling as though from facing a windstorm. Her beautiful face, unnaturally tinged by the liquidy light, glowed with the fullness of wonder.

One hand was outstretched, the crystal orbuculum cupped in her palm, the source of the radiating green light, offering the sphere to John Dee.

Blackwood stared, unable to comprehend. Orleanna had been catatonic, she had seemed hours away from certain death.

Was she dead now? Was this her spirit? Had she ascended to another form?

If so . . . why did she rush to John Dee?

She spoke to him in a strange low tone, the Enochian language. The idiom of angels. Why was she the one summoned by their invocation? Was she now speaking from the beyond?

Dee's face was suffused with adoration, engaged in spiritual congress with an astral being. He had achieved the impossible. He had bridged the schism between science and magic.

The spear fell from Blackwood's hand. He walked to the form of his wife, his Orleanna. Was she real?

"Orleanna!" he cried, over the hum of the weird light.

Dee broke his spell, speaking English. "No, Blackwood! No!"

Blackwood stood before her. Her eyes were lost in the green light swirling in the globe in her hand.

Dee yelled, "The angels have chosen her!" He was enraptured. "She is their messenger! She knows all!"

Blackwood looked at the glowing vision of his wife, his love. Lost to him now. Their life...their home, their future...any hope of children...all gone.

But as he mourned for her there, he sensed that it was not his Orleanna standing before him. He sensed evil, hidden behind a mask of beauty.

He looked away from her face. His eye was drawn to a window. Outside, before the grieving branches of a blighted willow tree, a figure in white, with raven-black hair.

It was his Orleanna, reaching for him as her form retreated into the darkness. Beseeching him. Warning him.

And then she was gone. He looked again at the figure before him.

She was a double. A fetch.

He reached out to her torso, the fabric of her dressing gown. She was insubstantial. His hand went right through.

Dee said, "Get away, barrister! The angel communes with me!"

Blackwood turned in a rage and shoved the old philosopher back against a shelf of books. He took

Dee's place, facing the fetch of his wife, only the glowing orb between them, nearly floating in her palm.

Blackwood gripped the orbuculum. A jolt of power surged through him, something he had never felt before. Pain ran through his joints and up his wrist into his forearm, but he held tight.

The bright-green light changed shades, becoming chartreuse, sickly and sour. The energy it emitted took more violent form, wind swirling around the famed library. A great tempest, knocking over books, ornaments, and occult instruments.

Blackwood saw deeply into the form before him. He saw his wife, the real Orleanna, and felt her suffering. She was not here in this room. She was trapped in some netherworld, banished for his transgression and the dark magic of Edward Talbot and John Dee.

Blackwood saw that she was to be punished for what he had done. In that moment was also revealed to him his solemn fate. His terrible destiny.

Save me, Hugo. Find me and save me.

The true face of the Orleanna fetch before him was revealed. Horribly smooth and nearly featureless, its mouth open in a groan.

Hands grabbed at Blackwood. Dee and Talbot, pulling at him. Ripping at his clothes, trying to shake him free.

The pain, having traveled up his arm to his shoulder and spread like a plague down his midsection to his legs, reached a crescendo. Blackwood's hand sprang open, releasing the crystal sphere, which dropped to the floor with the weight of a ball of lead.

The interior cracked but the globe held its shape. At once the sickly green emanant energy began to fade. The vision before him, the unnatural messenger from beyond, was grabbed by the swirling cyclone in the room, caught up in it, whipped around and around until it came apart, disappearing into the swirl of papers and mist.

Blackwood simultaneously felt the grip of extraordinary agony and a complete numbness—as though every limb had been cut away but he still experienced their pain. He fell next to the cracked orbuculum on the floor and suffered fits of convulsion, his body not coming to rest until the tempest in the philosopher's library spun out to nothing.

The history of barrister Hugo Blackwood ended on that day. His accounts were settled, but his property fell into disrepair over time and eventually was considered abandoned. The home, believed by some to be haunted, was razed; its exact location is now unknown, only its proximity to John Dee's address in Mortlake is known today. Both the parish register in Mortlake and Blackwood's gravestone are lost to history.

A pall was cast over Dee's own house and his career. Within the year, he had locked up his home, setting out rather mysteriously for Bohemia with Edward Talbot. Over the next six years, the two occultists led a nomadic existence, traveling abroad throughout Central Europe, Dee writing books and still attempting to communicate with angels . . . even as occult practices fell out of favor with the aristocracy, and the general public soon followed, unpersuaded by his florid accounts of magical entities.

It is not known why Dee remained in exile for so long. After splitting with Talbot, he finally returned to England in 1589, only to find that his home in Mortlake had been broken into and vandalized. His famed library had been looted in his absence, his rare books on the occult and unnatural practices stolen, along with his instruments for divining and spellcasting. His deep scholarship of necromancy and the supernatural arts was believed lost. What few possessions he had remaining, he sold off, piece by piece, living his final years in poverty in the same decaying mansion. The once-renowned astronomer, geographer, mathematician, royal court adviser, and occult philosopher died in Mortlake at the age of eighty-two.

Odessa sat in the spacious backseat of the Rolls-Royce Phantom, Mr. Lusk at the wheel, Hugo Blackwood sitting at her side, motoring through Queens. The bank branch was not far east of the hospital, on the other side of Flushing Meadows Park, on 108th Street.

Odessa said, "We can't cruise in to the crime scene riding in a Rolls-Royce. I don't know what we can do, to be perfectly honest, but I know we can't do that. We also can't go in there with a bunch of roosters. What do you expect we can achieve here?"

Blackwood watched out the window, unusually distracted.

"Well?" she said.

"Solomon never spoke to me like that before," said Blackwood.

Odessa said, "That's because his mind is going. The fungal infection that caused the stroke is affecting his brain."

Blackwood said, "That is why I am worried. It leaves his mind vulnerable."

"Vulnerable to what?"

The Phantom took a hard corner and then abruptly stopped. A traffic cop standing before a blue NYPD sawhorse was frantically waving cars along, trying to prevent gridlock. The main police barricade was another block down, a bottleneck of safety vehicles with lights flashing.

"Keep going," Odessa told Mr. Lusk. "Pull over as soon as you can."

He did, and Odessa sprang to the curb, Blackwood following. She doubled back to the traffic cop, finding another police officer blocking the sidewalk. Odessa showed him her badge and credentials.

The cop waited for Hugo Blackwood to offer identification. "Who's this?" he asked.

Odessa said, "He's with me."

They pushed on through. Odessa hustled ahead toward the staging area the New York Police Department's Crisis Intervention Team had established. They had a mobile command center truck parked outside the barricade, and a portable video surveillance tower elevated off its mobile stand, a twenty-foot-high vantage point.

Odessa immediately made the FBI contingent on the scene, a knot of four men in suits conferring near an unmarked Ford Fiesta. The Bureau was on scene because it was a federal crime to rob any member bank of the Federal Reserve System. The FBI used to investigate each and every bank robbery in the country, but that changed after 9/11, when resources were redeployed to antiterror investigations and homeland security concerns. Now the Bureau focused its attention on serial offenders, robbers who crossed jurisdictional boundaries, and the most violent bank crimes.

Odessa steered clear for fear of being recognized. She led Blackwood to the edge of the blocked intersection, their best angle on the Santander branch on the opposite corner of the next block. Odessa could see movement inside, the branch manager moving back and forth deep within the bank, but they were too far away to make out anything clearly.

"We have to get closer," said Blackwood.

"We are not getting any closer," Odessa said. "They've got this block locked off on four sides." She looked around, noting the level of precaution. "Must be a bomb threat."

She eyed a pair of NYPD detectives in plainclothes, one talking on his phone, the other, younger one scrolling through his. Odessa approached with her badge in hand.

"Excuse me," she said, "who can give me an update here?"

The younger detective looked up quickly, dismissively, then looked up again, the double take a response to the surprise of being approached by a younger female with FBI credentials.

"Not a lot is known," he said, affecting a casual air. "Original bank alarm seemed like a robbery. Maybe it still is. But it's the manager who took over her own bank. Busted robbery seems unlikely. They think she just snapped. Been emptying drawers and the vault and dumping the cash and coins on the floor. She's lost her damn mind."

"No demands?"

"Not that I've heard. I know the crisis negotiator can't keep her on the phone. Couple of customers ran outta there when she started ranting, before she locked them in. They said she made bomb threats. We're treating it as such—"

Two loud reports, like balloons popping, silenced the barricade.

"Jesus," said the detective. "She's shooting it up randomly. This ain't gonna end good."

Odessa said, "Is there a plan to go in?"

"Well," said the detective, "the other option is to stand out here while she shoots her employees and customers one by one."

"Right," said Odessa. "Thanks."

"You look familiar," said the detective, ignoring his ringing phone. "You work out of the B-Q here?"

"Federal Plaza," she said, lying, letting him take his phone call.

Blackwood overheard most of the conversation. "She wants the confrontation," he said. "The Hollow One wants her to be killed."

"Yeah, I know," said Odessa, impatiently. "What is it you think I can do here?"

Blackwood looked around. "We can't let it jump into another body."

"So tell me how," she said. "It's completely out of my hands."

"You have seen what it can do," he reminded her. "Other lives are at stake. You have to try."

He was right. Odessa did not want any other cop or FBI agent to be put in the position she had been in. Besides, what did she have to lose here: her job?

"Wait here," she said.

She walked to the largest of the mobile command center trucks set back from the perimeter and knocked on the door, opening it. She had her badge out, expecting to have to bullshit her way inside, but none of the half dozen cops even turned to look at her. Each of them wore headphones or earbuds, remotely monitoring the standoff via the truck's surveillance cameras and glass-penetrating microphones, or else spoke into a cell phone.

Odessa watched the video feeds on a bank of screens on the long side wall. The bank manager appeared behind the teller counter with a metal tray, a gun in her hand. She overturned the tray over the floor, dumping its contents, the camera dipping down to reveal a pile of paper currency on the floor.

The cop with the largest headphones was narrating her movements into a wire microphone, communicating with other cops. One high-angle view indicated snipers in position on the rooftops across the street.

"She's mumbling again," the man relayed. "Teller number three is sobbing and the suspect is running out of patience with her. Wait a minute... she's got some other object. It's a can."

Odessa saw the canister in the manager's hand. It looked like cleaning solution, or a can of air freshener from the bathroom.

The man continued. "She's dumping out customers' handbags on the counter... looking for something... oh man. I see it now..."

Odessa saw the manager flick a butane lighter. The woman walked over to the pile of cash.

"I don't believe it," he said. "She's burning it. She's burning it all."

The manager lit the spray, igniting the product, then turning the improvised flamethrower on the paper currency.

"Roger that," said the man, receiving other transmissions. "She's backing off now. We're going to get smoke alarms. She tossed the canister away. Still mumbling in a very strange voice. Over and over again. Something like, 'Blackwood...Blackwood...'"

Odessa was a moment processing these words. *Blackwood.* She said loudly, *"What?"*

Heads turned her way. Then another screen came on, a new video source, a body camera having been activated. The jerky perspective made it difficult to understand what was being seen at first. Odessa made out officers being strapped up in tactical gear, buckling helmets and performing weapons checks on assault rifles. It was the NYPD Emergency Service Unit, their SWAT team squad, preparing for a breach assault on the bank.

"You're going to do a dynamic entry?" said Odessa. "Hey, guys, listen to me. She's going to force a shoot."

One man pulled his phone away from his ear in aggravation. "Who the hell are you again?" he said.

"She's drawing you in," said Odessa. "She wants this."

"Holy Christ," said the man with the headphones. "Who is this now?"

Odessa scanned the monitors until she saw what

he was referring to. A person was walking down the middle of the street from the barricade heading toward the bank. A person wearing a finely tailored dark suit.

"Shit—"

Odessa burst out of the police van, racing around it, cutting between two blue sawhorses, running toward Blackwood before the police gunned him down. She waved her credentials wildly, hooking Blackwood's arm and yanking him back.

"What the hell are you doing?" she said. "They're going to shoot you."

"I'm the only one who can stop this," he said.

"I know that," she said, tugging on him, though he wouldn't budge. "She's asking for you. *It's* asking for you."

Blackwood was not surprised. "Yes," he said. "It drew us here."

"Drew us...?" said Odessa. And then, further refining her confusion, she clarified, "Drew us?"

The sound of shattered glass turned their heads toward the bank—and then two loud and brilliant detonations staggered them.

Flash-bang grenades led the charge into the bank. A phalanx of Emergency Service Unit tactical officers advanced on the doors with a battering ram, forcing their way inside the smoke-filled bank. The ensuing gunshots and screams were barely audible under the ringing in Odessa's ears caused by the concussive grenades. Uniformed officers spilled into the street from the barricade, prohibiting any further advance by Odessa or Blackwood.

Smoke streamed out. No other people exited the bank. Then the news arrived, relayed to police officers via their radios: "Shooter down! Shooter down!"

Odessa and Blackwood had to wait while the incident scene was secured and the smoke was ventilated. The street filled with police personnel. The injured would be evacuated, and then the crime scene processing would begin.

"What do we do?" asked Odessa. "Is it jumping into someone else?"

Blackwood said, "Most likely."

"It could be anyone," she said. "How can we know? What do I look for?"

Blackwood said, "I will sense it."

Odessa pushed forward, getting them as close to the bank as possible. FBI agents clustered on the street outside the entrance, waiting for the air quality inside to improve. Odessa had to stay back from them.

ESU members began to exit onto the street. They removed their helmets once they got outside, many of them coughing, chugging bottles of water to clear their throats. This gave Blackwood a clear line of sight to their faces.

Odessa didn't know what they were going to do if he identified the body the Hollow One had seized. Especially if it had jumped into a tactical agent with an assault rifle—as she assumed was its goal. She didn't even have a handgun with which to defend herself. She was looking back and forth between their faces and Hugo Blackwood, awaiting some reaction from him.

The ESU members regrouped, then began filing out for a debriefing. Blackwood watched them go with concern.

"Nothing?" Odessa said.

"No," he said. "We have to get inside that bank."

"Never going to happen," Odessa told him.

They moved up another few steps, Odessa looking in past the breached front doors, through the ATM vestibule into the main lobby. The smoldering pile of scorched cash had been soaked with water, many thousands of dollars mutilated and irredeemable.

Straining, she eyed the teller windows, and the open gate through which the bank manager had moved back and forth with cash. She saw what could have been an arm and a shoulder of the dead manager. A dark patch of blood on the floor struck something in her.

"Where are the wounded?" she said.

They had been so focused on the weapons-toting tactical officers, she hadn't seen the wounded tellers and customers being brought out.

She and Blackwood hurried wide around the edge of the perimeter, finding some of the exhausted hostages seated on the sidewalk curb, telling their stories to police detectives, a few being treated for cuts and bruises.

But nothing more serious than that. Odessa spoke to a young female EMT taking a middle-aged man's blood pressure. "Were there wounded customers?"

"Two customers and a teller," she said. "Nothing life threatening."

"Where are they?"

"Ambulance," she answered. "Already en route to the hospitals." Odessa glanced back at Blackwood. He was concerned.

Odessa said, " 'Hospitals' plural?"

"Three ambulances, three hospitals."

"Which ones?"

The EMT was getting annoyed at her. "The three nearest ones. That would be Flushing, Jamaica Heights, and NewYork-Presbyterian."

Odessa straightened. "Presbyterian Queens?"

"Of course," said the EMT.

The hospital they had just left.

The hospital where Earl Solomon was a patient.

She looked at Blackwood. He didn't have to say anything. His earlier words came rushing into her head.

No coincidences. Everything is connected.

"Oh my God," said Odessa.

Earl Solomon lay in his hospital bed, fighting sleep. The television was covering the hostage taking at the Santander bank, which apparently had ended in a police raid and the shooter's death. That was what the words beneath the news anchor said, but the screen swam a bit in his vision, and he wasn't sure. They had no camera at the scene, and kept looping the same footage of police vehicles and traffic cops pushing people back.

The television was on mute, no sound but the whirring and beeping of his machines, and his breathing, which went in quiet but came out loud. Solomon wanted to reach the television remote control wired to the wall behind his bed. But his arms were numb. They didn't move as well as he liked. It was easier just to lie still.

Sirens wailed outside, pretty much an all-day occurrence, but these ones sounded close. He heard a crash that seemed to reverberate up the building, as though the foundation had been shaken. Or maybe it was all in his head.

Now they had cell phone footage from somebody in one of the buildings across the street. Two flash-bangs that Solomon saw but did not hear, followed by a tactical entry. Fuzzy because of the distance of the phone owner from the bank...or maybe because of Solomon's vision.

Goddammit. He was tired of all this waiting. The bed had him now. He didn't think he'd ever get vertical again. That was a sorry thought. What was the point of waiting? What was the point of being a man in a bed who was never getting out of it again? Maybe it wasn't his vision drifting, maybe it was his mind.

All the things he had seen in his days, all the things Hugo Blackwood had shown him. Challenging his presumptions at first, shaking his view of the world and beyond. But even still, like any person, he never truly focused his attention on what was at the end. He knew there were other things out there. He had seen them. And most of what he'd seen was dark and malicious. But maybe there was something else. A peaceful place.

He thought back to Blackwood releasing the possessed boy in the graveyard that night so many years ago. Young Vernon Jamus, and how Blackwood stood over him, cleansing his soul. Freeing him. But to what? That was what Solomon wanted to know. This was one mystery Hugo Blackwood could not help him with, one case the occult detective could not solve.

There was no peace for Hugo Blackwood in this world, but maybe, just maybe, there was for Earl Solomon in the next.

Blackwood.

Solomon heard a familiar voice not his own.

Hugo Blackwood.

Solomon closed his eyes to purge the voice from his head. But it wasn't in his head, it was there in the room with him. Solomon squeezed his eyes tightly shut, wanting it not to be true. He turned his head, rolling it on the pillow until it was blindly facing the hallway door. And then he opened his eyes.

His vision was split, doubled, and took a moment to come together and focus on the boy standing inside his door. Little Vernon Jamus. Solomon was afraid, as the boy came into his sight, that he would be the evil Vernon, possessed by the demon that used him as its instrument of conjuring to raise the spirits of the dead Mississippi Delta slaves.

But it was cleansed Vernon who had come for him. Bare-chested, wearing the same pants he had almost sixty years ago.

Solomon's memory had summoned the boy. Invoked his spirit. Solomon's waiting was over.

Vernon had come to take him away.

But if so...

Why was he saying Hugo Blackwood's name?

As Solomon stared, a heavyset man turned the corner from the hallway into his hospital room. He wore a bright-blue shirt with a medical patch on the sleeve, and a cap with the name of an ambulance service on its crown. Below the brim, a thick trail of dark blood ran from underneath the man's hat down his cheek to his chin. His eyes were vacant, hollow.

Solomon's body seized up in terror.

Without another word or change of expression, Vernon Jamus simply disappeared, the ambulance driver stepping into his place.

The Phantom arrived at the NewYork-Presbyterian Queens Hospital to a chaotic scene. An ambulance had crashed into a building support pillar just outside the emergency room entrance. The nose of the van was punched in, the front hood buckled, the ambulance tipped to one side on the curb.

Hospital staff attended to the accident scene. Odessa and Blackwood raced from the Rolls-Royce, pushing through the crowd of onlookers. The back doors were open. An ambulance attendant was being strapped onto a spinal board, unconscious, her neck and head in a cervical collar. The stretcher was on its side, empty. The body in the front seat was covered with a sheet, deceased.

Odessa showed her badge to one of the attending emergency room doctors to facilitate questioning. "Where is the patient who was in the back of the ambulance?"

"That's her," he said, pointing to the driver's cab. "Impact of the crash sent her into the front."

"Dead?" said Odessa.

"Dead on arrival," said the doctor. "They said the ambulance was doing fifty and gaining speed when it shot through the parking lot and rammed the building. Driver must have lost his mind."

Odessa had an image of the wounded bank customer attacking the driver in the front seat and taking the wheel.

"But if that's the patient..." said Odessa. She looked at the ambulance again. "Where's the driver?"

They rode up to Solomon's floor, Odessa imploring the elevator to rise faster. The doors opened and she ran the short distance to his room. A red light over his door was flashing.

Inside, two nurses knelt on either side of the ambulance driver, lying facedown on the floor. Solomon's bed was empty.

"Where is he?" asked Odessa.

The nurses were still in shock at what they had found. One of them stood. "He's dead," she said, referring to the ambulance driver.

Odessa gripped the nurse's shoulder. "The patient in this room," she said, "Earl Solomon. His bed's here. He's not."

The nurse looked at the empty bed, slow to understand.

A male nurse came running to the door, drawn by the red alarm light, stopping when he saw the ambulance driver's body.

The nurse said to him, "Earl Solomon. Patient in this room. Where is he?"

The male nurse backed out of the room, looking up and down the hall. "Stroke victim, right?"

The nurse said, "He couldn't have gotten far..."

Odessa stared at Blackwood. She was terrified suddenly, desperately afraid for Solomon, and starting to panic. "Did it come here for him?" she said.

"We need to find Solomon," said Blackwood.

"Did it come here specifically for him?" she said.

The nurses looked at her strangely. Blackwood grasped her wrist and guided her out of the room, a few steps down the hallway, before she shook him off.

"Answer me," she said.

"We need to find him."

"*There are no coincidences*," she said, with a sharp edge, feeling hysteria creep into her voice.

"It came here for him," admitted Blackwood. He looked a little shaken himself. "We need to find him now."

"And *then* what?" she said—but Blackwood pulled her toward the stairs rather than answer.

★   ★   ★

"He could be *anywhere*," said Odessa as they rushed down the final flights, back out into the first floor. It was still bedlam due to the ambulance crash. Police were on the scene, dealing with hospital administrators as they tried to restore order. Blackwood followed signs for the emergency room, which was still taking patients despite the presence of news media.

Odessa stopped to talk to a cop in the middle of the hallway. "Have you seen an elderly black man in a hospital gown go past here?"

The cop nodded. "Yeah, lady, like seven of them." Then his radio squawked and he reached up to bring his shoulder-clipped handset closer to his ear in the crowded, noisy hall. "Holy shit!" he exclaimed in response to what he heard, and took off running for the door.

Blackwood looked at Odessa. They followed him outside, past the crashed ambulance, into the parking lot, running toward the street. They were just in time to see a police cruiser careen out of the lot, swerving wildly into a passing SUV, impacting it with a terrific crash, the SUV ramming into a parked mail truck and rolling backward across the two-lane street—where it was struck by another vehicle unable to brake in time.

The police cruiser avoided the pileup, fishtailing down the street with roof rack lights spinning, its siren wailing into the distance.

A few cops ran into the street toward the accident to assist victims. Others, like the cop from the hospital hallway, jumped into their vehicles to start a pursuit—the cruiser obviously stolen—but the multiple-car accident blocked both lanes of the avenue, preventing them from giving chase.

Blackwood and Odessa moved into the street, watching the cruiser getting away, swerving in and out of traffic.

Blackwood said, "We must follow him!"

As they looked up the street, a black Rolls-Royce with gunpowder-gray styling nosed out of a cross street just beyond the pileup.

Blackwood said, "Good man, Lusk!"

Odessa ran with him, past the traffic accident, hurrying to the idling Phantom. They leapt into the back and Mr. Lusk pulled away before their door was closed.

Mr. Lusk said, "The driver of that police vehicle…"

"Yes," said Blackwood. "It's Agent Solomon."

"His eyes…they weren't right," said Mr. Lusk.

"Get after him," said Blackwood. "Do not let him get away."

The Phantom's engine rose from a purr to a growl, lifting the vehicle forward. The cruiser moved with great speed, but its lights and sirens made following it easy—as did the trail of cars left in its wake, either parting for the onrushing police vehicle or run off the road by it.

They raced through Jackson Heights, passing collisions and weaving around fender benders on the trail of the screaming car. At times they would see the blue lights spinning ahead; the Phantom was neither gaining on the police cruiser nor losing ground.

Blackwood watched out the window, his manner intense but cool. Odessa was distraught about Solomon, and Blackwood's steady demeanor pissed her off. With anger came a sudden clarity.

"The Hollow didn't come for Solomon," she said. "It's coming for you. Using him to get to you. And you knew it."

"Did I?" he said, without looking at her.

"You knew he was vulnerable."

Blackwood turned his head her way, still not meeting Odessa's eyes. "I suspected it," he admitted. "Nothing like this ever occurred to me...until I saw him in that hospital bed."

"It's drawing you out. All this...the Peters shooting, the Long Island spree...there was no pattern. It was designed to summon you...to bait you into coming out into the open. Thanks to me. Thanks to my letter."

Blackwood met her gaze finally. No words, but it signified that she was right.

"And you've seen it this whole time. You knew it was wanting a confrontation...and you didn't care who got in the way. Even Solomon, a dying man, now leading you to your *appointment*. You wanted him taken."

"Don't be ridiculous."

"But you were okay with it. So long as it got you where you need to go. So long as you can catch your fourth Hollow and install it in your trophy room."

"Your oversimplification of this matter is absolutely astounding," said Blackwood. "Have you learned nothing? Or is this simply a willful attempt at imposing guilt?"

"I'm learning plenty," Odessa said. "Solomon tried to warn me about you. He said you'll let nothing and no one get in your way. He saw it coming but he was too frail to stop it. Well, I'm not going to let him go out a casualty of some horrible supernatural imp. You need to save him. You can't let him die like this."

Blackwood said sharply, *"You assume I have a choice."*

The flash of anger in his face was startling. Odessa became quiet, her eyes staying on him, wondering what sort of monster she had gotten herself paired up with.

The Phantom swerved hard left past a head-on

collision in which one vehicle's engine had burst into flames. Mr. Lusk said, "He's heading for the Queensboro Bridge!"

They trailed the wailing cruiser by at least a full city block, all the way onto the upper-level, two-lane inbound side of the bridge. The blue lights swerved madly up ahead, the Phantom snaking around spun-out automobiles left in its wake, crossing the East River over Roosevelt Island into Manhattan.

Odessa gripped her seat, bracing her shoulder against the side of the car as they careened off the bridge, emptying onto Second Avenue and continuing a block west before turning hard left, heading south on Third Avenue, driving the wrong way.

They rode against traffic, using every one of the five lanes of the wide avenue, filling the lane of destruction left by the runaway police cruiser. Some ten blocks down, the cruiser cut off a semitrailer, turning sharply right at about 46th or 45th Street. Mr. Lusk spun the Phantom's polished wheel madly to avoid the truck as it slid to a stop diagonally across the intersection, costing them some time. When the Phantom finally negotiated the turn, the cruiser's lights were no longer in sight, though its path of disruption was easy to discern.

The Phantom wheeled left, and at once screeched to an abrupt halt. Odessa, used to the bright-blue spinning lights, did not understand why they had stopped. Then she saw the cop car, side doors and rear fender crumpled from multiple impacts, its front grille smashed, steam rising out of the tented hood from the overtaxed engine. At first she thought the cruiser had broken down, but its lights had been switched off, as had its siren.

The Hollow had reached its destination.

Blackwood immediately exited the vehicle. Odessa followed, getting her bearings, craning her neck to the early-evening sky. She recognized a portion of Grand Central Station by the way the building disrupted the traffic pattern, so rare in the Midtown grid of New York City. The building nearest them was fenced off from the street, much of its twenty floors covered with scaffolding and safety netting, undergoing a substantial renovation. It looked currently abandoned, however; no lights in the glassless upper windows, no work being done. A city sign on the fence warned away trespassers, citing a shutdown of the work site per order of the city of New York.

"What is this place?" asked Blackwood.

"Maybe they ran out of money," said Odessa, looking up at the sandstone façade. Suddenly its proximity to Grand Central sparked a memory. "Wait," she said. "This is one of those university clubs. They were converting it into a big hotel here at Grand Central but they had to shut down the project. It was in the news about a month ago—big finding, then a scandal. They were excavating the club basement some thirty feet down and discovered centuries-old remains. It turned out to be part of a potter's field for dead slaves."

Hugo Blackwood turned and looked at Odessa with a look of astonishment. "Slaves?"

"It stopped construction. Now there are lawsuits flying back and forth. Trying to decide if they can reinter them or put up a plaque or if this kills the entire project." She noticed Blackwood was still staring at her. She realized this meant something more to him than it did to her. "What?" she said.

Blackwood regained his composure, to the extent that he had ever misplaced it. "Devilry," he hissed, producing his leather kit from inside his jacket, loosening its ties with sudden urgency. "Mr. Lusk?" he said.

Odessa turned to Mr. Lusk, who was still behind the wheel of the idling Phantom. He dialed a number on his cell phone and put it to his ear, replying, "I will give him the location."

"Who?" said Odessa, confused. "Give who the location—to what?"

But when she turned back to him, Hugo Blackwood was already gone.

O dessa heard the canvas-covered security fence shaking, and realized Blackwood had climbed up and over it. Angry at having been left behind, she found a supporting pole to reduce the fence's flexibility and scaled it. Two lengths of barbed wire topped the fence, angled toward the interior. She made sure her phone was secure in her pocket before vaulting high over the top wire to the fence on the other side, gouging out a bit of material from her jacket sleeves but no skin.

On the ground, she quickly crossed a plaza of crumbled asphalt to the entrance of the structure, ducking under plastic tarp billowing in the breeze. The door contained another warning sign, but a window to the right of it was missing a long, vertical glass pane, and she stepped right inside.

She did not see Blackwood, and decided against calling his name. She started down a wide stone staircase that split into two staircases doubling back. She got to the bottom and brought out her phone, turning on the flashlight, looking for more stairs. The modern-day island of Manhattan was built on the shoulders of previous centuries. She knew that the rule of thumb of Manhattan landfill was: Ten feet below ground level took you to about the beginning of the 1900s, where you might find poured concrete from the turn of the century; another five or so feet below that took you to roughly 1800, with walls of brick and mortar, where you might find surviving pieces of ceramic and domestic artifacts; twenty to twenty-five feet below street level, you were in the 1700s.

She ran out of stairs with Blackwood nowhere to be seen. Then her phone found a hole in the temporary wood floor, a ladder sticking out. She climbed down quickly, shining her light around.

"Put that thing away."

It was Blackwood, directly below her. She descended the last few rungs into a passageway floored by craggy rock.

He was shielding his eyes. "I need stealth. And you are ruining my night vision."

She killed her phone light, returning it to her pocket. Now her eyesight was shot. She relied on Blackwood, following him closely as she waited for her vision to adjust. Blackwood appeared to be following a trail of some kind.

"This has to do with the grave robbing?" said Odessa, her voice low.

"Slave graves are hallowed ground," said Blackwood, "as places of great pain always are. Their innocent spirits are a repository for great suffering, trapped in limbo for centuries. Harnessed and released into the city, they could wield a potent malevolent force."

Past some excavating tools, Blackwood slowed at an exposed stone support. Odessa's eyesight had recovered enough that she was able to discern a geometric pattern carved into the rock. It was no mere directional symbol. It was a sigil.

Blackwood stopped, looking ahead. He mumbled some words to himself in Latin, Odessa realizing it was another spell of protection. When he finished, he turned to her.

"You must leave."

"What?" she said.

"You should go no farther."

"You let me come all the way down here to tell me to leave?"

"There is nothing you can do here. You could only be used against me."

"*Against* you...?" She saw Blackwood staring into the darkness ahead. "You're going to need help with Solomon." Then she realized: "Are you sending me away because of what happened to him?"

Blackwood did not answer.

"Look," she said, "I don't know what to do down here. All I know is, we can't let that Hollow get at you. If it jumped into an immortal being...or at least a person who can never be maimed, murdered, destroyed...it could run wild forever. And that's after releasing the other three Hollows into the world. You would be the ultimate being for one of those things to possess."

Blackwood said, "That is why I cannot allow that to happen."

"But you know this is a trap."

"Yes."

"Then why walk into it?" she said. "Never mind walk into it alone?"

"There is another presence here," Blackwood said. "Another fiend. One I must face. An adversary I have faced many times before."

Odessa was bewildered. Two entities? "Who?" she asked.

Blackwood straightened out his suit jacket. "My wife," he answered.

Blackwood walked on into the dark underground. Odessa remained behind, thrown by his comment, and unsure what to do. He was right, she had little to offer against any otherworldly being, but going into this alone seemed foolhardy. She did not know what to do.

As she stood there, she heard a familiar voice call to her.

"Odessa," the voice said.

Hugo Blackwood followed the low-ceilinged stone cavern around a blind turn, emptying into a chamber that presaged a wider, airier vault. He heard an accented female voice incanting in Caribbean Spanish, her voice amplified by the ancient acoustics into a forceful, mesmerizing drone. A dim but luminescent violet glow was apparent in the stirred motes of centuries-old dust and soot.

He heard also a sharp snarl and the snapping of jaws. An onrush of animal paws; he could not tell from which direction they were coming. He imagined massive beasts, the exaggerated volume indicating a monster many times the dimensions of the chamber, an impossibility.

They slowed and rounded the corner, two pit bull canines, their faces contorted with ferocity. Inhabited beings, vicious hounds. Blackwood remembered the botanica owner's house, the grave robber saying that their two pit bulls had run off.

Here was where they had run to. Blackwood knew their owner was very near.

They advanced, stalking him, all shoulders and sinewy muscle, ravenous drool spilling from their gnashing fangs.

Blackwood extended his empty hand, palm forward, muttering a spell of compulsion. His eyes met theirs, and as he slowly rotated his open hand, as though adjusting a large dial, the beasts' eyes softened, their lips eased back over their black gums, and their bristling fur lay down flat.

As the dogs stood there locked into his spell, Blackwood removed a vial from his kit, dabbing a bit of oil on the tip of his right middle finger. He approached the animals with his hand extended, and gently swiped the oil vertically along each dog's philtrum, the indentation splitting the nostrils, running down to the upper lip.

Two or three breaths and the animals sank onto their hindquarters, falling onto their sides, slipping into a deep sleep.

Blackwood stepped between the slumbering watchdogs, rounding the corner as the incantation grew louder. There he saw a woman wearing a white robe wrap and a white headdress, presiding over a crypt of chalky soil, out of which rose an ethereal violet mist. The cold vapor assumed the form of the long-dead people buried there, some two and three deep: forty or more men, women, and children, silhouettes rippling, wisps of purplish steam slipping from their hair and their shoulders like heat from cooked meat, dissipating into the stale air.

At the low, moaned urging of the conjurer Juanita, the violet spirits turned and faced Hugo Blackwood from the loamy floor of the unearthed crypt.

Odessa looked for the source of the familiar voice, fearing it was Solomon.

"Odessa? Honey, it's me."

She watched her father walk out of the shadow, a grateful smile on his face. He wore one of his old cardigans over a Lands' End oxford, like he always did.

"Dad?" she said. Odessa was amazed to see her father, and yet his presence here in this subterranean catacomb in the center of New York City felt completely normal to her. In fact, his presence put her gently at ease. "Where did you come from?"

He stopped a few steps away from her, a hesitant smile on his face. "Why did you stop visiting me, honey?" he asked.

Odessa was suffused with regret, but at the same time, she welcomed the opportunity to explain herself and clear the air between them. "I couldn't do it anymore, Dad," she said. "You betrayed your clients. You betrayed your family. You betrayed me."

Her voice cracked on the last word. She went on.

382

"*Me*," she said again. "Of all people. I stood by you. I sat at your defense table in court. I vouched for you with everyone in town. You made a fool out of all of us. But especially me. You broke my heart."

"I know," said her father, nodding, taking a tentative step closer. "I know I did. But you don't…you can't know how lonely it was in prison."

"I'm sorry, Dad," she said. "I love you, but…"

"Can you forgive me, Odessa?" he said, taking another step closer, holding out his arms to her. "Please?"

Blackwood unfurled his leather kit, hands selecting an ampoule by touch, his eyes never leaving the misty forms. They were advancing toward him, legs not moving, but rather all of them drifting in the same direction like a patch of sage caught in a breeze. The conjurer Juanita had sent them forth, expecting him to resist their assault, to repel them and exhaust himself in the fight.

But Blackwood did not prepare a countering spell. He uncapped the ampoule of green glass and slathered a generous dab of a tincture of white rose petal on each hand, returning the vial to its place and sliding the kit into his jacket pocket.

Rubbing his fingers into their respective palms and intoning the spell in its original Enochian language, Blackwood extended his arms and opened his hands toward the slave spirits. A fine gold vapor was emitted by his palms as though exhaled. It formed a nimbus of honeyed light around his body as his arms spread wide. The slave spirits moved faster as they reached his form, lowering their heads in attack.

Blackwood's body was rocked as he welcomed these tormented spirits, taking them into himself. Instead of giving them the fight they desired, he absorbed their swarming pain, their fear, their bitter anger, their angst. He assimilated their energy, pulling their agony into his own heart.

He felt the conjurer Juanita pulling at them. Filling them with darkness. Driving them toward evil.

Blackwood could not heal their spirits. He could only commune with them. He could only speak to their souls.

You were exploited in life. You must resist being exploited by evil once more.

Odessa's eyes welled with tears. She wanted to forgive her father. She had always wanted to forgive him.

But she couldn't. Some crimes—especially the personal ones, the emotional ones—can never be forgiven.

"Dad," she said, "I...I can't."

His expression moved from befuddlement to disappointment... and then anger.

And then it was no longer her father standing before her. It was Earl Solomon. He swung his right arm very quickly and violently, catching her across the face with a backhanded smack that sent her stumbling backward and crashing hard to the stone floor.

Odessa looked up, stunned, her jaw aching, ear ringing. She looked around for her dad until she realized what had happened. It was as though a veil had been pulled away.

Earl Solomon, wearing a hospital gown and padded socks, ran at her with a face-twisting sneer and weird strength. He jumped for her, coming down socks-first, aiming to crush her throat.

Odessa rolled away at the very last second. Solomon collapsed on top of her, fists flailing, kidney punches pummeling her torso and sides. She covered up defensively at first, but Solomon's possessed body had stamina to burn, and she realized he would beat her to death if she let him.

She kicked herself over, throwing him off her and scrambling away. Separated from him again, she responded to the image of Earl Solomon, a man she respected, a person she liked. "No!" she implored him.

But it wasn't him. It wasn't Earl Solomon.

The Hollow One sprang to its feet, preternaturally agile for an elderly body, and ran at her wildly, arms waving over its head. Odessa got up but stayed low, using her weight to duck him and throw him off her hip. The Hollow One went sprawling over the bare stone ground with an ugly scraping noise.

Odessa was crying, tears of anger, tears of despair. "Don't," she said, pleading with it as it got up from the ground and started back at her. "Don't make me do this!" she said, but it came at her in a run, and she couldn't sidestep it cleanly. Their bodies collided, both of them falling away.

"*Stop!*" she screamed.

It wouldn't. She saw that. It was rabid dog and psychopath and Terminator all in one. It got to its stocking feet—and Odessa saw the pile of loose boards and tools beyond it.

The Hollow One came flailing at her, one hand catching her face, fingers digging deep into her cheek and temple, trying to blind her. Odessa let it spin her around, then kicked out at its knee, pulling free and staggering backward, landing on the boards.

She felt around for a weapon, unable to take her eyes from the Hollow One. She gripped the handle of a hammer. She rose to her knees as the Hollow One came at her, low—kicking the hammer from her arm. She rocked backward, grasping at the toolbox as the Hollow One grasped at her, feeling a familiar bulbous wooden handle in her fingers.

It rolled her around and bared its teeth, trying to get at the soft tissue of her face. Like a mad dog, it snapped at her, and Odessa dug her left forearm up under its chin, into its throat, to no avail. It bore down on her.

Through gritted teeth, Odessa said, "God forgive me." And then: "Solomon…forgive me—"

Her right hand dug the steel end of the awl into the base of the Hollow One's skull and drove it downward. With all her strength, she pierced the muscle of the upper neck, finding the brain.

The Hollow One's eyes went wide. Its tongue lolled out of its mouth, swelling, inches from her face. With a yell and a heave, she shoved it off her and crabbed away from the twitching form.

She watched in misery and relief. Her face and hip and kidneys and knee all hurt. She slumped to the stone floor for a moment, dizzy from hyperventilating, catching her breath.

She pulled herself up to a sitting position, then got to her feet. In the weird gloom of the chamber, she saw the shape of the thing lying still at last.

As she watched, a wavy emanation arose from it, like a trick of the shadows. A tinge of burnt solder reached her nostrils before she remembered about the Hollow Ones. She threw up both arms to shield her face, backing away—but then was gripped mid-step by a spasm, her body going taut, spine arched, head thrown back. An excruciating seizure of pain . . . and then her muscles ceased quivering, and her limbs and her mind relaxed.

Blackwood's body and soul were racked with the agony of the arisen slave spirits. By not resisting them and embracing their distress, he neutralized the conjurer's hostile intent.

Juanita, the priestess, the *mayombero*, grew enraged. As she fought to regain control over her risen ghosts, the dark being that inhabited her appeared. Out of her form arose the white-gowned, black-haired figure of Orleanna Blackwood, projected spectrally. Hugo Blackwood faced his depraved love, her fierce, dark eyes boring into him from within the burial chamber. A tug-of-war for the souls of the woken slave spirits.

Blackwood had allowed them to envelop him, and now he grew stronger in spirit, while his body weakened.

Return, he implored. *Return*.

Blackwood's body quaked as the hazy violet beings began to swim back into the chamber.

The ghastly image of his long-lost wife emitted a harrowing scream.

Let them sleep, commanded Blackwood. *Give them peace.*

She would not release them. She fought their spirits, one final attempt to excite their vengeful natures, wanting the powerful energy of their timeless suffering for herself.

The violet haze swam to her, overcoming her, staining her flowing nightdress purple, then darkening to black. The haze grew dense and suffocating, pulling her down into the aged soil with it, settling into the ground.

Blackwood's knees gave out and he collapsed onto one hip. He watched weakly as the last of the oily mist returned to the earth.

Blackwood regained his equilibrium, pushing himself up onto his feet. His body was like a hive that had just been evacuated of a thousand angry bees. But the underground vault was quiet once again.

"My darling."

The voice froze Hugo Blackwood. Over the past 450 years, very few things had made the hair on the back of his neck stand up, but her voice did. Trembling, Blackwood turned away from the crypt to the catacomb behind him.

Out of the darkness walked Orleanna Blackwood. Not as a demon. Not as an evil spirit. But as she had been in marriage, her skin fair, her eyes lively, her gossamer nightdress flowing.

"Orleanna," whispered Hugo Blackwood.

"You saved me," she said. Her smile was beatific, her arms open, waiting to be received by him. "*Finally, my love. We can be together once again.*"

"My dearest love," said Blackwood, the words catching in his throat like a sob.

"*Take me,*" she said. "*Embrace me. And again we will be one.*"

"Yes, my dear," said Blackwood. "Yes. But let me...allow me to look at you." His healthy, young wife. She looked ravishing. "Give me this moment, dear."

She tried. She angled her shoulders ever so slightly, smiling, a portrait of beauty, of youth, of health and happiness.

"*Oh, Hugo,*" she said, unable to hold herself back, "*we must be together. Take me. I can wait no longer.*"

Orleanna rushed to him, arms open. Blackwood opened his arms to receive his one true love, but at the last moment, just before she reached him, he grabbed her fine throat.

He squeezed it tightly, crushing the muscles of her neck, closing off air. Orleanna's face contorted in pain and confusion.

Blackwood's eyes went from soft despair to baleful anger.

Then the illusion faded, Orleanna's face becoming that of Agent Odessa Hardwicke.

Blackwood was shocked a moment, appalled, expecting to see Earl Solomon.

And in that split second of distraction, the Hollow One broke Blackwood's grip, using his arm to spin him into the stone wall.

Blackwood came off it dazed. Odessa came at him, her eyes wild. A demon. A Hollow.

It came at him with disorienting speed, grabbing him and throwing him with banshee strength. Blackwood landed hard against a ledge near the graves. The Hollow came at him with its arms waving, its mouth open but silent. He caught it with his shoe, a thundering blow to the midsection. With his other leg, he jettisoned it away.

Blackwood got to his feet and quickly produced his leather kit. He unfurled it and selected one of the instruments inside, a narrow-bladed steel dagger. He would eject the Hollow and hold it here with an immobilizing spell until help arrived.

The Hollow struck him bodily from the side, sending both of them flying, the kit and its contents falling from Blackwood's hand. He fell along the stone floor, face-first, rolling over just in time to catch the Hollow in wild flight, landing atop him.

One hand gripped the Hollow's throat, holding it at bay. Blackwood's other hand held the dagger.

The Hollow pounded on his face and chest wildly, slowing only as Blackwood's grip tightened around its neck. Its eyes saw the steel blade as Blackwood raised his hand behind the Hollow's head, blade pointing down.

"I am sorry, Agent Hardwicke."

He pressed the steel point against the base of her skull, ready to slay the unfortunate victim. But his hand held. He hesitated, and then experienced a vision. Odessa's face appeared as Orleanna's again. But this vision was not, he determined, the Hollow's doing.

It meant something to Blackwood.

But again, this hesitation cost him. The Hollow slammed his head against the stone floor, disengaging from his grip. It slammed his head again, dazing Blackwood, the Hollow thrashing about. At once, it snatched the dagger from Blackwood's hand. It turned the blade around, pointing it at its own throat, and with a crazed smile stabbed upward.

Blackwood just caught its wrist. The Hollow's strength was prodigious, and Blackwood had been weakened in his duel with the conjurer. His hand shook as the blade tip neared Odessa Hardwicke's neck.

He was losing her.

Then a flurry entered the crypt from the catacomb, a gust like the wind from the beating of great wings. Two big hands pulled at the Hollow, wrenching it off Blackwood, tearing the dagger from its hand.

Joachim, the tattoo artist and Hollow Ones' jailer, watched the Hollow spin away from him, still a crazed look in its eye, getting ready to charge him.

At once Joachim flexed his chest, and his shirt ripped apart at its back seams. A pair of wings unfolded, twice as wide as they were high, the patterns of their scales painted with structural color patterns to rival that of the rarest butterfly. It was an angry flex, stunning the Hollow, freezing it in its tracks. Joachim lunged for it, grasping it by the neck, his wings retracting.

In a flash, he spun the Hollow around, one arm beneath its chin, the other atop its head. He was making to snap its neck.

"No!" yelled Blackwood.

Joachim looked up, surprised. Blackwood picked up his fallen leather kit and went before the squirming Hollow, looking past its ferocious sneer to the eyes of Odessa Hardwicke behind it.

Joachim held it tight, his arm moving back from the top of its head. Blackwood intoned the incantation, placing both hands on the sides of the Hollow's head. His arms shook with the effort, the Hollow struggling in Joachim's grip.

The body convulsed. As Blackwood withdrew his hands, an image of the Hollow's head appeared between them, as though Blackwood was pulling it out. The Hollow's large mouth howled in either pain or reluctance, but Blackwood could not yank it free. He was losing his grip on the nasty imp, until...as though the result of a great push from within Odessa Hardwicke, the Hollow was ejected, Blackwood staggering back with the foul, baying spirit in his hands.

Joachim released Odessa, letting her body sink to the floor. He grasped the Hollow One, seizing it from Blackwood, gripping the squealing, mewling imp by its throat.

Blackwood went to Odessa, kneeling before her, clearing the hair away from her face. Her skin was deathly cold to the touch, but then her eyelids fluttered, her lips moving.

She was coming around. Blackwood helped her up into a sitting position. She looked at him dumbly, wondering why he looked so happy to see her.

"What happened?" she said, her tongue stiff, her mouth tasting of ashes.

"You...you fainted," said Blackwood.

She saw the mustached Mexican tattoo artist, Joachim, his shirt torn, holding a wrinkled old Hollow One, its mouth-face open and groaning.

Then she remembered: Earl Solomon. She reached out to Blackwood's shoulder, gripping the fabric of his jacket.

"Solomon," she said.

Blackwood helped her back through the catacomb to the smaller chamber. There lay Solomon, the bulbous wooden handle of the awl sticking out of the back of his head.

Odessa covered her mouth, stricken by horror at what she'd done. Blackwood dropped to one knee near Solomon, looking over his body, curled on its side.

Blackwood said, "Look away a moment. Please."

She did, and he removed the awl blade, tossing it aside. He straightened Solomon's body, fixing the hospital gown neatly, setting his arms straight down at his sides—just as he had once done with Vernon Jamus in another slave graveyard.

Odessa had turned back, tears running down her face now.

Blackwood opened his kit. "I am going to commend his soul to peace," he said.

He performed a sort of funeral rite, cleansing and releasing Solomon to the ages. Odessa paid little attention to his ministrations, weeping through it. At the end, Blackwood staggered to his feet, exhausted.

Odessa caught him, helped steady him. Blackwood nodded, returning his implements to his kit, and the kit to his jacket pocket.

Odessa could not believe it had come to this. But as she stood there mourning the death of the man whose body she had killed, she remembered watching the Hollow-as-Solomon twitch and die.

The emanation. Something had floated out of him, just like the thing she'd seen rise out of Walt Leppo when he died.

"Wait," she said, looking around. "How did I get from here into the crypt?"

Blackwood did not answer her. Something wasn't right.

Joachim entered the chamber, the Hollow One firmly in his grip. He paused near them, looking down at the body of Earl Solomon.

"I need to get this one up to Providence before something else goes wrong," he said. "He can join the other three. You did it, Hugo."

Blackwood nodded without joy. "Your timing was impeccable."

"Well, it was a long ride down from Providence. Nice work to you, too, Agent Hardwicke."

"Oh, I didn't..." Odessa started to say, but never finished the thought. As Joachim walked away with the Hollow, she thought she saw, before he disappeared into the shadows, folded against his broad back, a pair of beautifully inked angel wings.

Odessa returned to the crypt, trying to remember how she'd gotten there. She looked down at the centuries-old grave site. Blackwood entered behind her.

"This port island was one of the colonies' largest slaveholding communities in the early eighteenth century," said Blackwood. "African and Caribbean slaves constituted one-quarter of the workforce in New York."

"Unbelievable," said Odessa.

Blackwood said, "If past wrongs are not addressed, and dealt with honestly, dark spirits will erupt through the unhealed seam. It is the same for cities and towns as it is for people."

Odessa remembered the image of her father then. And something else came back to her. "While I was out," she said, trying to remember, "I had a dream. I saw a woman."

Blackwood turned to her, captivated. "Tell me."

Odessa reached deep into her memory. "Black hair. Black eyes. She wore a white dressing gown..."

"Yes?" said Blackwood, with quiet urgency.

"She wanted to help me. To wake up. I think she...she sent me back. Does that sound crazy?"

Blackwood didn't answer. He was lost in thought.

"You mentioned your wife," said Odessa.

Blackwood came back from his reverie. "The invading spirit revealed itself to me as her. She is trapped in a netherworld, waiting for me to rescue her. If I can complete my tasks, and save the world from these dark forces enough times, I believe I can free her from limbo."

Odessa understood then. Hugo Blackwood had been slaying projections of his beloved for four and a half centuries in a quest to save her. That was what made him the prickly creature he was.

Odessa was still unaccountably sore. Aside from her cuts and bruises, and the pain in her jaw, it felt like something more. She reached around to rub the back of her sore neck, and felt something strange there, beneath her hairline.

A raised vein. Fading now, but she probed it with her fingertips, and remembered...

A sigil. The mark of the Hollow Ones.

She looked at Blackwood, and saw that he knew then that she knew.

Odessa jumped back and clawed at her arms, sick at having been inhabited by one of those disgusting imps.

"My God!" she said. "That thing was in me?"

Blackwood did not say yes, and he did not say no.

"What did I... what did it make me do?" she said. She saw dirt on Blackwood's suit, a missing button. "Did I go after you?"

"You did," he admitted.

"But wait. I thought you said the only way to rid a body of one of those things...was to kill. You saved me." She was deeply confused now. "Why?"

Blackwood looked at her strangely, as though unsure of the answer himself. "Yes," he said. "Why indeed."

In the end, the FBI incident inquest never went forward.

The Office of Professional Responsibility, the Bureau's internal affairs division, declined to adjudicate the matter, based almost exclusively upon the surviving Peters daughter's sworn eyewitness account of what transpired on that tragic night.

Walter Leppo was determined to have perished in the line of duty, and his family received his full pension with incentive awards.

While her testimony absolved Odessa of any wrongdoing, due to the lack of a disciplinary hearing, Odessa was never formally cleared, and therefore her good reputation could never properly be restored. Her service weapon was reissued to her, but she was not returned to regular, active investigative duty. She was instead offered special assignment status, her position to be determined.

To Odessa, this reminded her of Earl Solomon's

unique and unusual arrangement with the Bureau throughout his career. She was resistant to this assignment, and determined she would voluntarily resign from the FBI.

Linus encouraged her not to do anything rash. "Give it a couple of days," he said. "Then decide what's right for you."

Odessa appreciated him standing by her through the entire process. But she couldn't help but think about what that old woman told her in the back room of that botanica.

He is a good man, and devoted. He has genuine feelings for you. You are his one true love. But he is not yours.

A few days later, while she was home alone trying to figure out her next life step, Mr. Lusk appeared at her apartment door. She was surprised by the sudden rush of excitement she felt at his visit.

"Blackwood?" she said, assuming. "He wants to see me?"

"Oh no, Ms. Hardwicke," said Mr. Lusk, in his theatrically mannered way. "I am here because of a legal matter."

She shrugged. "What would that be?"

"Specifically, the estate of Earl Solomon." Mr. Lusk furnished a sheaf of papers secured with a large black clip. "You have been named his executrix."

"I never...?" She flipped through the top pages. "I never agreed to that."

"Well, it's most convenient, in any event. Seeing as you are the sole beneficiary of his estate."

He handed her another sheaf of papers. She was shocked.

"His estate?" she said. She flipped to the final pages of the will, signed in Solomon's shaky hand, dated just a few days ago. The man whose life she had ended. "This doesn't seem right."

"I assure you, it is."

"So his house...I own a house now?"

"Once it goes through probate. But that should be essentially clerical. Good luck, Ms. Hardwicke!"

Mr. Lusk started back down the hallway. "Wait," she said, holding the door open with her foot, leaning out after him. "What about Hugo Blackwood?"

"Yes?" Mr. Lusk looked confused. "What about him?"

"Uh...nothing, I guess. Tell him I say hello."

"I will, certainly. If I see him."

And with a smile he was gone.

Odessa let herself into Earl Solomon's one-story house in Camden, New Jersey. She stood quietly inside the door for some moments, reflecting on Solomon, a man she barely knew, yet felt she knew so well. There was so much she didn't understand.

After a quick check of the house, she went out to collect the mail. Flyers and circulars and a couple of bills she would have to start taking care of. And a square package wrapped in paper and tied with twine—addressed to Earl Solomon, no return address.

She rushed back to the house and tore the package open. Inside were four boxed reels of Mylar recording tape, labeled: NEW JERSEY 2019 / HOLLOW ONES.

Odessa opened the back wall inside the narrow utility closet and accessed the secret room. She carried the boxes to the far end of the bookcases of cataloged recording tapes, filing the boxes onto the start of a new, empty shelf.

She returned to the first bookcase, pulling out the very first recording. #1001 / MISSISSIPPI 1962 / VERNON JAMUS.

Odessa threaded the tape into the reel-to-reel player atop the desk and slipped the old, comfortable, corded headphones over her ears, settling into the wide leather chair.

She switched the lever to PLAY. A few moments of hissing and popping, and then Hugo Blackwood's purring British voice began to speak.

EPILOGUE: The Box

Wall Street is a labyrinth. Canyons of glass and steel, occluding the sun and the sky. Night seems to fall earlier here than anywhere else in Manhattan.

But even then, the dark man in the long overcoat seemed to be walking only in shadow. He did so without effort or direction—shadows just collected around him, trailed him. And he dragged them along as he glided toward the unassuming mailbox.

The few people wandering the street avoided him—not out of fear, nor recognition, but because of an instinct imprinted in the most primitive part of their brains. Perhaps, in their fleeting observations, they noticed that he cast no shadow of his own.

The dark man approached the mailbox and extended an impossibly pale hand toward the mail slot. He deposited a small, letter-locked paper. It was addressed to Hugo Blackwood and sealed in wax with the symbol of a radiant, all-seeing eye.

This letter had taken hundreds of years to reach its destination, and with it, it heralded The End.